MURDER ON THE OLD ROAD

MURDER ON THE OLD ROAD

Amy Myers

This first world edition published 2010
in Great Britain and in the USA by
SEVERN HOUSE PUBLISHERS LTD of
9–15 High Street, Sutton, Surrey, England, SM1 1DF.
Trade paperback edition first published
in Great Britain and the USA 2011 by
SEVERN HOUSE PUBLISHERS LTD.

British Library Cataloguing in Publication Data

Myers, Amy, 1938-
  Murder on the Old Road.
  1. Marsh, Peter (Fictitious character)–Fiction. 2. Marsh,
  Georgia (Fictitious character)–Fiction. 3. Private
  investigators–England–Kent–Fiction. 4. Fathers and
  daughters–Fiction. 5. Detective and mystery stories.
  I. Title
  823.9'14-dc22

ISBN-13: 978-0-7278-6952-4   (cased)
ISBN-13: 978-1-84751-283-3   (trade paper)

All Severn House titles are printed on acid-free paper.

Severn House Publishers support The Forest Stewardship Council [FSC], the
leading international forest certification organisation. All our titles that are
printed on Greenpeace-approved FSC-certified paper carry the FSC logo.

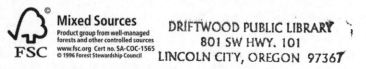

Typeset by Palimpsest Book Production Ltd.,
Falkirk, Stirlingshire.
Printed and bound in Great Britain by
MPG Books Ltd., Bodmin, Cornwall.

AUTHOR'S NOTE

The Old Road of the title is generally known as the Pilgrims' Way, running from Winchester in Hampshire through to Canterbury in Kent. Much of it now forms part of the North Downs Way, which has followed the earlier route as far as was possible by the time it was established. By walking it, it is still easy to imagine what it was like for pilgrims making their way to the shrine of Archbishop Thomas Becket. The village of Chillingham, however, the central setting for this novel, is fictitious, as are its inhabitants and the pilgrimage. Apart from that of the three peacocks, the legends surrounding the Old Road and St Thomas are 'real' ones, including the story of Seivia, which can be found in the books of St Thomas's miracles written a few years after his death in 1170. I have taken the liberty of transporting the miracle from a nameless location to Chillingham, however. St Thomas, Canterbury Cathedral and its treasures provide an inexhaustible source for imagination to build upon fact, and the genesis for this novel was one such fruit. Some years ago a short story of mine called 'The Pilgrim' was published in *Ellery Queen Mystery Magazine* and later in *Best British Mysteries IV*, edited by Maxim Jakubowski. Then I began to think, But what happened *next*? This novel is the result.

It would not have been possible, however, without the help of Christopher Maude – who, as well as sharing his knowledge of the Cathedral, recommended to me the fascinating book by John Butler, *The Quest for Becket's Bones*; the Reverend Dr E.V. Binks; and Mike Cockett, my discussions with whom about Hilaire Belloc's *The Old Road* first gave me the idea of linking the Pilgrims' Way to the Becket story in this novel. My thanks also go to my ever inspiring agent, Dorothy Lumley of the Dorian Literary Agency, and to Severn House for their patience and expertise.

ONE

'**W**hat on earth's going on?'

Georgia Marsh blinked as she pushed open the gate to the Three Peacocks garden. As this was a pub in a remote village on the Kentish North Downs, she could hardly have expected to see thirty or forty people, young, middle-aged and elderly, mostly clad in long rust-brown robes with full sleeves and big hats, caps or wimples. Some sported short tunics and tights, a few were adorned with crowns. The grass was littered with hefty sticks, and music played a part in this gathering, judging by the number of lutes and recorders lying around.

'Maybe it's one of those mythical villages that only appears once in a hundred years,' Luke commented.

'Morris dancers,' Peter grunted. Not his favourite spectator sport.

'No bells on their legs,' Georgia reassured him. Anyway, Morris dancing didn't seem likely at a Thursday lunchtime, even if it was June. This was the only pub in the small village of Chillingham, and it was so crowded that she had to look hard for a table that had enough space not only to accommodate Luke and herself, but also her father's wheelchair.

'Come and join us.' A hand of hearty welcome shot up. A long table was only half occupied by the 'elite'. No russet gowns here. This was apparently the crowned 'King' himself, a tall sturdy man probably in his forties, who was booming out his welcome. Sitting next to him, also crowned, was his 'Queen', an elegant dark-haired petite woman, wearing what looked a rather smart medieval grey job designed to match the King's dark green tunic.

Their companion was a suave-looking silver-haired man, perhaps in his early sixties, who seemed annoyed at their arrival, which amused Georgia, although to do him justice the frown was quickly quashed. Instead of a crown, he was sporting a rather splendid golden tea-cosy on his head, matched by a full length golden cape.

'Murder's off the menu today.' The King laughed heartily at his somewhat unusual declaration. 'I won't be slaughtering anyone until we get to Canterbury, so do feel free to join us.'

No choice but to obey the royal command, and so, weird though it was, Georgia surrendered. In any case, Peter, always one for the eccentric side of life, was already eagerly propelling himself to the table. She followed with less enthusiasm. She never trusted control freaks, and the King had every sign of being one. Luke, as usual, seemed more tolerant.

'Who are you planning to murder?' he enquired.

'My dear brother, of course.' The King indicated Mr Teacosy, who glared back at him. 'Also known as Archbishop Thomas Becket, who will be foully done to death by this merry band in due course.' A lofty arm indicated the peasants busily tucking into their sandwiches and pints of beer.

Dear brother? The tension between the two men was all too obvious. Little fraternal love there, Georgia thought, and a big age difference. There seemed to be two battles going on here, the spoken and the unspoken. Luke must have felt it too, as he rose rather hastily to go into the pub for food and drinks.

'I'm looking forward to my fate,' Becket replied smoothly, before delivering his put-down. 'And even more to your subsequent humiliation, mighty majesty.'

'Well worth it.' Another guffaw from the King.

The Queen quickly stepped in as peacemaker. 'We're the Chillingham Drama Group,' she explained sweetly. 'We're staging our play in Canterbury in two weeks' time. Do come. It's at the Stour Theatre.'

'*Murder in the Cathedral* – T.S. Eliot's drama?' Peter sounded merely polite, but Georgia could see his eyes were gleaming in curiosity – and not just over the play. She'd worked with him for a long time and could read the signs.

'No. It's the Tennyson play, *Becket*.' Becket's languid drawl – surely affected – began to grate on Georgia's nerves, and the King's loud bluster was little better.

'Chillingham likes to be different,' Becket continued, 'especially as the Archbishop was one of Henry Irving's great roles. Much neglected masterpiece. It adds another dimension to the familiar story, doesn't it, dear *half* brother? Not only the power struggle between the King and Becket, but the domestic triangle of the King, his mistress Fair Rosamund – and the poisonous Queen Eleanor.' A grin at the Queen. 'Ah, we happy band of actors.'

No doubt about it now. For whatever reason, Georgia realized, they had walked into the midst of a family 'situation' – one that had obviously been running for a long time. The fact that they were only half brothers made more sense of it. The King looked as if he'd like to carry out Becket's murder personally here and now. Becket himself was clearly bent on provocation – and the Queen? Georgia wouldn't mind betting that the real power lay in her hands. If, as implied, she was playing the poisonous queen, then not much acting would be required. This lady was made of steel.

'You're here for a rehearsal?' Peter asked blandly, although Georgia was sure he had picked up exactly the same vibes as she had.

'Far from it. Today sets the whole venture in motion.' The King then recollected his *noblesse oblige*. 'Let me introduce ourselves. My wife Aletta, my half brother Valentine Harper, and I am Julian Wayncroft—'

'Lord of this manor,' Valentine finished for him in deeply grave – and mocking – tones.

Aletta pointedly ignored him. 'Our plan is to walk to Canterbury today, then take our hired coach to Winchester for our first performance tomorrow evening. And then begins the great pilgrimage on foot back to Canterbury over the next two weeks, followed by five performances.'

Aletta had been blessed – or cursed – with a high, rather tinkling voice, and her general air of sweet condescension made Georgia instinctively recoil. Her mind boggled at the sheer scope of the undertaking. A two-week walk from Hampshire and *then* put on a play? For an amateur drama production it seemed a challenge, to say the least, and Peter clearly agreed with her.

'A pilgrimage *before* your murder, Archbishop Becket?' he joked to Valentine.

'This pilgrimage of yours. You're taking the Old Road?' Luke asked, having returned with the drinks.

Julian jumped in to take ownership of the conversation before his brother could reply. 'All the way from Winchester to Canterbury, the old Pilgrims' Way, trodden for thousands of years. That's a comparatively modern name, of course, as the track was used long before pilgrims set foot on it – and, as you say, colloquially called the Old Road, notably by Hilaire Belloc in his book of that name.'

'See my edition thereof, price fourteen pounds ninety-nine, available at all good bookshops,' Luke joked. 'I publish local history books. My wife Georgia, her father Peter Marsh, and I'm Luke Frost.'

'Marsh?' Valentine glanced from Peter to Georgia. 'Of Marsh & Daughter? The true crime book series? Old murder cases?'

As Peter nodded, Georgia saw Julian stiffen. 'Is that why you're here today?' he shot at them, with an attempt at a laugh that didn't work. Why would that be? she wondered. Only a few minutes ago he'd been joking about murder himself. He seemed to be a man of swift-changing emotions, and in a power struggle she would put her money on smooth-talking Valentine.

'Good heavens no. Better brains than ours have studied Becket's death.'

Peter's light-hearted remark dispelled the tension, and Georgia relaxed. She was probably imagining a situation that did not exist. After all, sibling rivalry was hardly an unknown phenomenon. Nevertheless, she wondered how Aletta fitted into this uncomfortable relationship. Was she peacemaker or partisan?

She reproved herself for letting her imagination roam out of control and smiled across at a young man who had just joined the table. His likeness to Julian was so apparent that this must surely be his son. No princely splendour for him, although he cut a dashing figure, with a shock of black curly hair peeping out from under a sort of chain-mail beret, a mock chain jerkin, black tights – and trainers, which rather spoiled the effect.

'When are we off, then?' he demanded of his father.

'My son Sebastian,' Julian said, introducing him briefly, then glanced at his watch. (On a Plantagenet king's wrist?) 'The coach arrives at two o'clock. Finish our lunch, load the coach and up to the North Downs Way.'

'Why are you walking to Canterbury?' Peter queried. 'Not taking the coach?'

'The great god Publicity.' Sebastian grinned. 'That's what this pilgrimage is all about. There's a reception organized to greet us as we stagger down into the city with our banners. We want to be *overwhelmed* with—'

'Seb—' his mother broke in warningly. 'Obviously media presence. Desperately.' She turned apologetically to them. 'That's why we're opening the play on the day of Becket's traditional anniversary on the seventh of July. Silly, really, since he actually died on the twenty-ninth of December. But I suppose that month wasn't so good for pilgrimages, so July was chosen instead, the anniversary of the day his bones were moved to the shrine in Trinity Chapel.'

'Or not, as the case may be,' Seb drawled. 'That man has more bones scattered around than a can of sardines.'

'Seb—' Julian said sharply.

Not a man she would like to cross, Georgia decided, but his son only laughed. 'Don't worry, Pa. I'm all for it. Can't wait to get to Canterbury this afternoon.' He yawned ostentatiously, and Julian's face grew even darker.

'I'm still grappling with the idea of you all marching the whole of the Pilgrims' Way,' Georgia put in hastily, seeing yet another family situation erupting. 'You'll all be exhausted by the time you come to perform the play itself.'

'It'll be a doddle,' Seb replied blithely. 'Even Ma can manage it.' Aletta awarded him a cool smile.

'Tim Hurst suggested Georgia and I share the doddle with you this afternoon,' Luke said. 'What do you think, Georgia? It's only four or five miles to Canterbury. We've got our walking gear in the car, and Tim says the coach that's taking them on to Winchester can drop us off on the way back.'

What did she *think*? The idea seemed horrific. Nothing she had so far seen of the main players in this pilgrimage recommended a longer acquaintance with them. Unfortunately Tim Hurst, who was the co-owner of the Three Peacocks, had once worked with Luke, and Luke was obviously thinking that they should support him. Perhaps Tim had some role in the play. If Luke went, she should too. After all, all drama groups had their tensions, and this was only for an afternoon.

'Fine,' she said bravely. 'If you don't mind, Peter?' She turned to her father.

'I'm relieved to say this wheelchair isn't footpath friendly,'

Peter replied blithely, 'so don't worry about me. I'll drive home and read a good book.'

Georgia deduced from this that Peter was silently egging her on for some reason known only to himself. A reference to good books was usually a euphemism for research, either by Internet or through his vast collection of reference books. If a new Marsh & Daughter case was on the horizon it meant the starting pistol had been fired. If the case then developed they would work on it to the point where they could write it up for their true crime non-fiction series. But at the Three Peacocks there was no case – or even the sniff of one, unless Julian's odd reaction to the name Marsh & Daughter counted. Marsh & Daughter usually investigated past mysteries, but there had been no mention of one so far except for Becket himself, and even Peter wouldn't have the gall to rush in where so many learned historians had trodden before. So what could have caught his attention? True, the Wayncroft family situation was highly charged with emotion, but that was no concern of Peter or hers. Yet that gleam in Peter's eye clearly said: Trust me, something wicked this way comes.

She must have missed something, she decided, so she surrendered gracefully. Marsh & Daughter were between books at present, always a difficult time. Their last case had been completed and written up, and Luke, their publisher, hoped to get it on the market in time for Christmas.

'Why's Tim going on the pilgrimage?' Luke said to Julian. 'Does he have a role in the play?'

'Nothing important. He's merely our all powerful director.' Julian grinned, good humour again to the fore.

'I'd no idea Tim was keen on drama.'

Luke had been surprised to re-meet Tim Hurst earlier that year. Georgia remembered the day well. They'd come here by chance and discovered that Tim ran and owned the pub with his partner Simon Bede. They'd lived here six years and were trying to turn the Three Peacocks into a combination of gastro pub and village community rendezvous. Not as yet, she and Luke had gathered, very successfully.

Georgia had immediately liked Tim. In his mid-thirties, he was outgoing, quick-witted and talented. A bundle of nerves, she guessed, and he held his body like a coiled spring. Simon was older by, she guessed, about seven or eight years. He was the sturdier of the two, both physically and mentally, and was affable without being extrovert, but so far as their relationship was concerned, it seemed to be he, not Tim, who was insecure. He looked the perfect 'mine host' for a tavern, and Tim the inspirational cook, but in fact it worked the other way round. Simon was the chef, Tim the business and outside man.

As departure time drew near and Georgia saw the coach draw up, there was a general move inside the pub to pick up luggage. She saw Tim emerge with Simon, who was carrying what looked like a rolled up banner, presumably to advertise the play.

'No pilgrim's garb, Tim?' Luke joked.

'My robe's in here.' Tim flourished a backpack. 'I didn't wear it behind the bar in case any normal people dropping in for a pint took fright.'

'Are you both going?' Georgia asked. Tim was clearly pleased that she and Luke were to accompany them, even though Tim looked strained, and his light banter had a false note.

'Just me,' Tim replied. 'Can't both be away two weeks. Simon doesn't mind, do you, Si?'

'Simon does, in fact,' he answered wryly, 'but we bow to necessity. We need the publicity.'

'Badly.' Tim pulled a face.

So they expected the play and pilgrimage to help the pub as well as the drama society. Georgia remembered Seb's talk of the great god Publicity – more, surely, than the need to cover costs in a local production would require. There had been real emphasis on it, and Aletta had even used the word 'desperately'. Was there something here she wasn't getting? The subtext of village life was seldom available for strangers to read, but this particular subtext disturbed her. Had it had that effect on Peter too? It might explain why he was keen for her to join the merry band this afternoon.

'Tough times for pubs now.' Simon pulled a face. 'The Three Peacocks is in every pub guide we can break into, but we really need word of mouth local trade as well.'

Georgia felt guilty that she and Luke had come so seldom since their first visit. The Three Peacocks' prices were far from cheap, however. Gastro food demanded gastro rates, and she wondered how long it might be before standards – or menus – had to be downgraded.

'Can you cope on your own, without Tim?' Luke asked.

'Should be able to,' Simon replied. 'Derek Moon comes in to run the bar, and his mum Lisa will give me a hand front of house and in the kitchen. We'll manage.' He didn't look happy at the prospect.

'It's worth it, Simon,' Tim said quietly.

'*If* it works.' The reply was even quieter and obviously destined for Tim alone.

If what works? Georgia wondered. It couldn't be the play, because if Tim were directing it, Simon would surely never suggest it might fail. The pilgrimage? Perhaps. Or was this a different subtext altogether?

There was an awkward silence, which Peter broke with a jovial, 'So, the lord of the manor and a pub owner are going on a pilgrimage today. Don't you need to complete the village establishment with the vicar? Is he blessing the pilgrimage with his presence?'

Another pause, then Tim replied quietly, 'She has to come. It's a village event, isn't it?'

'Good thing we keep our trainers in the car boot,' Luke said, opening it up.

Was it? Georgia's misgivings had returned. Perhaps, she told herself, her personal problems were beginning to cast their pall over daily life – and if she were not careful they would suck Luke in too. So far her lack of success in conceiving a child had seemed to affect only her, but where Luke was concerned she could never be sure. He was a past master at disguising his true feelings – admirable in a publisher, but it could be tricky in a husband. This afternoon she would force herself to push the personal aside, however, and concentrate on what might, after all, be an enjoyable walk.

In the two years she and Luke had lived at Medlars they had walked most of the local footpaths, including most of the old Pilgrims' Way. Medlars was only a mile or two from here and quite near the track. Their walks had always been towards Old Wives Lees or Charing, however, not eastwards to Chartham Hatch, probably because of the urban sprawl as

Canterbury was approached, and so this stretch of the Old
Road was unfamiliar.

The name 'the Old Road' had a touch of magic about it,
Georgia thought, giving it an atmosphere of its own, at times
almost creepy and at times comfortably humbling. It brought
back an age when travelling was an experience to be enjoyed
in itself and a pilgrimage a devotional journey that added
meaning to life. It could also be a holiday, it could be made
for penance, it could be to pray for the restoration of health,
it could even be an escape from paying taxes, since pilgrims
were exempt from such burdens – let the Chancellor put that
one in his Budget! It could be for all those reasons that pilgrims
took to the road. When a shrine was visited, they could buy
badges and other signs to fix to their robes or hat, as proof
that they'd visited the saint. They rode if they were rich, they
walked if they weren't. They went barefoot if seeking penance.

Georgia had a fleeting image of Julian Wayncroft hobbling
along barefooted and falling on his knees in penance once he
got to the shrine. King Henry II had done so after he ordered
Becket's murder, and the relations between Julian and
Valentine seemed to lack as much cordiality as those between
the King and Becket.

She began to cheer up as the group moved off from the
pub, heading for the track that ran along the top of the village.
When it was established in the 1970s, the North Downs Way
followed the route of the Old Road or Pilgrims' Way, where
that was still possible. If she remembered correctly, the route
of the Old Road was unclear between Chilham, Old Wives
Lees and Chillingham, but from this point on the new track
was following the original one. The group even began to look
a merry band, with the banner held aloft, the hum of voices
and even singing to the lutes, not to mention a peculiar
clanking, which came, she was told, from the wooden balls
attached to the tops of the walking staffs.

'Very traditional,' Luke remarked.

'Are you two new recruits?'

Georgia turned round at hearing the unfamiliar voice behind
her. It belonged to a woman perhaps in her early fifties, whose
identity was easy to guess. She was wearing a long black
cassock, presumably the nearest she could get to a medieval
pilgrim priest's habit.

'Very temporary.' Georgia stopped to wait for the vicar to catch up. 'We're merely hangers-on for the afternoon.'

'Splendid. Very medieval. I'm sure that's what the villagers must have done in the old days. Turned out to follow the pilgrims, and then went back home when they were tired – thus winning both ways.' The vicar was having to shout over the noise now. 'Anne Fanshawe,' she introduced herself. 'Vicar of Chillingham, together with several other parishes in the neighbourhood.'

Georgia introduced herself and Luke. She liked the look of Anne Fanshawe. A strong face, but a kind one, she thought. 'Luke's a friend of Tim's,' she explained, 'so he couldn't resist joining in.'

'Luke Frost? You're the publisher, aren't you?'

'I am. Currently planning a new book on tea shops for pilgrims,' he joked.

Anne Fanshawe didn't laugh. 'That would be good. The Old Road's a shivery experience at times.'

'Is that why Fright Wood got its name?' Georgia had been studying the map, and she had seen the name on the way to Chartham Hatch. The track was running along the hillside, and at first there had been apple orchards on their right, and in the distance the blue haze over the fertile Weald of Kent. Now they were walking past woodland, little changed, Georgia imagined, over the centuries, save that it must have been much thicker on both sides then. Apart from the Old Road, this hillside would have been impenetrable.

'I doubt it,' Anne replied. 'This is Peacock Wood.' She seemed disinclined to say more, and at that moment the music stopped and there was silence, save for marching steps. And no bird sang, Georgia thought uneasily, remembering Keats' creepy poem – and no pilgrims either. Just an eerie silence, broken at last by one solitary bird's warning call.

Luke went ahead to chat to Tim, and Anne fell back to talk to someone else, leaving Georgia briefly alone as the woodland closed in on both sides. Trees were arching over the path to form a tunnel, with the sun blotted out. As the trees began to thin out she could see open countryside ahead. But then it happened. Her stomach churned, with a sickness that seemed to be stifling her. The path turned a corner, and the woodland was almost behind her. Ahead, however, the line of walkers looked misty, almost unreal, as though they were the pilgrims who had trodden the Old Road in the past. Luke was not far in front, but even so she felt isolated, nauseous and choking with no reason. She recognized these symptoms all too clearly as she forced herself to stumble onwards. They had nothing to do with lunch, and everything to do with the place through which she was walking.

This path, that wood, smelt of decay and evil. Somewhere near here violence had taken place in the past, with the victim crying out for justice. His emotions had been stamped like 'fingerprints' on the atmosphere for those who followed to pick up. She'd met them before, and now they were engulfing her again. Before the gunshot that had put Peter in a wheel-chair, he had been in the police force, and there he had acquired a reputation for 'intuition' that sparked off investigations into past cases. It had not been intuition, however, it was their shared gift – if gift it was – for sensing fingerprints, and now they put it to good use in the cases taken on by Marsh & Daughter.

Just as she could stand it no longer, the nausea passed, suddenly and completely. The misty sun cleared, and she could see Valentine Harper ahead with Aletta. She could hear Julian's loud bray, she could see Tim Hurst. They all seemed united in one common purpose, and she was an outsider, caught up in a situation she did not understand. But that was today's dark puzzle, not the reeking claws of yesterday she had experienced while walking out of that wood.

She ran to catch Luke up, and he turned to grin at her. The grin faded as he saw her face.

'What's wrong?'

'I'm OK now.' That was because she was clear of that wood. Luke didn't believe her though, and he put his arm round her.

'Life getting to you, sweetheart?'

She wondered if he meant their personal problem, but it wasn't that. Not today.

Luke knew only about Marsh & Daughter's cases, not about what sparked them off. She could never bring herself to tell him, since their cases stood up by themselves and the reasons for their choices lay between herself and Peter. She sometimes thought Luke might suspect that there was more to the selection than she told him, and that he might feel excluded. She would tell him one day, she told herself. But not today.

She began to breathe more easily now, but Luke was still anxious.

'We'll go back right now,' he said.

Back to that wood? She couldn't, even with Luke's support. She clutched at him as he turned round, and Anne Fanshawe, coming up behind them, must have noticed something wrong. 'Nasty place, Peacock Wood. It always gives me the shivers. It must be the murder.'

So she had been right, Georgia realized without surprise. Violence had taken place there. 'Murder?' she repeated.

'Years ago, of course,' Anne said hastily. 'Another age, another country. I've only been back in Kent seven years, and only four of them as vicar of Chillingham, so I don't feel personally involved.'

Anne was clearly sorry she had ever mentioned the word murder, and Georgia felt torn between a need to know more and her instinctive desire to get as far from this place as possible. 'Was the murderer ever found?' she managed to ask.

'No.' Then, perhaps feeling she had been too abrupt, Anne continued, 'Look, I'm no historian, and I don't know that much about it. I've three other churches to look after besides Chillingham.'

Did the lady protest too much? Georgia must have looked as disturbed as she felt, for Anne looked at her doubtfully. 'You're still a bit white. I'll drive you both back to the village after we've seen the jolly troupers off at Canterbury. My car's in the car park there.'

Simon was getting ready for the evening trade when Georgia and Luke arrived at the Three Peacocks, but he was eager for news of Tim and abandoned his kitchen duties. 'How did it go?'

'Good send-off,' Luke told him. 'The pilgrims duly received a public blessing at the Cathedral entrance with at least three press there, plus local TV News.'

'Tim do OK?' Simon asked. 'He was pretty wound up about it.' Tim had planned and given a short speech after the blessing.

'Fine,' Georgia told him. 'After that, one of the pilgrims tripped over a cable, and somebody who said he was Herbert of Bosham and doubling De Brito got his sword tangled up in his cloak.'

Simon laughed. 'That'll be Matthew Moon, Lisa's elder son. Derek, who's looking after the bar for me, is the younger. Rotten typecasting. De Brito's one of the chief villains, and Matthew's the gentlest soul in the village.'

'Looks as if Becket's life may be spared after all then,' Luke commented.

'Take my Matthew away from his carpentry and he'd trip over his own feet.' A pleasant looking elderly lady – perhaps in her late sixties, and with a cloud of white hair around a round rosy face – emerged from the kitchen area into the bar. Simon introduced her as Lisa Moon. Despite the stereotyped farmer's wife appearance, Georgia was aware of shrewd eyes busy summing her up.

'You're not in the play then?' Georgia asked.

'Bless you no. Matthew's in it, and my granddaughter Tess is too. That's enough for one family. The rest of us get on with our work.'

'The Moons pretty well run this village,' Simon joked. 'Matthew's wife Christine runs the village shop, Matthew's the carpenter, Derek decorates and builds. Been here for centuries, haven't you, Lisa?'

'Clive was the Moon, not me,' she replied. 'My husband, he was. As for me, I was an incomer way back. Lived all of six miles away, I did. Just about accepted now.'

'Tess, Lisa's granddaughter, is playing Fair Rosamund, the king's beautiful mistress, whom the wicked Queen Eleanor tried to poison, just like Snow White,' Simon said. 'Lisa—' Simon broke off, perhaps aware that Lisa wasn't laughing.

'Long time ago, Simon,' she said.

Georgia watched them curiously. There had surely been a note of warning in Lisa's voice. More subtext?

TWO

'Can we look in on Peter before we go home?' Georgia asked.

Luke's car was still sitting in solitary state in the Three Peacocks' car park when they left, and that did not look good for pub trade this evening. They debated whether to eat there themselves, but she was impatient to see Peter. She had a childish instinct to share her experience in the wood, and to tell him that there had indeed been a murder there. Perhaps even, she ruefully acknowledged, she had a suppressed hope that her father would assure her that there was nothing mysterious about Peacock Wood and that she need have no nightmares over it.

Luke nodded. 'Fine by me. Will Janie be there?' Janie was Peter's fiancée, but the relationship was an up and down one. Luke was certain that Janie and Peter would make a successful long term relationship, whereas Georgia was none too sure.

'Try prising her away.' She spoke more sharply than she had meant to, and when Luke looked surprised, she regretted it.

Sure enough, though, as she rang the doorbell, then used her key (as was their standard arrangement), she saw Peter in his office on the left and a glum-looking Janie watching TV in the living room on the right. In her late forties, Janie was about ten years older than Georgia, but they got on well, which was surprising given how different they were in most ways. Janie favoured the romantic approach to life, although that hid a very practical side indeed, while Georgia was aware that she herself took life head on, hiding her own romantic side. She longed to sweep around in floating romantic dresses as Janie did, but never had the nerve.

'Hi,' Janie got up to greet them. 'Come to join me in my solitary confinement?'

'I need a word with Peter first,' Georgia said apologetically, knowing she would be delaying him even longer. That was easy enough, and she wondered how many evenings Janie spent like this. She wasn't living here permanently, and therefore had to travel over each time, only to find, no doubt, that all too often Peter considered the computer more interesting – as Janie must view it.

Peter tore his gaze away from the offending computer as Georgia went in. 'Ah,' he said complacently, 'I wondered if you'd pop in. Fingerprints?'

'So you knew.' Georgia was indignant, but not greatly surprised. 'You might have warned me about that wood.'

He looked hurt. 'I *didn't* know. Anyway, if I had warned you, it wouldn't have been a fair test.'

'What of?' She knew all too well the answer to that one, but would make Peter pay for not confiding in her. 'That unsolved murder?'

'So *you* knew,' he said accusingly.

'That's *all* I know. Tell me.'

'Murder on the Old Road in 1967. A new one on me, although we live so near to it, but I didn't move here with your mother until after that. You were a mere toddler. I've spent hours on the Internet since I got back, checking *The Times* and everything else that I could click on or read.'

'What set you off?'

'Simon, our friendly but desperate publican.'

'Desperate about trade or Tim, do you think?'

'The former more obviously. And the murder—' Peter paused for effect.

She had to know. 'Whose was it?'

'Hugh Wayncroft, lord of the manor and Julian's father.'

She hadn't expected that, and found it astonishing. This afternoon Julian had been marching in pilgrimage right past the place where his father had been murdered. True, it was forty years ago, but even so, how could he bear to go there? Then she did her arithmetic. Julian would scarcely have been born or would have been only a toddler when the murder happened, and so his father had no physical reality for him. But for his half brother? Hugh had been his stepfather, and in 1967 Valentine would have been about Sebastian Wayncroft's age today. Was that significant or was she building without bricks?

'No one was charged,' Peter continued, happy now that he had taken her by surprise, 'and now you confirm there were fingerprints. Wouldn't that suggest there are still outstanding issues? Where did you feel these fingerprints?'

'At the far end of Peacock Wood – that's the first one you come to on the Old Road going towards Canterbury. You can see it from the village. Was he killed there, do you know?'

'Yes.'

'Shot during a shooting party?' she asked. That might explain why no one was charged – it could easily have been an accident. Then she realized Peter was looking smug, which meant he was holding something back.

'No. Strangled, and on a pilgrimage.'

'*What*?'

'Just like the one you joined today,' Peter told her. She could see he was enjoying winding her up. 'In 1967 there was a pilgrimage from Winchester to Canterbury to stage Tennyson's *Becket*.'

'They have this pilgrimage and play every *year*?'

'No. It's the first time since 1967.'

'But that really is creepy.' Too creepy, she thought with foreboding.

'Someone had the bright idea that it would be good to recreate it. The pilgrimage and play presumably, rather than the murder. The plan is to put the village on the map, rather than just to promote the play. They had an identical plan in 1967, which doesn't seem to have come to anything. You'd think the murder would have achieved that by itself, but everything went quiet. The sixties pilgrimage, as is this one, was to celebrate the July anniversary. As Aletta said, winter is not a good time for pilgrimages, and my guess is that the monks realized that it wouldn't attract so many pilgrims as the summer date. And we think *we're* publicity conscious. In 1220, fifty years after Becket was murdered, his tomb was moved from the crypt to the Trinity Chapel, and fifty years after that came the first Jubilee remembrance of it. I wonder if the 1967 Chillingham pilgrimage was some sort of trial run for a really big do in 1970?'

'Was there one?'

'Not so far as I can see.' Peter frowned. 'Strange that. The excitement all died down again, along with all reference to Hugh Wayncroft's murder. Chillingham seems to have sunk back into slumber again until this year.'

'Because of the murder, do you think?'

'Perhaps. But, if so, why the repeat performance?'

'Doesn't Simon know why?'

'I didn't ask. Of course, he wasn't in Chillingham in 1967.'

'Nor was the vicar, the Reverend Fanshawe.'

'Oh yes, she was.' Peter looked smug at pulling this new rabbit out of his hat. 'Her name was then Anne Riding, daughter of the village historian and teacher Bill Riding. She was ten years old and played the role of Geoffrey in *Becket*, the small son of Fair Rosamund, the king's mistress.'

Again, Georgia was taken aback. She was sure Anne had made no mention of that, only that she had been back in Kent seven years. Perhaps there had been no intention to mislead her, and yet every antenna Georgia possessed was waving as furiously as a hazel twig in the hands of a water-diviner. Was there a conspiracy of silence in Chillingham? Or had life simply moved on after a tragic episode? But if the latter, surely some people must still feel the wounds.

'Go ahead. Tell me,' she said.

She could see Peter was itching to spill out the whole story, and she wanted to hear it. Hugh Wayncroft had been murdered over forty years previously, but the family was still at odds with itself, and perhaps Chillingham itself was too. In a small village unrest could spread from the centre out.

At the back of her mind she registered that Janie would be fuming if she and Peter stayed talking much longer, but consoled herself that, far from being annoyed, it was possible Janie might be grateful. This puzzle, virtually on his own doorstep, might distract Peter from his other preoccupations, which she suspected were also driving Janie crazy.

Peter needed no urging. 'Let's start with Hugh Wayncroft's murder. He was forty-five, married, with a small child, Julian. His body was found in woods close by the Old Road – or, if you, prefer Pilgrims' Way – which at that point is now the North Downs Way. He was still clad in his Becket costume, but the pilgrimage was nearing its end. The company had walked the whole length of the Old Road from Winchester to Canterbury, so far as was possible, because by 1967 parts of it had long disappeared. Tennyson's play had been performed in Canterbury, and on Sunday, the ninth of July, the happy pilgrims had walked the last few miles back from their triumph to an intended celebratory welcome in the Three Peacocks.'

'I wonder who sparked off the notion that repeating it would be a good idea. And what happened to the final celebration? Was it still held?'

'As to the first question: no idea. As for the second, yes, in a way. With the largish cast, and all the production staff and so, over forty people were involved. Only some time after they had reached the Three Peacocks, where the publican Fred Miller had arranged for the welcome home, was it realized that Hugh Wayncroft was no longer with them. When it was discovered he hadn't returned to Chillingham Place either, a search party set out and found his body. He'd been strangled, and there the matter rests.'

'What do you mean, *rests*? There must have been a police investigation. Motives? Passing tramps? MI5 plot . . .?'

'I haven't had time to consult Mike yet—'

'But you will,' Georgia said resignedly. Mike Gilroy had been Peter's sergeant for some years before Peter's enforced retirement, and Peter was under the happy impression that Mike liked nothing better than to break off from the pressure of being Detective Superintendent Gilroy and throw himself into the archives of his and other Kentish police areas in order to 'help Peter with his enquiries'.

'Possibly.' Peter's turn to be indignant. 'Neither the local papers nor *The Times* carried the story after the initial furore. That suggests to me that there was plenty of gossip, but it was wrapped up in the small local community of Chillingham and didn't wing its way beyond its boundaries.'

'So for motive – first, look at the family,' Georgia said. 'Is eagerness to grab the estate on the cards?'

'Dear cynical daughter, I have clearly trained you well. Money is usually the root of all evil. But not, it seems, in this case.'

'Because Julian was only a year or two old, and therefore unlikely to be planning a murder,' she chimed in. 'Valentine as a stepson would not inherit. What about Hugh's widow, anxious to get her hands on the property while she could rule in Julian's name? Or come to that, as Valentine would have been twenty-odd in 1967, maybe the widow saw her chance to set her first son up for life as well as her son by Hugh?'

Peter looked smug. 'Good one, but here's where the family history really kicks in. Hugh was the *younger* brother of Robert

Wayncroft, who only died two years ago. Robert seems a mysterious character. The Wayncroft family has lived in Chillingham Place probably since medieval days; certainly they were well installed by Tudor times. They are, or were, staunchly Roman Catholic in religion, and must therefore have come not only under Tudor pressure, but also under even heavier oppression during the Civil War. Nevertheless the Wayncroft family somehow managed to hang on to its lands, probably because it's not a sizeable estate.

'Robert Wayncroft inherited the estate from his grandfather unexpectedly young; it was during the Second World War when he was a lieutenant in the army. He survived the war, but after it he seems to have had some religious conversion or calling, because thereafter he devoted his life to charitable work, much of it overseas. In 1957, therefore, he decided to give the manor and estate to his younger brother Hugh, who had recently married one Jessica Harper, a widow with a small child – our Valentine.

'There was only one proviso,' Peter continued, 'and that was that if Hugh predeceased him then the whole estate would revert to Robert. Accordingly, when Hugh was murdered in 1967, the whole caboodle did revert to Robert. He never married or had any known children, and therefore after Hugh's death he bequeathed the bulk of the estate, including Chillingham Place, back to Hugh's descendants, currently represented by Julian and his son Sebastian. It passed to them on Robert's death two years ago. Until then Hugh's family had lived in the manor house for a peppercorn rent by courtesy of Robert; the house had been turned into several apartments. For the last five years of his life Robert lived in one of them, Hugh's widow Jessica in another, and Julian another. I gather from Simon that Valentine left the village for many years, and only returned on Robert's death. He, too, now lives in Chillingham Place, courtesy of Julian – presumably.'

Georgia grappled with this oddity. 'So the widow's eagerness to grab the estate is ruled out as a motive for getting rid of Hugh, as is Valentine's. They needed to keep Hugh alive in order to be sure of their future there. Robert could have turned them out lock, stock and barrel when Hugh died, for all they knew at the time.'

'Talking of time . . .'

Georgia glanced up at Luke's voice to see him standing in the doorway, no doubt dispatched by Janie to hurry them up.

Peter was too engrossed to take note of the warning. 'Even Mitchison's *Village Murders* doesn't mention the case, except that it was unsolved. Odd.'

'Maybe the publishers took it out for libel reasons,' Luke intervened in a voice heavy with meaning.

Peter glared at him. 'Quite possible. Publishers are notoriously overcareful in such matters.'

Luke grinned. 'They have some crazy idea that they'd prefer to stay in business.'

Peter brushed this aside. 'It's a question of where we go next.'

'To join Janie and me. There's a question of supper.' Luke's pointed remark was again ignored.

'Mrs Moon strikes me as a possibly entry point to the village community,' Peter continued blithely.

'I agree. Simon said the Moon family rules Chillingham.'

'Did he tell you she played Fair Rosamund in the 1967 production?'

'No.' Georgia was intrigued, trying to imagine the Lisa she had met as a young and beautiful blonde. It was hard to do so. Her involvement in the production must have been what Simon had been about to mention before Lisa stopped him. Why though? Lisa would surely have been proud of it. 'Did she tell you anything about the murder?'

'Not a whisper. I found out about it from the local newspaper review of the play. Our Mrs Moon obviously believes in keeping a very tight mouth indeed.'

Unlike Janie, who blew in like a storm cloud to join her protest to Luke's. 'What on earth's keeping you, Peter? I thought David was a workaholic but you beat him hollow.'

'My fault, Janie,' Georgia said immediately. 'I shouldn't have come.' Who was David? she wondered.

'Yes, you should,' Peter shot back. His expression conveyed the message that Janie didn't own this house – or own him. Georgia's heart sank. There was trouble ahead.

Janie cast them both a scathing look. 'Peter doesn't need any encouragement to glue himself to the computer.'

'Why don't we all go out to the pub?' Luke quickly suggested. 'Then none of us will have to cook.'

Thank heavens for Luke. Georgia clutched at this solution, especially as she saw Janie's face lighten. Battle lines were being drawn all too quickly between her and Peter. Something was clearly amiss with their relationship, but Georgia knew better than to intervene. If she did, both of them might turn on her. Far better to go to the pub!

The White Lion in Haden Shaw always produced excellent food, and once they were established inside the familiar bar, Georgia felt she could relax. Tempers resumed their normal levels, and at least a truce seemed declared.

On the short walk back to Peter's house, where Luke had left their car, however, Janie raised the subject again. 'Sorry, Georgia. My fault. Things have been bad ever since we got back from Linz. I thought if I went there with him, it would not only confirm what happened to your brother, but lay it to rest for good, so that Peter and I could start with a clean slate. It hasn't worked that way. He's still obsessed with Rick, so if you and he are embarking on a new case, I suppose I should applaud it. At least I could put my oar in from time to time. Up till now he's been emotionally living in Austria, and he doesn't want company there. Not mine, anyway.'

Georgia froze. The mystery of her brother's Rick's disappearance in France many years ago had at last seemed solved, and so it had been as far as she was concerned. Not for Peter, however. He had insisted on travelling to Austria to visit the relevant authorities and demand physical evidence of how Rick had died. Mental certitude was not enough. Georgia should have been accompanying Peter herself, and she still felt guilty that she had not been able to do so. Even though Luke kept pointing out that she could have done nothing else, it still hurt, and in her darker moments she felt she had betrayed both Rick and Peter.

By terrible coincidence the date for her second round of IVF treatment had unexpectedly materialized for the very week the Linz trip had been booked and travel, hotels and appointments fixed. She had agonized over whether to put off her own appointment, but that meant more waiting when the clock was already ticking so loudly on her ever conceiving a child. Keep your appointment, said Peter. He would go with Janie.

Keep your appointment, said Luke. Didn't that suggest that
he was as hell-bent on having children as she was? Every
time she asked him he denied it was that important, but she
argued to herself that he could have been saying that for her
sake. So she *had* kept her appointment, and Janie had stepped
into her place eagerly, it had to be said. Result? Georgia was
no further forward on her own desired result, but Peter returned
from Austria with as much evidence about Rick as there would
ever be. Short of going for permission for exhumation of
several unidentified bodies there was nothing more they could
do. They had, Janie told them, even been shown the records
of the Omega Seamaster wristwatch he had been wearing, but
Peter had insisted Rick's had been a different model, a De
Ville, and was adamant that further enquiries should be made.
Where, when and what? she had asked. He had no idea, but
the subject was not closed, and Janie was clearly at breaking
point.

'It will pass, Janie.' Georgia sounded more confident than
she was. 'I'll talk to him.'

Janie shrugged. 'You shouldn't need to. If it is not now,
yet it will come. Isn't that what Hamlet said? David—'

'Who is this David?' Georgia asked curiously as Janie broke
off.

Janie flushed. 'The new head of the Fernbourne board of
trustees. He's making things happen at the museum. It's
exciting now. I've got the go-ahead to follow up my own
ideas too.' Janie ran the Fernbourne Museum, which was
devoted to the works of the Fernbourne Five, a group of
writers and artists working in the years before, during and
just after World War II.

Georgia put all the enthusiasm she could muster into her
reply. 'That's good. It could make all the difference, your
having such support there.'

Janie wasn't fooled. 'It does. But I love Peter, Georgia.'

THREE

C ould a village really be as peaceful as Chillingham appeared? Georgia parked her car in the church car park, having decided on a peaceful ramble round the village before deciding on her next move. No community was ever as tranquil as it appeared to the outsider. It was possible the murder of Hugh Wayncroft might still be leaving its mark on the village, but it was equally possible that the tensions of today might be due to some completely different reason. It was her job to weigh up whether past or present was ruling Chillingham, and from that Marsh & Daughter could decide whether or not to look further into his death. The subtext – that word kept cropping up – was all important.

'People don't change,' Peter had said. 'Despite all the new houses and incomers, there's always that bottom layer waiting to be discovered if you dig deep enough. As with people. All of them, all of us. So find out what makes Chillingham tick, Georgia.'

Mission understood. How to put it into practice, however, was rather more problematic, she had thought wryly.

Now she was here it seemed even more difficult. She'd left this visit until after the weekend in the interests of not appearing to be on a witch-hunt, but on a Monday morning, Chillingham almost seemed to be mocking her as it slumbered in the sunshine. You can't get at me, it seemed to be saying. How could you hope to – you're an outsider.

Well, she could and she would. In a place this small, she would begin with the church, which was dedicated to St Thomas. She presumed that was Thomas Becket, rather than the apostle or St Thomas Aquinas. Given its situation, there seemed little doubt, even though, from its late medieval architecture, this building might not have been standing at the time most of the pilgrimages took place. It was positioned on a corner of the lane that led up through the village to the North Downs and an even narrower lane that followed the boundary of the Chillingham estate and eventually wound round to Chilham.

Inside the church it was cool and calm. It was secure in itself; it had seen centuries and people come and go. The Queen Anne arms were painted on a panel above the door as all churches had at one time to display, as if to declare that the earthly monarchs come and go, but the church of God endures. There were monuments to the world wars and at the far end a Wayncroft chapel, with the splendid full length Elizabethan tombs of Sir Edward Wayncroft and his wife Cecilia. Interesting, she thought, that somewhere the Sir had become lost over the years. There was also a brass on the floor to a Sir Geoffrey Wayncroft, who according to the inscription had died in defence of his faith. This, too, was Tudor. She remembered that the Wayncrofts were Catholic, but at some periods of British history they would have had to have kept that very secret indeed. The most recent memorial was to Hugh Wayncroft, a simple brass plaque with only his name and the dates of his birth and his death inscribed on it.

She wandered into the churchyard to see if she could find Hugh's grave there, but there was no sign of it, although there were some later Wayncroft tombs. Nevertheless, it was a helpful guide to the families that had dominated this village for a long time. Moons were prominent, so was another family, the Painters, and there were plenty of Millers to be seen. Hadn't the Three Peacocks publican in 1967 been a Miller? She found Bill Riding's grave and wondered what part he had played in the 1967 production. If Anne had played a role in it, her parents must surely have also been involved.

Her eye was caught by a wicket gate. Public footpath? There was no indication that it was, but it would be natural enough for a public footpath to lead to the church from the Old Road and beyond. The meadow on to which the gate opened looked as if it might stretch as far as the Old Road itself. A few sheep were grazing in it, and at the far end she could see some stone ruins, perhaps of a former barn. Curiosity made her walk over to them to have a closer look, with sheep scattering reproachfully from her path.

As she drew closer she could see that the ruins were more substantial than she had thought. There seemed to be two former buildings, one adjoining the other, and she changed her mind about their having been barns. The larger of the two had the remains of four walls at varying heights and was roughly twenty feet long and ten feet wide, with the entrance in the narrower wall. Not a barn, she decided. It was the wrong shape. The smaller building abutting it was in better shape, with an arched doorway still intact. She decided the larger one might have been a chapel, and from the look of the ruins it preceded the church in date. With its position so relatively near to the Old Road that was highly possible. She remembered St Martha's Chapel near Guildford, which she had visited once with Luke. Pilgrims needed not only wayside inns for physical refreshment but religious sustenance too.

What had this smaller building been used for, she asked herself, peering through its doorway. Inside the small enclosed area was a further arched wall, which sheltered a gated area covered with a modern grid. It was, or had been, a well, but Health and Safety had been at work here with a vengeance. No one was going to prise that iron grid off in a hurry, even if they managed to get through the iron gate.

Unusual, she thought.

She must have spoken out loud because a voice behind her made her jump. 'Isn't it just.'

It was the Reverend Anne Fanshawe.

'Sorry,' Georgia said. 'I hope I'm not trespassing.'

'Actually yes, but no problem. Everyone thinks they own this place, and who's to say they're not right?'

There was a note of bitterness in Anne's voice that made Georgia even more curious and, mindful of her mission, she pushed further. Anne Fanshawe was a lady who appeared easily able to resist pressure, if she wanted to.

'Both these buildings look interesting,' Georgia observed brightly. 'An old chapel?'

'Yes.'

Anne did not seem disposed to say more. Interesting in itself. There had to be a reason why not. 'A pilgrims' chapel?' Georgia pressed. 'Dedicated to St Thomas?'

'Possibly.'

Very dismissive. 'And the well?'

'Just a well.' Anne's smile took away some of the sting, but her message was plain.

Georgia ignored it. 'Like St Thomas's well at Otford? The one that, legend has it, he produced by striking the ground with his staff?'

'Legends say a lot of things, and there are quite a few wells all over England *said* to be created by Becket. The facts behind them are few and far between.'

There Georgia agreed with her, her mind switching over to Peter's desperate longing for proof about Rick's death. She forced it back again. 'Is there a village history published? Or a website? I'd like to read more about them.'

'Neither, I'm afraid.'

No doubt about it. The vicar, for whatever reason, was not talking. Very well. Georgia decided to press further. 'There must be information somewhere. I understand your father was the village historian?' Nothing except an obstinate set to Anne's mouth. Her best chance now, Georgia reasoned, was to say nothing, look enquiring and wait. It worked.

'Yes, he was,' Anne said unwillingly at last, 'but he died before he could publish anything. I left the village in the late seventies with my mother and for good, as I then thought.'

'But you came back.'

'As you see.'

Subject closed, and unreopenable, judging by Anne's expression. Very well, Georgia would use another tack. 'I heard you were in the 1967 production of *Becket*. Did you walk in the pilgrimage too? The one in which Hugh Wayncroft was killed?'

That must have hit a nerve. Anne flushed. 'I don't like fencing, Georgia. So let me be clear. I've read Marsh & Daughter's books. I like them, and admire what you've achieved in some cases. But Chillingham and Hugh Wayncroft's death are not going to form one of them. It's the last thing I need.'

I need? Georgia noted the emphasis. 'The murder was unsolved,' was all she said, 'and unsolved cases can have lasting effects, both on families and on communities.'

'Don't you think I know that?' Anne flashed angrily at her. 'But Robert Wayncroft *wanted* it to stay unsolved. And before you make assumptions, I'm not breaking any secrets of the confessional; his views were publicly known. So let Hugh rest in peace.'

'If you're sure he is.'

'You believe in ghosts?' Anne was furious now.

'No.'

'Then you've answered your own question.'

'You told me Peacock Wood gave you the shivers.'

Anne stared at her. 'I was trying to reassure you.'

'You said you don't like fencing.'

'Shivers are subjective.'

'But we shared them.'

Anne glared at her, and Georgia watched her as she walked away. She hadn't handled that too well, she thought ruefully. Then her hopes rose as Anne paused and came back.

'I'm not going to let you win, Georgia. I'd like to, but I can't. So I have to tell you a certain amount about myself. I warn you it will be the minimum necessary. Agreed?'

'Agreed.'

'I came back to Kent in 2002 when I was ordained. My husband had died and that had led me to take holy orders. I was a curate at St Edith's in Canterbury for a year or two and then came here as vicar.

'I met Robert Wayncroft,' she continued steadily, 'by chance in Canterbury. He returned to England in 2002 after many years away. I knew him, of course, from my childhood, and he told me he proposed to spend his remaining years in Chillingham Place. He was eighty-two then, and he lived on for another five years. He was a Roman Catholic by upbringing, but had a great affinity with the local church – naturally, since the living had been in the gift of Chillingham Place for centuries. I remained in touch with Robert, and he suggested I apply for it when the former vicar retired. So that's me. Anything more you'd like to know about him before I talk about the other Wayncrofts?'

Anne looked a belligerent figure . . . or was she merely defensive? Georgia wondered. 'No, and thank you,' she replied. She would have liked to have asked what had made her accept Robert Wayncroft's suggestion, but she couldn't probe that far too soon.

Nevertheless, Anne did add, 'We remained friends because Robert was, by then, living in his flat in Chillingham Place. I shared his views about development in the village. We both opposed it, and I still do.'

Anne was looking at her in such a challenging manner that Georgia decided to take that no further. Another put-down would be the result if she did and perhaps bring this tenuous communication to an abrupt halt.

'And Hugh's death?' she asked. 'Why did Robert want it to

remain unsolved?' Anne's body language was almost shouting 'no more' so Georgia added, 'Unless I understand that, Peter and I can't judge whether the reasons are sufficiently valid for us to leave the subject alone.'

'Because the murder was history by the time Robert returned here for good.'

'Fencing?' Keep your voice neutral, Georgia told herself, or you'll get nowhere.

Anne managed a grin. 'If I say nothing more, will you still go on ferreting?'

'Yes. I'd have to, don't you see?'

'Unfortunately, yes. So it's better it comes from me than you upset other people by barging in to a situation you don't understand.'

Thanks, Georgia thought wryly, but there was no point in arguing.

'Just now you said that unsolved cases can have lasting effects on communities. I presume therefore you think this is true in the case of Chillingham.'

'So far it seems to be.'

'If so, it goes back further than 1967, so my father explained to me. Until last century, the Wayncrofts owned nearly all the property in the village and ran its affairs, mostly fairly but traditionally. Even though property had begun to change hands, by the time the 1960s had arrived the village was a backwater and money hard to come by. What happened was that it became split between those who wanted to modernize it – such as Fred Miller at the pub, for instance and Clive Moon – and those who most definitely didn't.'

'Including the Wayncrofts presumably.'

'Yes and no. Hugh was a stickler for tradition, but young Val was a tearaway and joined the opposition. So did Jessica, Hugh's widow. His death stopped the opposition in its track, but Robert always feared it would rear its head again. It split the village.'

Georgia frowned. 'Sorry. I don't see how our finding Hugh's murderer could affect that issue.'

'Progress,' Anne explained. 'In the shape of Val Harper. He left the village for France in the 1980s, as it was clear – at he saw it – that the village was going nowhere. He had the luck to marry into the Bonneur family, and he settled in France for good. His wife was well-heeled, to say the least, and part of the old aristocracy. Typical Val, though. A keen eye for the main chance – only to make a mess of it. He played around and landed up divorced and penniless, so as soon as Robert, who couldn't stand him, died, back comes Val on his white charger, determined to rescue the village from oblivion. It's the one thing Julian and he agree on, although I suspect that's only because Julian's banking career may be faltering and Chillingham Place eats money. This current farce of a pilgrimage is one result of their so-called united front.'

'It was their idea?'

'Val's in the driving seat, I suspect.'

'But you don't approve.' Georgia was surprised. She had assumed Julian would be a staunch traditionalist. 'Sooner or later there are bound to be housing estates popping up here and goodness knows what else, so that would bring Chillingham into prominence whether it likes it or not,' she pointed out. 'Why do you feel so strongly about not supporting Val and Julian's plans? What do they have in mind?'

'Quite a lot,' Anne said firmly. 'I can't do anything about housing projects, but I can stop this tourist attraction nonsense. I *can't* approve the principle.' She must have caught sight of Georgia's astonished face. 'Robert asked me to oppose it, Georgia.'

Georgia grappled with this. 'Why you, not Julian? He's the heir.'

'Because Julian is all for encouraging tourism, and so is his mother. Robert was right. He said it would all blow up again once he was dead.'

Georgia clung to the one thing that seemed to make sense. 'His mother? Jessica? Is she still alive?'

'And kicking.' Anne paused. 'Ask the Moon family about St Thomas and the Wayncrofts, and tell them I sent you.'

Anne's amused look as she left had irritated Georgia. It implied she had only been allowed to see the tip of the iceberg where Chillingham was concerned. She supposed this was fair enough. She might have felt the same if a relative stranger had barged into her and Peter's private lives, but having told her some of the story, Anne should have concluded it. Georgia felt she was being manipulated, and she didn't like it. 'Ask

the Moon family' – why? Reluctantly, however, she acknowledged that it was in her interests to play Anne's game if this
were the open sesame to Chillingham. The Three Peacocks it
should be, then, in the hope that Lisa Moon would be on duty.

The pub was virtually empty as Georgia walked in, but on
a Monday this was not surprising, and it certainly suited her
purpose. She tried to picture the Three Peacocks full of gastro
diners, but the sight of those empty tables and the general
look of forlorn expectation of happier times made it hard to
do so. There was no sign of Lisa, and it was Simon who
greeted her cheerfully from behind the bar.

'You're the lunchtime rush all by yourself, Georgia. What
can I get you?'

Georgia ordered a cider, which seemed appropriate in
Kentish apple land. 'How's the pilgrimage faring?'

'Too soon to tell, but the signs are good. Tim said the play
went well in Winchester on Saturday night. A few first night
nerves and dramas, but on the whole a success. The local
papers and citizens gave them a good send-off when they
embarked on the St Swithun's Way yesterday, and Tim's hoping
that the pilgrimage might pick up some national media interest
when it arrives at the North Downs Way, a bit further along.'

'Are you going to meet them at any point?' Georgia knew
that some of the Chillingham pilgrims were in for the whole
two weeks, but others were joining for particular stretches
only.

'The vicar is.'

An odd reply, but Georgia was getting used to that in
Chillingham. 'But not you?'

'Only if I can get Lisa and Derek to cope for a day or two.'

A minor problem, Georgia thought sadly, if this empty pub
were anything to go by.

'I'd like to do bits of it,' Simon continued. 'The Otford to
Wrotham stretch for a start – and, of course, the walk from
here to Canterbury for the last lap. But Tim's laden with
leaflets encouraging residents along the way to join the
pilgrims and drop in here for lunch, so someone has to be
here to run the shop.'

'No problem, Simon.' Lisa appeared from the kitchens to
fetch a bottle from the bar. 'I can cook sausage and chips for
a day or two.'

'Very funny,' Simon grunted. 'Lisa,' he explained to Georgia, 'is a superb cook of everything from pie and mash to truffle soufflé.'

'No need to butter me up,' Lisa returned cheerfully. 'I've enough fat of my own.'

Georgia seized her chance. 'If the Becket tourist trade does increase, you should do well here. I take it that you're both keen supporters?'

'You'd take it wrong then, m'dear,' Lisa replied, not it seemed offended.

'I'm on one side of the fence,' Simon said wryly, 'and Lisa's fixated on the other, aren't you?'

'I need my job, Simon.'

He laughed. 'You can't deny you're all for keeping Chillingham a great big secret, can you?'

'Let sleeping dogs lie, that's what I say.' Lisa looked unfazed.

'As with Hugh Wayncroft's murder?' Georgia put her foot firmly into the playing ground. It was a safe bet, she reasoned, as Simon had not been in the village then, and it would hardly upset Lisa after forty years.

Mistake. Georgia realized that immediately as the atmosphere instantly cooled. 'I'll be seeing to those potatoes, Simon,' Lisa said, turning to go.

'But the vicar said I should tell you she sent me.' The words sounded ridiculously childish, even to her.

'Well, did she now? Fancy that. And now you've told me.' Lisa didn't even bother to turn round, but disappeared through the kitchen door.

'I seem to have upset her.' Georgia could have kicked herself.

'Old history,' Simon muttered uneasily. 'But I don't mind talking about the murder, if that's what interests you. I'm a newcomer after all, and I've always thought it strange that Hugh Wayncroft's death seems a no-go area. Whenever I raised the subject, I would get a polite answer and the conversation would be diverted, so I stopped asking. All I could pick up was that he was probably killed by an itinerant strawberry picker. There used to be a farm not far away.'

'Is that credible?'

'From what I can gather, no. But, as I said, no one opens up about it. It's just water under the bridge now.'

'Even to Lisa?'

'Especially to Lisa.'

'Deliberately buried?'

'The jury's out, but my advice is not to go digging.'

'On the murder itself, perhaps. But the vicar told me the village was split both then and now on the question of promoting itself, and as Hugh Wayncroft was opposed to it, it seems possible it could connect to his death.'

'Did she say that?'

'No. But nor did she explain why the issue seems to have polarized the village as strongly as she implied, both then and now.'

'It's simple enough,' Simon replied savagely. 'Chillingham is crying out to be put on the map, and if it doesn't succeed not only this pub, but also village life will die on its feet. The post office is under threat unless trade picks up, and if it goes the village shop will too, and so will the B and B business. What's left of the Chillingham estate would have to be sold, and the Three Peacocks can't survive much longer. Only the church would be left. The church usually survives.'

'So the vicar is a traditionalist.'

'Not the only one, alas,' Simon admitted.

'Do *you* think the split could be relevant to Hugh Wayncroft's murder? Anne Fanshawe implied it was just as fierce then as now.'

'I wouldn't know, but it seems possible. A lot of livelihoods were at stake, just as they are now, and Hugh Wayncroft was blocking their attempts to progress.'

'But now his son is in favour of it.'

Simon nodded. 'Julian, Aletta, Val and Jessica all are. You'd think the village would follow their lead, but no. And yet Chillingham is doomed to decay if it doesn't.' He paused. 'You know why this pub is called the Three Peacocks?'

'No.' It was an unusual name.

'There's a legend that Chillingham Place always had peacocks roaming round the estate, and that if their number fell below three, the village and Chillingham Place would be finished. Tim told me peacocks were once a symbol of resurrection, and later of the soul, hence the importance of keeping

them happy. Well, there are no peacocks here now, not in
Chillingham Place or in Peacock Wood. Not one. Every so
often Julian has a go at breeding them, but they always die
or disappear. It's mere folklore, of course, but it doesn't help
at a time like this. Chillingham Place eats money, and Julian's
income doesn't bring in enough to ensure its future or even
his. The only way forward is through the tourist trade, so let's
drink to jolly old St Thomas Becket.'

'Did he have specific connections with Chillingham? I
noticed the church is dedicated to him. Would that old chapel
also have been?'

Simon regarded her with some amusement. 'Didn't Anne
tell you?'

'No. I asked her if the well had any legends attached to it,
but she wasn't forthcoming.'

'What a surprise. Anyone would think she wanted to keep
the saint all to herself.'

'Explain please?' Georgia asked hopefully.

'With all the pleasure in the world. The village's future
depends on St Thomas. The ruined chapel and well are both
attributed to him. The medieval tourist trade ordered chapels
to be built after the saint's martyrdom, and the well in particular is a miracle site. St Thomas had a starring role in hundreds
of miracles. The first was reported only three days after his
death, and five years later the then Prior of Canterbury
produced his huge Book of Miracles, all ascribed to Thomas
Becket and taking place not only in Canterbury and the rest
of Britain, but also in France, Scotland, Ireland . . . Everyone
joined in. The Canterbury monks were all too eager to boost
the cathedral's tourist takings, and masses of miracles occurred
both locally and all along the Old Road. Chapels and wells
dedicated to him sprang up like mushrooms, including ours;
as wells and water are a vital part of any religion, so they're
often attached to chapels. So here we are in Chillingham
with a Holy Well of our own, undoubtedly attributable to
St Thomas.'

'With what evidence?'

'The Book of Miracles itself. There was a blind girl called
Seivia who was on her way to Canterbury and had a vision
of St Thomas at Chillingham. He told her that her sight would
be restored and that the first person she would meet would

be a young man called Robert. She should tell him that St Thomas commanded him to build a cross on the spot. Robert duly did so, St Thomas appeared again and struck the ground with his staff, and that's how our chapel and healing well came into being. From then on, the well was reputed to cure any ailment under the sun. As, indeed, for all I know it might have done. Faith can achieve miracles.'

Georgia was impressed. 'Anne kept quiet about Miss Seivia. I can see why you're eager to develop the village now. Even so, the ruins wouldn't attract too many coachloads on their own.'

'Ah, but a school of thought has it that St Thomas's bones are buried here.'

Now that really could draw the crowds. 'Does that have any validity?'

'That's the question. There's some circumstantial evidence that makes it a sporting chance they might be here. There are plenty of theses about where his bones are, or aren't, so I don't see why Chillingham shouldn't be represented too. At Chillingham Place if you're very privileged you can see the St Thomas figure, which was a sort of medieval wooden puppet worked from behind the scenes by monks in the chapel you saw. The punters thought the saint was speaking directly to them, so if he turned his head or the corners of his mouth down, it meant he disapproved of their offering and another groat or two had to go in the cash box. It gave the monks a lot of pocket money when St Thomas blessed the sick. So yes, Chillingham had something special.'

Georgia remembered Luke telling her about something similar. 'Wasn't there one at Boxley Church?'

'Yeah. But the Boxley Rood of Grace has vanished long since. Chillingham is luckier. Bits of the St Thomas figure are safely under lock and key.'

'I can see why Julian and Val Harper want to exploit it. But what would the masses today actually get out of it, apart from seeing the ruins and bits of wood? Even with the legend of the bones, it still doesn't seem enough to do the trick.'

'Believe me, Georgia, the minute the button's pushed for the go-ahead, we're off. Val has it all in hand. There are plans for visitor centres, books, websites, tours, walks, a theatre called Beckets to put on full-scale productions, including a short drama on the murder and miracles. Nothing overlooked – that will also be available on DVD. He's designed badges and tokens copied from the ones bought by the pilgrims at St Thomas's shrine. He's stopped short of providing phials of the saint's blood, thankfully, but all the other plans are in place. There's just one little snag.'

'The opposition party, just as in 1967?'

'Then led by Hugh Wayncroft, with the support of the vicar and half the village.'

'And on the 1967 pro side?'

'Jessica Wayncroft, which can't have made for domestic bliss. Val Harper, of course. Fred Miller, Clive Moon, and the other half of the village.'

'But with Hugh's death the way should have been clear to go ahead, so why didn't it?' Then Georgia realized the probable answer. 'Robert Wayncroft?'

'Precisely. The estate reverted to Robert, and he, too, was against it.'

'But he is no longer alive, so it's a different matter. However much people may object, the Wayncrofts can go ahead.'

Simon grimaced. 'Afraid not. Robert bequeathed the manor and estate to Julian, with one little exception. St Thomas's chapel and well, together with the field they are in.'

This grew weirder by the moment. 'So who owns them?'

'Anne Fanshawe does.'

So that was it. The last piece of the jigsaw, and it made sense of it all. *That* was the reason for the clear-cut split in the village. Anne was leading the opposition, and Val Harper and Julian the progress group. *That* was why Anne felt under an obligation to Robert Wayncroft. And *that* was why Anne had suggested she speak to Lisa Moon.

Who wouldn't speak to her. There was still one last strand to be tackled, though, and Georgia clutched at it.

'Could I talk to Jessica? If she's still in reasonable health?'

Simon glanced towards the doorway, where Lisa was standing, listening to them.

'Oh yes,' Lisa said neutrally. 'The old bat's going strong.'

FOUR

'The pilgrim returns.' Peter took his eyes briefly from the book he was reading.

'With honours.'

'Chillingham seems to be a mass of anthills,' he commented, when Georgia had finished relating both the fruits and aggravating dead ends of her visit. 'Fine on the surface, but stir them a little and the armies begin to march.'

'The queens might be living a whole lot deeper than I've dug,' she warned him. 'I've only scratched the surface.'

'You seem to have got the lie of the land, though,' Peter said approvingly. 'So far Thomas Becket seems the main link back to 1967, but it's not a bad start.'

Peter seemed remarkably enthusiastic, she thought with some surprise as she went to the kitchen to make some coffee. His carer Margaret had already left for the day, but Georgia noted that Peter had actually eaten his lunch. All too often he forgot all about it. Margaret had left a dinner ready for him to cook that evening, which was significant as that was usually Janie's province.

'Dining alone tonight?' she asked, when she returned to the office.

'Yes. I told Janie I was busy.'

Georgia knew better than to probe further. Peter was a past master at this game when it suited him, so it was best to ignore it. She wouldn't even ask him what he would be 'busy' doing.

'The hullabaloo over St Thomas must have died down after Hugh's death,' she commented, 'because Robert Wayncroft put his foot down. As he was living abroad most of the time, he was conveniently unobtainable for any lobbying to be effective.'

'Quite. And as soon as Robert dies, Val Harper gallops back and it springs up again. Moreover, some of the same personalities are around. An interesting situation, wouldn't you say?' He cocked an eye at her. 'Even dangerous? How about joining the merry band for a while?'

'Thanks a bunch. You mean that pilgrimage?' Her first instinct was sheer horror. The last thing she wanted was to be away from home at the moment when her chances of conception were reducing all the time. She had underestimated her father, however, as Peter continued briskly: 'Of course you can't go. Stupid of me.'

That made her struggle with the idea. 'Perhaps for a day or two.'

'Excellent.' Peter beamed. 'So that's settled.'

'Not quite.' Damn. As so often, she'd played into her father's hands. 'Are we *sure* we're taking this case on?'

'We are.' Peter looked at her in amazement. 'It's a challenge. We've never picked up the gauntlet with so little to go on.'

He must have seen her expression, because he flushed and turned quickly back to his book. Wasn't he doing the very opposite over Rick? All the evidence in the world wasn't going to convince Peter that Rick was no longer alive.

'Let him go, Peter,' she said quietly.

'How?' He didn't even look up.

It was a plea for help, but she had no answer. It had to come from within him.

'Not this week at least. No way. There's the new gazetteer to edit, plus I have to get ready for John Waites on Friday.' Luke looked contrite. 'Why don't you go though? Usually, you'd jump at the chance to get away from me.'

The joke didn't amuse her. The gazetteer was a big job, and John Waites was Frost & Co's distributor so Luke had justification on his side. Even so, he should think of *her*. 'Not now,' she said mutinously.

'Ah.'

Too late, Georgia fumed at her own stupidity. Bad enough to worry herself over the passing time, but the one thing she had vowed was not to involve Luke in her anxiety. That would seem as if it wasn't his company she wanted, only his part in the conception process.

'A few days away might help you relax,' Luke continued. 'Get involved in something new.'

A typically male response. 'Such as the Chillingham feuds?' she asked. She knew Luke was right, and yet . . . and yet . . .

He shrugged, which she read as a message that he couldn't
care less provided she left him alone with his precious work.
'Village feuds *and* sibling rivalry. If you and Peter are thinking
of making this a Marsh & Daughter case, the pilgrimage might
be just the place to immerse yourself in it. Take care though.'

'Over what?' she threw at him, irrationally annoyed that he
was so willing for her to go.

'Trouble looks as if it's marching right down the road – or,
in this case, the Old Road.'

'Trouble? Your chums Tim and Simon see progress as the
only way *out* of trouble.'

'Wait till the tourists arrive and they're still cooking chips
all day long instead of the gourmet fare they're dreaming of.'

That made her laugh. 'Not as bad as that, surely?'

'Worse,' Luke said mock-gravely. 'Look, I really am going
to be tied up this week so it's an ideal time for you to go.'

Compromise, she decided. 'How about my going just for
the day on the Otford stretch? Simon's planning to do much
the same. The group is only at Farnham as yet, and won't
reach Otford until the weekend at least. If you don't want to
come with me on the walk, you could come over to dinner
in the pub they're staying in and drive me home.'

'Thank *you*.' Luke's turn to laugh. 'I'll see how things go.'

'OK. I'll mug up on Otford and St Thomas. I seem to
remember he spent a lot of time in the manor house that
preceded the Tudor archbishop's palace. Isn't there a story
about his forbidding nightingales to sing because they were
disturbing his train of thought? Doesn't seem a very saintly
thing to do.' Georgia forced herself to be positive. 'I'd like
to check out the St Thomas sights in Otford. The well's not
open to the public, but the ruins of the palace can be seen.
I'll check it on the Internet.'

'You will not, woman! Not while I have a book at hand.
A *reliable* book, a *comprehensive* book, a book whose *pages*
turn flexibly and smoothly, a book that can be treasured and
studied, a book that can be admired, and best of all a book
that's published by Frost & Co.'

Georgia gave in. 'I grovel.'

'Good. That stretch is only about six or seven miles, and
you should be able to stagger that far.'

'Thanks. Got a book around to tell me the weather forecast?'

'Blast you, no,' Luke said amiably. 'So I grant you computers do have their uses. By the way, talking of Otford, I had a letter – a real one, not one of his twittering emails – from Mark. He's planning to return to England if he can get a job. He mentioned Otford, as that's where he grew up.'

'That's good news.' Georgia was delighted for Luke. Mark was his son by his first marriage; he was now in his early twenties and had settled in the States after university when he'd married a fellow student. 'Whereabouts is he looking?'

'It's dependent on where the jobs are, I gather. There aren't too many opportunities around.'

The ringing of the phone interrupted them, and Georgia went to answer it. It was Peter, and she was instantly worried because it was unusual for him to ring in the evenings. 'A problem?' she asked him immediately. His night 'turns' caused by Rick's disappearance had seemed in the past, but as he still dwelt on it so much it was possible they had returned – and they wouldn't be helped by the pattern of his up and down relationship with Janie.

'Far from it. I had a phone call from the lady herself.'

'The lady being . . .?'

'Mrs Jessica Wayncroft. She is not requesting, but *demanding* to see at least one of us tomorrow, and, sweet daughter, I nominated you.'

Demanding? Fine, Georgia thought. She, too, could be demanding. Hugh Wayncroft's widow must be well into her eighties by now. She conjured up a picture of Jessica, the 'old bat' as Lisa had described her, as a dowager in black, sitting upright on an ancient chair in a cobwebby room like Miss Havisham. Even though Dickensian days were surely over, this image would not fade. The word 'demanding' implied an imperiousness that went side by side with it. Why was Jessica *demanding* to see her? To tell Marsh & Daughter to steer clear of the subject of her husband's death? Probably, but that would only convince Peter and herself that there was something to look into.

As she drove into Chillingham, Georgia felt ready for the attack. No church car park this time. Instead, she passed it, and with a mental flourish turned right further along into the drive of Chillingham Place. A large B and B sign pointed with an arrow further along the lane, and a red-brick lodge stood to one side of the drive. It looked occupied, so she half expected a gateman to rush out and challenge her, but only a distant cow raised its head and gazed soulfully at her car. She followed the long winding drive through fields with grazing cattle, then through some woodland with late azaleas and rhododendrons; then came a lawn and the forecourt of the house itself. Chillingham Place was of pleasant Tudor construction, or so it looked from the outside. The inside might reveal remains of an earlier medieval dwelling.

Discreet bells by the old wooden door reminded her that this stately home had been converted into several apartments. With some trepidation, she pressed the bell marked Mrs Hugh Wayncroft, half expecting the door to fly open to reveal a parlourmaid clad in black with a white lacy pinny and headdress.

It wasn't. Nor was it opened by a Miss Havisham who had tottered to the door clad in black with clunking pearl necklaces. Jessica Wayncroft was definitely twenty-first century, not Dickensian. The formidable dowager proved to be a merry-eyed little lady about five foot high, lithe on her feet, slim of body and clad in bright turquoise designer trousers and silk tunic, which set off her snow-white coiffured hair admirably.

'Come in, come in – oh, what a pretty jacket. I wish I could wear red. Of course, I do sometimes. You're not a bit as I expected. I was quite in awe of Marsh & Daughter . . . but now I see you wear red, I do feel quite at home.'

Georgia laughed. 'As you are, of course.'

'So I am.' A giggle. 'Now follow me, Miss Marsh – or do you prefer Mrs Frost? I do so admire your husband's list. I believe I possess every single book he's published. And that includes the works of Marsh & Daughter. I am an addict for crime, Miss Marsh. I really am.'

Georgia heaved a sigh of relief. The worst was over. The words, 'Call me Georgia,' trembled on her lips, but she held them back. Softly, softly at first. This lady had charm, but behind the charm might lie a different picture. 'Thank you, Mrs Wayncroft. Luke will be delighted to hear he has a fan. And my father too.'

'Oh, but I told him that on the telephone last evening. Such a pleasant, polite gentleman. We had quite a chat.'

Georgia decided not to disillusion her that being pleasant and polite wasn't always top priority for Peter.

'I've made coffee,' Jessica continued. 'At least, I think I have. Sometimes it comes out as tea, you know. No, you wouldn't know. You're not old enough. But you will.' The giggle was more like that of a fourteen-year-old than an octogenarian, Georgia thought, beginning to warm to her. Not a Miss Havisham; more a Miss Bates from the pages of Jane Austen.

The large living room – surely a transformed medieval Great Hall – was full of a comfortable array of sofas, pictures and china. A dozen or so eighteenth-century Staffordshire dogs formed a watchful pack in the fireplace, which also held a modern stove in front of an ancient fireback of Adam, Eve and the Tree of Life. Photos on the tables, and paintings – including miniatures and silhouettes – made Georgia feel she could happily live in a room such as this. The coffee – and it *was* – took time to serve, and Georgia decided to wait for Jessica to make the first serious conversational move. This might pander to Jessica's desire to control, but it left Georgia freer to assess why her presence had been *demanded*.

'My son tells me you walked into the midst of our village revels last week and have become interested in Chillingham's affairs,' Jessica began. Her eyes were shrewd, and the faint smile on her lips made Georgia suspect that not only did she think she was in control, but also intended to remain that way. Which son? Georgia wondered. Julian or Valentine? And why was Marsh & Daughter's visit last week so important that whichever son it was had taken the trouble to tell his mother, presumably on the telephone?

Time to play enthusiastic visitor, Georgia decided. There was no indication yet of why she had been summoned. 'There's certainly a lot of history around here. Simon Bede was telling me about the legend of the peacocks, and the vicar showed me the ruins connected with St Thomas.' Nothing like starting a chess game with your queen.

'Indeed. The ruins are central to Chillingham's heritage. My son Valentine believes they should be nationally publicized. He has great plans for a theatre here. We shall become another Bayreuth, with a St Thomas festival every few years, perhaps even annually.'

Georgia blinked. It seemed a far step from an unbuilt theatre to emulating Wagner's world-famous opera venue, but there was no harm in thinking big, she supposed. 'Is Julian also involved in this theatre project?'

'Naturally. My sons support each other.' A sly look, as if Jessica herself were acknowledging that this wasn't always the case. 'And Sebastian too. After he graduates, he will play a big role in the St Thomas development. Julian will run the visitor centre, Valentine oversee the entire project, and Sebastian the theatre, website and marketing of Becket products. St Thomas's connections with Chillingham have to be recognized. After all, his bones probably lie here. It's a most exciting time, and I have decided not to die before the festival is established. I've been busy designing St Thomas badges – researching, I believe you writers call it. And also a special Peacock badge to denote a visit to Chillingham itself. And mugs. One must have mugs.'

'I understand you also have pieces of a medieval wooden statue of Becket with movable parts?'

She had stepped too far. Jessica's face froze for a moment, but then she laughed. 'Indeed we do. There were a few pieces of old decaying wood found in the chapel, and research into family papers suggests there was such a figure. There is no real provenance, but certainly they seem to be genuine.'

Georgia wondered about that, but let it pass.

'Hugh was the real historian,' Jessica continued. 'When first I came to this house I found several centuries of history were lying around and their weight was rather too much for me at first. My darling Hugh took his duties very seriously.'

'He was the younger Wayncroft brother, I understand.'

Jessica nodded. 'You have been doing your homework, Miss Marsh – or shall I call you Georgia? My name is Jessica, as I'm sure you know. So much pleasanter to be informal. Nevertheless, one did know where one *was* in the old days, when barriers were so easy to erect. With more formal customs in the interests of politeness, it was so easy to be impolite by intentional accident, if you see what I mean.'

'I do,' Georgia assured her. 'The art of the gentle put-down.'

'Quite. But now it's so much easier to chat, is it not?'

Provided, Georgia thought, one was sure of where one stood – socially, emotionally and psychologically – and with Jessica that wasn't yet clear. Jessica had not yet declared her hand.

'Hugh was only three years older than I was,' Jessica continued, 'but it often seemed to me that I was the elder. Of course, I had been married before, to Peter Harper. Peter died in December 1944, a few months before Val was born, and so I had to struggle on for many years as a single parent. But then I met Hugh. We married in 1956, but Julian wasn't born for another nine years. Such an emotional time, waiting and hoping. Do you have children, Georgia?'

Georgia was well used to this question, but this time it clean-bowled her and she had to fight for composure. 'Not yet,' she managed.

That should do it, and with luck Jessica would not enquire further. There was a thoughtful look, and Georgia held her breath. But there were no more questions, and she relaxed again. Too soon, perhaps, because Jessica took her by surprise with a forthright: 'I want to talk to you about Hugh's death.'

Approach with care. This had been planned. Hence the *demanding*, Georgia realized. 'You don't mind?'

'I do, very much. However, when I know enquiries are being made on the subject, either out of curiosity or because someone wishes to write about it – and you might, mightn't you? – I feel I have a duty to speak out. The wrong impression can so easily be gained. Julian was only a baby at the time of his father's death, and my Val a young man. Young men see things differently, but can change their views in later life. Everyone else connected with the murder has died. Dear Fred Miller, at the Three Peacocks. Darling Bill Riding – have you met his daughter? – oh, of course you have. Our vicar.'

'The Moons are still living here,' Georgia pointed out.

A pause. 'Ah yes. Dear Lisa is alive and well, but her husband Clive, who played such a big role in the 1967 production, the King himself, has now died. But she can have little to say on the question of Hugh's death. It was Clive who was so active.'

'On the stage or over the question of promoting Becket attractions? I understand the ruins belonged to you at the time.'

'They did, but alas no longer. Hugh was against what he termed their exploitation. So now, Georgia, I must tell you about my Hugh. When I came into this family it seemed to me that I had married not only Hugh, but also the whole Wayncroft family. I can introduce you to them. Do come.'

She sprang up with the liveliness of a twenty-year-old and led the way out of the room into a hallway with a grand staircase up to the next storey. Family portraits stared disdainfully down at Georgia from every point. They lined the walls of the staircase; they filled those of the hallway too. Mature Wayncrofts, Wayncroft children, Wayncroft women, military Wayncrofts, country squire Wayncrofts and aged, severe-looking, bewigged Wayncroft worthies.

'I see what you mean,' Georgia said. 'It can't have felt like your home.'

'Indeed not. And these are just the minor portraits. Julian has the important collection in his apartment, and Sebastian has one or two to remind him of his heritage, poor lad.'

'How would you define that?'

A keen glance. 'Plenty of families have lived in one house over the centuries, so what is so special about the Wayncrofts? I can only suppose it was the Roman Catholic connection, which kept a link with royalty in Jacobean times even after the Restoration.' She laughed. 'Plus a nose for self survival.'

Not in Hugh's case, alas, was Georgia's immediate thought. Perhaps Jessica read her mind, because she immediately led the way back to the living room. 'The Wayncroft Roman Catholic tradition has been somewhat diluted now, but Robert and Hugh held strongly to it. Nevertheless, they also felt an obligation to the village and therefore to the Anglican church here. After all, it is dedicated to St Thomas.'

'Is that why the St Thomas ruins now belong to Anne Fanshawe?'

Jessica sighed. 'The Wayncroft family sometimes had odd notions. Whereas Julian and Sebastian are in favour of fully honouring St Thomas, Robert and Hugh firmly believed that the best way of so doing was not to put them at risk from tourists and to keep the remains holy. Robert saw that as his duty, and so he left them to Anne and not to Julian, the foolish man.'

'But why to her personally, not to the church?'

'I have no idea. You will have to ask her that, though I have to say she is unlikely to tell you.' Jessica tittered. 'I presume Robert took that course because Anne shared his personal commitment to leaving the ruins undisturbed. How very foolish. In my view we should honour history, not ignore it. But Anne will not be moved. Just as Hugh, too, could not be so persuaded.'

'Did you never share his views?'

'I had a son of eleven when I married Hugh and a second son who was born nine years later,' Jessica said almost apologetically. 'With Julian to think of, as well as Val, I needed to see a future, and all I could see was a pile of mouldering bricks at Chillingham Place, which we could not afford to run. I also had a husband who seemed to believe more in history than in the need for educating his children. Without children I might have felt differently, but I did not then, and I do not now. There is the future of the family to consider. I am not as impetuous as I was once, when I could not understand Hugh's viewpoint. He was serious-minded – and that's what both infuriated me and drew me to him. I was such a flighty thing, and so was my first husband – not flighty exactly, I suppose, but Peter was a risk-taker. I met him in the special forces during the war; we married, and then came his death and Valentine's birth. Hugh was so different. A brilliant actor, but withdrawn as a person. He played Becket and I was Queen Eleanor, Henry II's wife – such a splendid part, such a *wicked* woman. And who knows, perhaps her scheming to kill her husband's mistress, the so-called Fair Rosamund, really did have bearing on Becket's murder, as Tennyson's play suggests. In it, Becket saves Fair Rosamund from my evil hands.'

'So far as I recall, legend-cum-history claims you managed it in the end,' Georgia said lightly.

Jessica smiled. 'Queens usually win. On the Sunday afternoon after clearing up the theatre, we marched back home along the Pilgrims' Way to Chillingham. There had been an after-show party on the Saturday night, so there was a bit of a mess, and as we were only amateurs there were no professional stage staff to do the dirty work. We arrived at the Three Peacocks about six o'clock for the celebratory evening that Fred had arranged. I thought Hugh had gone straight home for some reason and would be joining us, but he didn't arrive. Val and I dashed off to see if he was there, but he could not be found, and so we realized something must be wrong. All we could think was that Hugh had had an accident during the last part of the walk. He was inclined to straggle on walks, since he was a keen birdwatcher and often fell back because he had spotted something or other. I set off immediately with Val and Clive – and, I think, Fred. Others came along after us. We found Hugh – or rather Clive and Val saw him; they wouldn't let me near at first – lying at the edge of the wood. They told me to stay where I was because there was no doubt that he was dead.' She grimaced. 'They did not tell me how he died until later. Even from where I stood I could see he was dead from the way he was lying.'

She gave a little shrug, as if to say it was all a long time ago, but it didn't convince Georgia.

'I'm sorry,' she said sincerely. 'This must be very hard for you.'

'I relive it each time I think of it. Age doesn't change emotion, it merely hides it in a cupboard until one opens the door. But sometimes one has to do just that, to brush away the cobwebs. That's why I wanted to see you.'

'There must have been a full police investigation.'

'Of course. And an inquest too. Murder was the verdict. I was so shocked at the time that I couldn't take in all the details, but it must be on record somewhere and you could find it *if* necessary. But I hope it won't be – not for my sake or my family's, but for the village's. There are troubles enough around today without any need for delving into the past.'

'What would *you* like? To know more?'

'My dear Georgia – how odd, already I think of you as dear Georgia – I still would like to know who killed Hugh. I can't believe the truth would hurt now, but nevertheless, in the greater interest, I ask you to let it lie.'

'I have to ask why. Is it because you think the St Thomas issue was the motive for his death?'

Jessica bowed her head. 'It's possible; the village felt very strongly, then as now. All the more reason for not stirring old ashes.'

'Because whoever killed your husband was on that pilgrimage with you?'

Jessica hesitated. 'Probably, although many of the villagers turned out to welcome us home and came to greet us. It's possible that someone who hated Hugh lingered and killed him.'

It was time to enter difficult territory, and Georgia braced herself. 'Could there have been other, more personal motives for his death?' She could hardly name Val, but she wondered very much what the relationship had been between him and his stepfather, given their opposing views.

Jessica stiffened, very obviously reading the implication correctly. 'Hugh had enemies, because of his beliefs, but as a man everyone loved him. Valentine had his differences with him, as one would expect. He was headstrong and twenty-two. Hugh was gentle, but a martinet where the family and Chillingham were concerned. He saw Val as an outsider, but that was no reason for Val to kill him. In fact, Val had everything to lose and nothing to win. With Hugh's death, he, Julian and I were left penniless, and it was only thanks to Robert's generosity that we had Chillingham Place as a roof over our heads all those years.'

'And what about the rest of the cast? Would any of them have had reason to kill him?'

Georgia had been wary about asking so bluntly, but in fact Jessica laughed, perhaps because the main effort of speaking about Hugh had been surmounted. 'Have you ever belonged to a drama group, Georgia?'

'Briefly.' She had done so for one or two years, until Zac had come. He had swept her into marriage and refused to allow any distractions from her sole reason for existence as he saw it: to be devoted to him.

'Even brief experience should remind you that emotions run high in drama groups. One is thrust so closely together that private emotions swell up – often as a grand finale to the performance itself. Hence the attraction or otherwise of after-show parties in such groups. We were saving our real celebration for our return to Chillingham, but the after-show party was quite exciting. I seem to remember pouring a glass of very expensive wine over Lisa Moon's head. She was playing Fair Rosamund, and I fear I carried Queen Eleanor's vendetta from the play on too long. Hugh was very annoyed with me, and so was Clive. I do assure you Lisa didn't mind. She thought it rather amusing.'

FIVE

'**M**ike. This is a nice surprise.' That was only half true. As soon as Georgia saw him in the office, when she returned from Chillingham to see Peter, she feared the worst. Her father was calling in the heavy brigade far too soon. And Mike Gilroy was definitely heavy. Mild he might seem, a gentle ambling giant of a man in height, and patient. Up to a point. Peter didn't believe in keeping forces in reserve, however, and so far Georgia did not feel their investigation into Hugh Wayncroft's murder had progressed to the stage where Mike's help should be invoked.

'No surprise to me.' Mike greeted her with a kiss. 'The minute I heard Peter's voice on the phone, I knew I could abandon such unimportant matters as crime figures, terrorists and world emergencies.'

'Why not?' Peter returned, apparently astonished. 'Hugh Wayncroft's murder remains unsolved.'

'In 1967 I was one year old so I can't help you from personal experience.'

'Of course not. I'm not unreasonable. However, you do still keep files somewhere, don't you?'

'We do. Tucked away according to age, carefully tied up with red tape.'

'Very well. What did the Wayncroft case tell you?' Peter cut through any Gordian knots that might be presuming to threaten his path.

Mike capitulated. 'Not enough for you to set the hounds of hell loose, Peter. I do admit it looks weird on the surface. It took some working out just why it had been abandoned.'

'Because they knew the answer but couldn't prove it?'

'Probably. It was an interesting case, in fact. He'd definitely been strangled. The hyoid bone was broken, but there were no signs of a ligature being used, or anything definable as prints. What you might call a quick clean job.'

'Any signs of struggle?'

'Apparently not.'

'Taken from behind?'

'Unlikely. There seem to have been three lines of enquiry. One was a travelling fruit picker, who was traced but nothing could be proved. The second was a young man in the group called Valentine Harper.'

'Wayncroft's stepson,' Peter said. 'And the last?'

'A local carpenter, Clive Moon. Also in the group.'

'He's no longer alive. Evidence?'

'No DNA then, of course. Precious little trace evidence, and those most closely involved weren't talkative. As most of the village seems to have been closely involved that didn't help. There was heavy emphasis on the fact that odd-looking characters had been seen in them there woods around that time. Possibly true enough, but apart from the fruit picker they'd vanished like ghosts in daylight come the investigation.'

'What did they have on Harper and Moon?'

'Motive: Clive Moon had organized a village petition and march to the manor about some project to do with Thomas Becket, which didn't please Wayncroft. Valentine Harper marched with him – and was known to have it in for his stepfather.'

'Alibis?'

'I'm beginning to feel like your sergeant again,' Mike said good-humouredly. 'Unbreakable is the answer to that. Hugh Wayncroft had been dead an hour or two before he was found, during which time Harper claimed to have been firstly in the pub with his mother, and then to have walked back to Chillingham Place with her to see if his stepfather was there. Clive Moon was with his wife the whole time.'

'What about the last stages of the pilgrimage?' Georgia put in. 'I met Jessica Wayncroft, Hugh's widow, this afternoon and she told me Hugh often stayed at the rear of the column. He could have been killed, therefore, before anyone even reached the pub.'

Mike flicked through his notes. 'Harper said he was at the front of the column with his mother. Everyone testified to that; Lisa Moon swore her husband Clive was walking behind her with someone called Fred Miller towards the rear of the column.'

'Fred Miller's dead too,' Peter said crossly. 'Who else was interviewed?'

'Judging by the size of the file, everyone on the march.

There was a chap called Bill Riding; even his young daughter
Anne was questioned. Fred Miller, the vicar, and a local
gardener called John Painter.' Mike looked at them both. 'So
where does that take you?'

'To the word *why*, Mike,' Peter replied. 'Why is the same situation currently being recreated: the same play, the same
pilgrimage, the same two opposing factions, the same issue?'

'The same apart from the murder,' Mike pointed out.

'I only hope you're right.' Peter looked worried. Surely,
Georgia thought, he didn't seriously think there was anything
as threatening as that in the tensions they'd run into so far?

After Mike had made a polite escape, Georgia recounted
her interview with Jessica. 'Do you still think I should drop
in on this pilgrimage? Hugh Wayncroft's death isn't likely to
be a topic of conversation, and if, assuming the wild improb-
ability that you're right about there being a very dark cloud
over this whole venture, I wouldn't be able to stop any trouble
that gets stirred up.'

Peter considered this for more than the token protest it was.
'There's no guarantee you'll get any further,' he replied. 'On
the other hand, from what you've related of the not so formidable Jessica Wayncroft, plus the *hard work* I've put in,' he
added meaningfully, 'I'm fairly sure that even if we paid a
hundred more trips to Chillingham we would get no further
without pushing very heavily. Something that has been buried
for forty years or more needs dynamite to disgorge it.'

'Wrong word. We don't want to blow it to bits, merely
uncover any bones that might lie hidden.'

Peter looked at her quizzically. 'Do you speak metaphorically?'

'Metaphorically?' She was thrown for a moment.

'Thomas Becket's bones,' he reminded her gently. 'I believe
you mentioned a legend that they are hidden in Chillingham.
It's worth bearing that in mind.'

Georgia sighed. 'Even supposing it has a grain of truth in
it, or even that it is one hundred per cent correct, it would be
hard to prove whose the bones were.'

'Unless there was other evidence with them?'

'A certificate signed by the Abbot?' Georgia asked drily.
This was surely an avenue leading nowhere. 'Whatever the
evidence, it could never be conclusive.'

'It seems to me you lack the spirit for the hunt. Does not man's questing soul interest you?'

For a moment she was afraid Peter was right, but then she rallied. 'Not in this case.'

'Why not?'

'Because even if the bones were unearthed, it would be a diversion from Hugh Wayncroft's murder. And that's where *we* have to start.'

'Only if he was killed for personal reasons. If the motive was that he was standing in the way of others' plans for their own aggrandizement then it's very relevant. Now do you see the point of joining the pilgrimage?'

Standing on the platform at Chartham railway station waiting for the Victoria train with her backpack making an uncomfortable hump under her enveloping rainwear, Georgia could see no point at all. Why on earth was she standing here on a Saturday morning in the drizzling rain? It was not only damp, but also chilly for the end of June; nor was there any sign of Simon, although she had arranged to meet him here. Anne Fanshawe, who would also be walking this stretch of the pilgrimage, had left for Otford yesterday evening, but Georgia and Simon preferred to join the group near the ruins of the Archbishop's Palace. Simon had told her Julian had fixed a press interview at nine thirty.

'You'll be fine,' Luke had assured her, secure in the knowledge that he at least would not be walking in the rain.

At last she saw Simon's car drive past towards the car park, and he joined her just as the train pulled in. Georgia struggled out of her rainwear and sank thankfully on to the seat. 'Will the walk go ahead if this rain continues?' she asked hopefully.

'Come rain or come shine, Tim says,' Simon told her gloomily. 'If it's a real downpour before it starts then it's agreed we can leap into the coach and do it the easy way. If it's just drizzle, hard luck. We walk.'

Usually, Georgia had no problem with walking in the rain. Out on the Yorkshire or Cornish moors with Luke it never seemed a hindrance, but today, when her job was not to enjoy Mother Nature, but to work with all her antennae operating at full strength, the prospect was far from appealing.

'Are you in for the duration?' she asked Simon, 'or coming back with us tonight?' When she'd spoken to him on the phone yesterday he'd been undecided whether or not to accept her offer of a lift back home with Luke, who had been persuaded into joining her at the pub that evening.

'Daft I may be, but Lisa's picking up my car later on so that I can stay on for another day,' he told her. 'I had an SOS from Tim this morning; he needs support.'

That didn't sound good. 'Mutiny in the ranks?'

'In spades, but nothing to do with the play. That's what is infuriating Tim. Our darling vicar arrived yesterday evening and told them flatly that she's going to speak out at Julian's press interview if there's one word said about our plans to develop Chillingham. He can only talk about the play and pilgrimage, decrees our vicar. Julian won't cancel, and he's hardly the diplomat that Val can be, so the fireworks may be starting early in the day.' A pause, then: 'I'm damned glad Lisa isn't coming.'

'Why?' Georgia was genuinely puzzled. 'Because she'd be support for Anne?'

Simon flushed. 'No. Lisa's too gentle a soul to get mixed up in a verbal punch-up before the cameras. She'd feel bound to voice her views – and where would that leave Tess and Matthew? They're looking forward to the play, not the infighting en route.'

Lisa Moon, gentle soul or not, seemed to Georgia well able to cope in any situation. She would state where she stood, nothing more and nothing less, so Simon's explanation failed to convince Georgia. She decided to move on to safer ground, as she and Simon would be viewing the central battle at closer quarters all too soon.

She was correct. The short walk down from the station to the remains of the old palace was a brief respite (except from the rain) before joining the pilgrims, and even in this weather the ruined tower made a good backdrop for an interview about a pilgrimage to Canterbury. Even as she glimpsed the bedraggled group standing on the grass, clad in modern rainwear over their robes and hats, it was clear there was tension. It was already divided into two camps. Anne was standing in the smaller group, together with a pleasant-looking middle-aged man and a pretty girl, so far as Georgia could judge under the waterproofs.

As she and Simon walked up the lane towards them, she could see and hear Julian in full flow before the TV cameras. She caught the words 'part of a greater plan in honour of St Thomas Becket' and her heart sank. Julian was igniting the fireworks already, and she watched Anne Fanshawe with foreboding as the interviewer turned to her and a hiss of disapproval ran round the pro-group. She could not hear all Anne's words, but those she did set the fireworks off. She caught the phrases 'plans admirable in themselves . . . ruins of St Thomas's chapel and Thomas's well . . . private land not open to the public . . .'

As Georgia listened to the shouting match that then broke out, no doubt captured by the cameras, she hardly dared look at Simon. Would he think that any publicity, bad as well as good, would help his cause, or grieve for the probable damage to Tim's production?

These ruins must have seen plenty of strife in their time, no doubt seeming just as insignificant in the great scheme of things as this issue surely was. Very little remained of the palace to suggest its former grandeur, apart from the tall tower that still stood, and some pieces of the outer walls now in cottage gardens. The old manor house that had preceded it would not have rivalled it in splendour, but now both buildings were chiefly stones and memories. If, as legend had it, Thomas Becket had lived in the manor house, he, too, would have wrestled with strife, been depressed by the rain and had his daily battles to struggle with – those unruly nightingales who had persisted in irritating the saint now made a much more convincing story. So did the story of the Chillingham well, Georgia thought. Rain and drizzle were water, which was the staff of life, whether dropping from the sky or gushing out from a well spring.

Eventually, with a grin all over his face, the interviewer thanked the warring parties and the pilgrims were free to set off.

'Are we really walking in this?' Simon asked Tim, who had come over to join them.

'Val says yes,' Tim told them gloomily. 'I'd have plumped for the coach, but he's in charge of this – um – side of things.' He'd clearly only just refrained from using more explicit words and chosen the stiff upper lip. As the unhappy band of pilgrims rejoined the road to the station, passed the pond and walked over the railway crossing towards the Old Road, Georgia fervently wished that she could leap on the next passing train, no matter where it was going. Judging by the silence of her fellow travellers she was not the only one.

As they turned on to the Pilgrims' Way path, however, and began the climb to the top of the downs, the atmosphere began to feel less tense, and damp or not, people were beginning to spread out and talk. Simon and Tim were working their way to the front of the column, but Georgia decided to remain near the rear where she might have more choice over whom to approach. There was a group of youngsters behind her, and their laughter made a welcome change in this gloomy weather. Issues such as the future of the village would not weigh so deeply with them, and it helped her keep this pilgrimage in proportion. The girl in the bright red waterproof with fair hair straggling from beneath her hood, caught her up.

'You were talking to Seb Wayncroft just now,' Georgia said lightly.

The girl grinned. 'Yes. Don't tell Grannie Moon, she doesn't approve.'

'That row at the palace won't be good publicity for the play.'

'Seb says there's no such thing as bad publicity.'

'Not too sure about that. Are you Tess, by any chance?'

The girl nodded. 'You're that journalist, aren't you?'

'Almost right,' Georgia replied lightly. 'I gather you're playing Fair Rosamund. It must be hard to concentrate on that with all this uproar about the Becket ruins.'

'Yes. I get sick of it,' Tess said frankly. 'Goes on at home all the time too. Uncle Derek's all for it, so he and Gran are always rowing. Dad's against it, but he keeps out of it. Can't wait to get to uni in the autumn.'

So Lisa Moon wasn't always as calm and gracious as Simon had suggested. The Moons were a divided family. 'There are always two sides to a question,' Georgia replied diplomatically.

Tess seized on this. 'That's what I say to Seb. It's the vicar's land. She can do what she likes with it.'

Unfortunately, not everyone here took that view. Georgia could hear raised voices in front as the group came to a halt at the top of the downs. One shrill woman predominated: *'What do you want, Vicar? To put us all out on the streets?'*

'That's Sue Smith,' Tess muttered. 'Helps Mum in the shop.'

There were more people than Sue Smith involved though. Georgia could see Anne, boxed in by Val and Julian, and she was clearly having a hard time – and perhaps vice versa. Anne appeared to be taking the rebellion in her stride, luckily, and was making some diplomatic reply that Georgia could not hear. She was much relieved when the situation seemed to calm down, whether through Anne's diplomacy or the sheer glory of the view from the top of these Downs. Such sights should dwarf human battles, but rarely seemed to do so.

When Tess rejoined Seb, Georgia made her way forward to catch up with Anne, thinking she might be isolated.

'And what might you be here for?' There was only a slight barb in Anne's voice.

'What do you think? Reconstructing what might have happened in 1967.'

Anne shrugged. 'Not a good idea to stoke up the fires.' Then she grinned. 'I suppose one might say I've done that myself.'

'You've every right to do so.' Georgia hesitated, but she'd get nowhere that way. 'I still don't understand, but today's battles are not my business.'

'Good. I seem to recall, however, that I've already explained my reasons to you.'

'You told me the general area of your concern.' Keep it cool.

'That's as far as I go. It's not my decision to make. Thanks be,' Anne added wryly.

Georgia asked no more. If Anne was still convinced it was Robert Wayncroft's decision not hers, she would get no more out of her. Nevertheless, she itched to know why he had been so set against development that he'd partly disinherited his own family. Marching along in waxed rain jacket and trousers, Anne didn't look in the least fazed either by the spat that threatened this pilgrimage and play or by Georgia's presence – even though both implied a reawakening of tragic events in which her father had been involved, and indeed she herself as a child. Anne had the confidence of one who knew she was in the right, and no earthly voice was going to change her mind.

Anne went ahead to talk to Simon, and Tim promptly fell
back to take her place, obviously having overheard some of
her conversation with Anne. 'See what I'm up against?' he
whispered.

Georgia responded cheerfully. 'You know what drama
groups are like. Everyone's suffering from pre-performance
nerves, even though it went well at Winchester. When the
curtain goes up again, everything will calm down.'

Anne and Simon were striding some way ahead now and
Tim watched them gloomily. 'If it was only Anne and the
Moons, I'd agree. But there's a whole body of opinion in the
village that thinks as they do. I'm all for development, as you
know, but I wish everyone would consider the play at the
moment and not how much they'd like either to ring Anne's
neck or raise her to sainthood.'

Time to play disinterested observer. 'Perhaps she'll come
round once the play is over.'

'I'd love to think so, but no way. Even if we managed to
get her out of office, what's the point? She owns that land
personally. The first sign of someone in that field without
permission and she'd whip an injunction out.'

'Is compromise possible? Maybe she would open the ruins
a few days a year?'

'Sounds good, but she's not the compromising type.'

Which, Georgia thought, is one of the reasons Robert
Wayncroft might have left her the land. Again she wondered
what the others might have been. Could it have anything to
do with her family background? 'What was her father like?'
she asked.

'Bill Riding? Si and I never knew him of course, but he
seems to have been generally popular. In his teaching career,
he taught half the village, and no one has an ill word to speak
of him.'

'Wouldn't his daughter have inherited some goodwill?'

'At first she did. But Bill's long been dead, and now she
has to earn it for herself. Bill was a historian, he loved those
ruins, and he and the Wayncroft brothers were good friends.
It would have made some sort of sense if Robert had left the
ruins to him, but apparently it was only when he returned
to England in 2002 that he changed his will and left them to
Anne.'

'It's odd, isn't it?' Georgia frowned. 'I see why Robert might have left them to a historian friend such as Bill Riding – because Jessica certainly isn't a fan of history, and Julian probably showed no signs of interest either, as he grew up. But why leave them away from the family after Bill's death, especially since he clearly took his duty to the Wayncroft family seriously?'

'I suppose that is odd,' Tim replied with surprise. 'Si and I have got so used to the idea of their belonging to Anne now that we hadn't thought it through. It's bugged us so much in the last couple of years. You could have knocked the village down with a feather when Robert died and the bequest became public knowledge. The surviving Wayncrofts were not pleased. Quite a furore there was, but Madame Vicar just sailed through it. It's my guess she knew about it in advance. Maybe it was even her idea. Since then she's blocked every move we've made to try to get even limited public access.'

'Are the ruins listed?'

'Sure. But that's all the more power to her elbow.'

'Even if she fails to maintain them?'

'Ah, but she does maintain them. Matthew Moon went in to do some restoration work on them last year.'

'I thought he was a carpenter, like his father.'

Tim laughed. 'He is. A brilliant one. But the Moons can turn their hands to anything in the building trade and most of what else needs to be done in the village. Derek Moon is the same, and young Will looks as if he's in the same mould – except that they don't have quite Matthew's skill at the lathe, do they, Matthew?' He turned to the pleasant-looking man ambling behind them, whom Georgia had noticed in the crowd at the Otford palace.

Matthew grinned as he caught up with them. 'As the Good Lord giveth, Mr Hurst. Tess has a good eye for a piece of wood too, so maybe she'll be chipping and carving away one day. You'll be Miss Marsh then?' He nodded at Georgia. She was struggling with her waterproof hood, which kept slipping off, and Matthew came over to achieve the impossible by persuading it to stay in place over her head. One clip and it was secure.

'Thanks, Mr Moon.'

'Mum told me about you,' he replied. There was no hint of blame or curiosity in his voice, just acceptance – and Georgia liked that. He was, she thought, a man who would make up his own mind, a good father for Tess.

'I'm afraid I upset your mother. I'm sorry about that,' she said as he caught hold of his daughter's hand as she swung past them with Seb.

Tess laughed. 'Easy to do, isn't it, Dad? I wanted her to tell me all about her playing Rosamund way back in history, but she wouldn't even do that. Told me I had to find my own way through the dratted thorn bushes.'

'Are you enjoying playing Rosamund?' Georgia asked. They were catching up with Anne again now, and concentrating on the play rather than village affairs seemed a good idea.

Tess nodded vigorously. 'Bit hard pretending that I've got a ten-year-old kid though. I'm only nineteen.'

'There's drama groups for you,' Tim commented. 'There's never anyone the right age with the right talent.'

Anne must have overheard because she turned round to joke: 'I offered to play my old part. You said I was too old, Tim.'

Good humour seemed to have been restored, Georgia thought thankfully. Something about the presence of the Moons perhaps, a placid acceptance of life's foibles. Matthew was one, and Tess another. And Lisa? Perhaps if she found the right way to approach her, Georgia thought. But ahead of her she could see Julian and Val striding ahead, two dark figures against the hill's horizon.

'Hostilities halted?' she asked Tim.

'Let's hope so.'

'No way.' Tess giggled, at which Anne gave her what Georgia interpreted as a warning glance. 'Not till hell freezes.'

'Why not?' Georgia held her breath, hoping that tongues might be loosening.

Luckily Tess wasn't put off by the vicar's presence. 'Naughty old Queen Eleanor. She had a thing going with Becket years ago, and King Julian didn't like it one little bit.'

'Legend or history?' Georgia asked.

'Legend,' Anne said quickly.

'History,' Tess said simultaneously. 'Even Seb knows that's why Val got out of town and Aletta married Julian. He was the better bet.' She gave a nervous glance at Anne, in case she'd gone too far.

Maybe she had, but Georgia was glad of it. In compensation she switched to a safer topic, the play, although her mind was still on the antipathy between the two half brothers despite their present common cause. Where did Aletta stand in this? Val was in his sixties, but he was still a personable man, and old attractions might die hard.

By lunchtime, the rain had ceased. Half the party split off to walk down the hillside to a pub, while the others took advantage of a lull in the rain to eat sandwiches where they were and enjoy the view. Georgia opted for the latter. There'd be enough joint community eating this evening at the Dog and Duck pub, the far side of Wrotham, where some of the party were staying. The rest, she gathered, were either camping or had been fixed up at B and Bs, but for dinner everyone would be at the pub.

Anne had also chosen to enjoy the view, and she and Georgia perched on a rock in amiable companionship. 'I didn't lay the drama on this morning just for you, you know,' Anne dropped casually into the conversation. 'Or for the cameras.'

'Wasn't it avoidable?'

'Regrettably not, more's the pity. I'd have liked to have enjoyed today.'

'The pilgrimage experience, or the Old Road itself, rain and all?'

'Both. You can't think I wanted to have our differences aired before the cameras.'

Georgia considered this. 'I'll plump for no.'

Anne made a face. 'Public sympathy usually lies with the underdog, and I don't seem to be doing too well in that respect. Cranky old female vicar thwarts village wishes.'

'That bad still? I thought I saw you talking to Val and Julian quite amicably earlier.'

'Val perhaps. He and I are old sparring partners,' Anne said. 'Julian's another matter altogether, not to mention his wife. But Val and I used to dance in the dew occasionally before I married and moved away.'

'Serious dancing?' Georgia found it hard to imagine suave Val and down to earth Anne having even a mild fling together.

Anne laughed. 'On his side – and not entirely honourably.

I was a lot more attractive at twenty-one than I am now and not so obstinate. In his younger days, Val was a man of the world, and I could see we wouldn't suit, so he got a quick brush off. But we do still get on well – or did.'

'Did?' Georgia queried.

'Before this Becket division arose. Val always rushes in where angels fly away screaming.'

'There's gossip that he made a play for Aletta before she married Julian. The two brothers and the lady in-between make the kind of story that, given several centuries of folk history, would turn into a legend.'

'Legends are dangerous things, Georgia –' Anne turned to her impulsively – 'but some, at least, are based in truth. The problem is that faced with the truth of a legend, what does one do? One holds it in one's hands and looks at it, too scared to take the next move and say this is not fiction, this is real. That step has to be taken, and Robert Wayncroft knew that.'

'Which legend, Anne?' Georgia asked quietly. Anne wasn't speaking of Aletta now.

Anne seemed to regret having spoken, because she laughed. 'Only speaking generally, of course. Just generally.'

There was a silence, which Anne was evidently not going to break. 'Are you staying overnight?' Georgia asked eventually.

'Yes. I managed to get a bed in a local farmhouse. So I'll eat with you all in the pub first of course.'

The Dog and Duck, on a minor lane on the slopes of the downs between Wrotham and the hamlet of Delmont, proved to be large and comfortable, with a garden, outside tables, dogs roaming around, and an extensive interesting menu. For a moment Georgia regretted her decision to leave that night, especially as the youngsters in the group were larking around and it seemed the whole atmosphere of the day was about to change. They had arrived mid-afternoon and had plenty of time to enjoy it. She watched Seb and Tess playing a game of croquet in the garden. Romeo and Juliet she thought. 'A plague on both your houses': the Wayncrofts, who thought it their right to brush away all obstacles to their goal; the Moons, firmly established in tradition. The Wayncrofts would win – were it not for Anne Fanshawe standing shoulder to shoulder with the Moons. And yet, in the late afternoon sunshine that had grudgingly appeared, it seemed possible that the tension of the morning would vanish.

'Hi.' Luke appeared from nowhere and bent over her shoulder to kiss her. 'Survived all storms and tribulations?'

'The rain or the dramas?'

'Either.'

'Both – I hope.'Even now she could not be sure she was right. The afternoon had been a mere lull in hostilities, not an ending. People came and went as they checked into their varying accommodation facilities, but by seven o'clock they were all gathered in the pub's dining area. Seated at a table by the window overlooking the forecourt and lane, with Luke, Tim and Simon, Georgia was relieved to be away from contentious issues, and it was easy to hope that the rest of the group was similarly contented.

It was not. Voices raised above the otherwise cheerful buzz of conversation quickly told her that. Three tables away, nearer the arc of the bar, Anne Fanshawe by bad management – or perhaps someone's design – was sitting with Aletta, Julian and Val, and at the next table were Seb, Tess and Matthew. As the general buzz halted for a moment, Anne's voice rang out loud and clear:

'No chance. No chance now or ever that I would agree to open the ruins to the public. *Any* public. I'm sorry, but there the matter rests.'

Georgia could see her sitting there on the far side of the table. Everyone was very still. There was a red flush on Anne's cheeks, and she looked very angry. The Wayncrofts were watching her in silence. Then Georgia's attention was diverted, and when she next looked Seb had gone to join his parents, leaving Tess with her father. The Wayncrofts and Anne seemed to be talking very earnestly but quietly now, and she could hear nothing.

'Phew.' Tim let out a long breath. 'Now reassure me that *that* will blow over, Si, and that harmony and light will prevail for the good of the play. Still believe that?'

Simon did his best. 'It might.'

Luke tried too. 'These outbursts could just be the effect of the pilgrimage. Actors are selfish by nature. Once they get on stage, all else but them, their part and the play is wiped out.'

'Any other time, any other play,' Tim muttered, 'perhaps. But not this time. Stay on, Si, will you? Until we get back to Chillingham?' He was looking desperate.

Should she stay over too? Georgia wondered as Simon reassured Tim. No, she decided. Her task was to concentrate on the last pilgrimage, and everyone here was far too intent on the disputes of the present one.

As she and Luke left, there was a general movement towards departure, and as they reached their car Anne passed her, obviously on her way back to the farmhouse where she was staying.

'Want a lift?' Georgia called as Anne said goodnight.

'No thanks. I need some air. See you in Canterbury, if not sooner. I imagine your bulldog approach means you won't be abandoning Chillingham yet awhile?'

Georgia laughed. 'No way. Too many interesting sticks for Peter and me to chase.'

She watched Anne set off along the road before climbing gratefully into Luke's car. Anne looked a lonely figure as she walked away from the light of the pub and forecourt and into the dark lane with only the flickering light of a torch to guide her. See you in Canterbury, Anne had said. And what would that bring forth? Georgia wondered. It seemed that, just like the pilgrims of old, they were all making this pilgrimage for differing reasons. What was Anne's?

SIX

George struggled to open her eyes, as somewhere a phone was ringing. Whose? Luke's mobile? Hers? The landline? It was only seven thirty in the morning, for goodness sake, and the previous evening they had arrived home late from the Dog and Duck. Thankfully, Luke must already be on his way to answer it, as the ringing stopped, and she sank back into sleep again. Not for long. It was only an instant before something in his voice as it drifted upstairs made her register that something was wrong. Peter? Immediately, she was fully awake, just as her own mobile began to ring. She sank back in relief because it was Peter's voice at the other end.

'Georgia? Thank heaven. Where are you?'

'In bed.' It took a moment or two for it to dawn on her that something was indeed wrong.

'Then get up. I've just had a call from Val Harper.'

That didn't make sense. 'What on earth did he want?' But almost as soon as she'd said that, she knew it must be bad news. 'What's happened?'

'Anne Fanshawe – she's been found dead, and not from natural causes.'

Dead? 'But I was talking to her yesterday,' was her inane reply. Shock makes idiots of us all, she thought as she struggled with the enormity of what Peter was telling her. Her forebodings over this pilgrimage had been proved right. 'How?' she asked.

'He didn't say. They need you and Luke over there as you were at the Dog and Duck last evening, and I'm coming too.'

Of course they must all go. All Georgia could think of was that last image of Anne walking off into the dark night. No point in questioning Peter any more. It would wait. She thought fast. 'I'll pick you up in half an hour.' Her car was adapted to take Peter, and there was room for Luke too.

Even as she switched off, Luke came back into the bedroom. One look at his face told her he'd had the same news. 'So you know,' she said.

'Yes. Call from Tim. Yours?'

'Peter – he's had Val Harper on the phone. Peter wants to come with us, so we're picking him up in half an hour. What did Tim tell you?'

'He was all but incoherent – in a complete panic. I couldn't make much sense of what had happened. He just said we should get back to the pub. The police are there and will start questioning everyone soon. Did Peter tell you any more?'

'Nothing apart from the fact that it wasn't natural causes. It could be a car accident, or she might have fallen downstairs in the farmhouse.'

Luke's silence reinforced her own lack of conviction in these explanations. Eventually, he said, 'From what I could glean from Tim's gabbling, I don't think that she died in the farmhouse. Wherever it was, she was found early this morning, and the police roused the farmer, who directed them to the pub.'

One scenario after another rushed through Georgia's mind as she could well imagine the chaos there must be now amongst the pilgrims. The sooner they got going the better.

Luke had not been exaggerating. When they arrived at the Dog and Duck Tim looked even worse than he had yesterday evening. His nervousness was stamped all over his face. There was no point in wondering whether this arose from the murder or the uncertainty that must now hang over his play. He probably didn't know himself.

As if in mockery of the dark horror that had befallen the group, the day was fine, and when they arrived Georgia could see the party was spread out across the terrace and gardens. The pub would not officially open until twelve, and so the Chillingham group had it all to themselves until then, although with the camping contingent having joined them again, there were so many people gathered here it was hardly quiet. The coach, baulked of its purpose of picking up luggage, was still in the car park. There was also a police car there, but there was no sign of SOCO or control vans nor of a police cordon, which suggested Anne must have been killed some way from where Georgia had last seen her. She could see two constables sitting apart from the rest of the group, however, no doubt busy with recording details of potential witnesses. The rest must still be at the scene of crime together with all the SOCOs.

Simon disappeared to fetch some coffee for them – very welcome, as breakfast at Medlars had been non-existent except for a snatched slice of bread – and they found a table on the terrace outside. Julian and Aletta were not far away, but it was Val who came over to them, looking very drawn, with Julian and Aletta following him.

'Good of you to rush over to help in our little local difficulty.' Val tried to make it sound light-hearted, but failed miserably, which was hardly surprising in the circumstances.

Julian and his wife seemed in shock, naturally enough. 'She was strangled,' he told them. His face was drained of colour, and his voice held nothing of its usual heartiness. 'She was found by a local dairyman early this morning in the lane leading to the place where she was staying.'

Murdered then, Georgia thought; the last doubt had to be dismissed.

'There's nothing else on that lane but the farmhouse, so the police tried that first,' Julian continued. 'The woman who runs it recognized who she was and told them she was part of the group at the pub.'

'So here we are,' Aletta added shakily, 'awaiting the police's pleasure. They arrived just as we were getting up at about eight and told us to stay put. Since then it's been nothing but phone calls for all of us. There's the next of kin issue, of course.'

'Who is her next of kin?' Peter asked.

'Her daughter. I've met her once or twice.'

Aletta was usually one of those cool women, Georgia thought, who despite the worst fate could throw at them always looked immaculate, not a hair out of place. Today her calm had deserted her, even though that was evident more in her voice and body language than in her appearance. She still seemed in control, however, as she laid her hand on her husband's arm and persuaded him to sit down.

'Do you know where the crime scene is and how far it stretches?' Peter asked.

'From the farmhouse, up to where that lane joins the one running past this pub,' Val said. 'They'd have liked to have closed part of this road too, but some traffic has to get through somehow. No doubt about it, though, we're all suspects until proved otherwise.'

His usual suavity had deserted him, and he, too, was clearly in shock. Georgia remembered Anne saying that he and she used to dance in the dew together, which suggested there could still have been a tie between them.

'It might have been an opportunist murder,' Georgia said. Always a good starting point, even though she didn't believe that was likely in this case.

'Of course. But meanwhile we're all on the list.' Aletta laughed nervously. 'Remember that production of *The Mikado* you produced, Val, back in the early eighties? The Lord High Chancellor who had a little list of those who would not be missed. That's us. We'll all be dragged in one by one.'

Val smiled at her, but Julian's face, caught off-guard, suggested he did not appreciate his wife's attempt at light-heartedness.

'Do you know who's the senior officer yet?' Peter asked him. Georgia guessed Wrotham would come under Darenth Area, which was not one Peter knew well.

'DI Whitton,' Val replied promptly.

That could be good news at least. There had been a Will Whitton who had been Mike Gilroy's sergeant at one time. Georgia remembered him as having a cheerful easy-going manner, a rosy cheeked complexion and a sense of humour. Unusual qualities in an ambitious sergeant, and they hid an astute mind. Mike had said he'd go far. Luckily for them, he seemed to have gone no further than Darenth Area.

Them? Georgia realized with some surprise that she was identifying herself with the pilgrimage, which must mean she felt a sense of unity with it, more than her obligation to be present as perhaps the last person to see or talk to Anne – apart from her murderer.

This must have struck Luke too because he went over to the police table to announce their presence. A woman PC turned round to look at Georgia appraisingly, as if sizing her up for a grilling. Fine, she thought, she would help all she could. Even the short time Georgia had known Anne had been enough for her to realize that they were on the same wave-length, if not always in accord, and that she felt personally involved in the hunt for her murderer.

Tim and Simon brought the coffee over to them and sat down at the table as the Wayncrofts moved away. 'Dare I ask what difference this makes to your pilgrimage plans?' Luke asked. 'Or don't you know yet?'

'No idea,' Tim replied helplessly. 'I'm hoping we can move on tomorrow, if not tonight, using the coach to catch up for lost time.'

'What if one of us is arrested?' Simon said matter-of-factly.

Tim looked so appalled at this prospect that Georgia hastily tried the rational approach. 'Just because there was tension between Anne and quite a few of you here, that doesn't mean the police will assume that one of you killed her. They'll need evidence.'

'I suppose so,' Tim said, but there was no conviction in his voice.

Peter added his dose of common sense. 'The investigating officer has to assess the evidence first, and see where it's pointing. That could take time. They can't hold you all here indefinitely, so my guess is that it will be up to you whether you go on with the pilgrimage or disperse.'

One look at Tim's face made Georgia realize this was an aspect he hadn't considered.

'They'll be looking for other answers to this, not just from us,' Simon said reasonably, and Tim looked slightly consoled.

If only Anne had taken the offered lift to the farmhouse, Georgia thought. No, that way of thinking would lead nowhere. She had not yet thought of Anne as a friend, but after yesterday, she had been coming to think they *could* become friends. She thought she understood her, and although they were very different in character, they shared common ground. Perhaps it had been partly the Old Road that had brought that about. Its sense of having been trodden over so many years, by individuals and groups just like theirs, was a unifying one. In a way, the past provided fingerprints on the Old Road other than those that had led to the Marsh & Daughter cases. There were good vibes imprinting themselves on the atmosphere as well as those of violence and injustice. Tranquil fingerprints could survive even the jungle of modern so-called civilization, which was encroaching ever more steadily. It was these she might have felt with Anne yesterday.

'Has there been any gossip about shady characters in the area?' Luke asked.

'There's hardly been time,' Tim replied, 'but the landlord told us about a dog walker who had a scare a week or two ago, and he reckoned he'd had one or two odd casuals in the pub.'

'Then fix your thoughts on them, not on your flock,' Luke advised.

'My flock?' Tim grimaced. 'You can guess what we're all secretly thinking, but don't dare to put into words. And it isn't the play. Si and I haven't even got as far as that.'

'It's natural enough,' Georgia said. 'I imagine you're wondering what will happen to the Becket ruins.' Someone had to name it, because of the terrible possibility that Anne had been killed because of them. She shrank away from thinking this through though. It was too soon, much too soon.

Tim nodded. 'They'll probably go to her daughter. And that's the trouble.'

'Why? Have you met her?'

'Yes. She's a chip off the same block as Anne, but worse.'

By lunchtime the pub's clientele was swelling visibly, both inside and out. News had obviously begun to spread, and media representatives were gathering. With the weather remaining fine, by unspoken assent the Chillingham group remained close together outside. Periodically one or two would peel off or be collared as likely prospects by the media to be interviewed as witnesses. Georgia was beginning to find it unbearable. Through TV and the press, the whole nation was going to hear what a wonderful person Anne Fanshawe was, and what an inspiring vicar Chillingham had lost. All probably true, had not the issue of Thomas Becket come between her and her parishioners. Today, however, that subject would be taboo, conveniently sidestepped.

At last more police cars arrived, and Georgia saw the guardian PCs going out through the garden gate to greet their colleagues. Now it would start. Now it would become real. She recognized Will Whitton right away, although he looked older. So must she, of course. All too old. A sudden stab reminded her of the pressing decision she and Luke still had to make over whether or not to go ahead with a third course of IVF. She made herself put that aside. Anne Fanshawe deserved all her concentration now.

Will Whitton must have had prior warning that Peter was here, as he immediately came over to their table, and Tim and Simon took the hint by moving away. Will greeted Peter like a long lost friend, despite the fact that by the time Will had joined the force Peter had already left it (officially). Their subsequent acquaintanceship had been through Peter's periodic eruptions into Mike's working life.

'I gather you were here last night, Peter,' Will began, after the personal chat was over.

'Not me. Georgia and Luke were.'

'Remember me, Inspector?' she asked.

Will grinned. 'Who could forget the dashing Georgia Marsh?'

'Now a dashing Georgia Frost.' She introduced Luke.

Friendly relations established, he got down to business. 'Tell me about Anne Fanshawe.'

'We were recent arrivals on her scene,' Peter explained. 'You need Chillingham residents to talk about her.'

Will wasn't having that. Georgia knew all too well that he might look like a cherub, but angelic he was not, when it came to his job. 'You knew her, and you know who was here. I'm told you were the last person to talk to her, Georgia.'

'Probably. I offered her a lift just as she was leaving. Luke was unlocking the car in the car park, and I saw her walking past. She turned it down.'

Will looked at her sympathetically. 'You must feel badly about that. But life and death can turn on small decisions. What did you do then?'

'Drove back to our home near Old Wives Lees, not far from Chillingham. That meant we turned right out of the car park here, and then left down to join the A20, which meant that we didn't pass Anne again. As you know, she turned left out of the car park.'

'Did you see her walking along the road?'

'Yes. I watched her for a few minutes before I got in the car, to be sure she didn't want to change her mind. She had a torch, but it was a dark night, so she disappeared from sight quite soon. She had a dark dress on too. I suppose that's not the reason . . .'

'No chance,' he said briefly. 'She was definitely strangled, not run down, and her body was dumped in the ditch. Did you pass any other traffic going that way?'

Georgia glanced at Luke. 'I don't remember anything, do you?'

'No. And I would have done because this road and the one to the A20 are mostly single track.'

'Was she robbed?' Peter asked. 'Could that be the motive?'

Will gave him an amused look. 'That's loaded, isn't it? I take it you'd like that simple explanation. Well, the jury's out. Or rather I am. No sign of a coat, but the night was warm. Her bag was chucked in at her side, credit cards missing, but cash left in it. No signs of sexual attack. Could be robbery therefore, but unlikely.'

'No credit cards at the farm?'

'No, so at present I'm not giving odds. My turn: was the victim popular with this group, would you say?'

Georgia decided to take this one on. 'She wasn't walking the whole pilgrimage with them, only the odd day.'

'Why was that?'

'She had four churches to look after so her job was the main reason, I imagine. Also she wasn't in the play, only a supporter. And – ' she knew she had to say it – 'she wasn't popular with everyone.'

'Thanks for that. It's the impression I've got, or rather my trusty team has. Choice of words and tone of voice can tell one a lot that doesn't register on the written witness statements. You'd know that, Peter.'

'All too well,' he agreed.

'Care to tell me the reason for the victim's non-popularity?' The very mildness of Will's manner seemed to Georgia to underline the fact that he wasn't going to be sidetracked, but she still hesitated.

Peter did not. 'The vicar was at the centre of a row over village development, chiefly because she owned the land and buildings that were the key to its success.'

How straightforward that sounded, Georgia thought, grateful she had left it to him. If she had been the one to tell Will, she would probably unwittingly have conveyed more of the angst invested in that subject. From Peter's lips it sounded a perfectly logical dispassionate situation. To listen to him, the heightened emotions towards Anne might not have existed.

'I take it that as she was the landowner she was keen for development,' Will said.

'Far from it. She led the opposition,' Georgia said.

Will looked surprised. 'Strange,' he commented. 'Usually it's the landowner who wants to make a killing—' He broke off at this unfortunate choice of words and made a face. 'Sorry.'

So he had already sensed that Georgia felt emotionally involved. 'Not in this case. She believed her duty was to oppose it.'

'Duty to whom or duty to what?'

'Twofold. The late Robert Wayncroft and Archbishop Thomas Becket.'

He groaned. 'Say no more. I can see why matters clearly got heated. Feeling duty to the past, especially to a saint, is difficult to fight. Just give me a rough idea of who was on her side and who wasn't.' He must have noticed her look towards Peter for guidance. 'This development,' he added, 'I take it the Wayncrofts, being the bigwigs of the village, were also against it.'

'No.' Luke took over to Georgia's relief. She didn't feel up to dealing with this. 'You'll have to ask them, but basically they were in favour of it.'

'Again, that's weird. Traditionally, the bigwigs fight tooth and nail to resist change. Or,' Will added dispassionately, 'in this case perhaps they fought with hands.'

Georgia froze, not understanding why she felt so torn. She wanted Anne's killer found, and yet feared it coming too close to home. Someone here, someone she'd talked to, could have done this. She was getting too emotionally involved, and perhaps Luke realized because he stepped in again.

'I assume it's a man you'll be looking for.'

'Not necessarily. If the victim was taken by surprise from behind, it's possible it could have been a woman, although it's less likely. Now tell me what you were doing here yesterday, and why you're here today, Peter. None of you lives in Chillingham, so are you on a case, Peter?'

She had almost forgotten Hugh Wayncroft, Georgia realized guiltily. He, too, had been strangled. Was that coincidence? It must be.

'Hugh Wayncroft,' Peter explained, 'was murdered in Chillingham in 1967 on a stretch of the nearby Pilgrims' Way, north of the village, at the end of a pilgrimage just like this one. He had played Becket in the same play as that scheduled for next week in Canterbury by this group. His murder was never solved. Ask Mike Gilroy.'

A long pause. 'Most interesting,' Will said at last. 'I will ask him. Indeed I will. Any connection between the two murders, do you think?'

'I've no idea,' Peter replied levelly. 'Coincidence has a long arm.'

'So does the law,' Will replied. 'It seems we should pay particular attention to exactly what was happening during the pilgrimage yesterday, and the dinner yesterday evening. We know about you two, Georgia. Could any others have left the pub about the same time and caught her up, without your seeing them or without being noticed by the others?'

'I didn't see anyone, but it's possible.'

Will looked at her. 'Anything happen during the evening?'

He'd picked up her reluctance to talk, and so she had no option. 'Another row broke out, but . . .'

'Tell me,' he said when she stopped.

'She refused point blank to open up the ruins of St Thomas's chapel and well to the public.'

The phone rang yet again, but to Georgia's relief Luke went to answer it. Will Whitton had released them to return home late in the afternoon, although the pilgrimage party was still being kept at the Dog and Duck. On the way home, Georgia had suggested to Peter that he should stay with them at Medlars overnight, and rather to her surprise Peter had agreed. She had in mind that it had been a long day for him, but he, apparently, had other ideas. They could discuss Anne Fanshawe's death in relation to that of Hugh Wayncroft.

Georgia had rung Janie to suggest she joined them there, but to her dismay it turned out that Peter had forgotten to tell her that he'd be out all day. The museum was closed on Sundays and Mondays, and so today had been a free day for Janie. She had come over to Haden Shaw, had had a wasted journey, and, when Georgia rang, informed her that she had no intention of setting out again.

If it had not been for the fact that Anne Fanshawe was dominating her thoughts, Georgia would have tried harder to persuade her to change her mind, but she lacked the energy. There was always a question mark over including Janie when the primary cause of a meeting with Peter was work, chiefly because Janie would go to such lengths to make it clear that she didn't mind one bit being excluded from the conversation. That made it all the worse. How complicated relationships could get, Georgia thought. Another reason that she hadn't talked Janie into coming was that Peter had a face like a thundercloud when she suggested it.

Luke had been busy preparing his special spaghetti in the kitchen when the phone had rung.

'What's the news?' she called when she heard the receiver replaced.

'It was Tim.' Luke appeared in the kitchen doorway. 'They've just been told they'll be free by tomorrow evening, and so they can carry on with the pilgrimage on Tuesday. That's the Cuxton stop, and on Wednesday they'll be crossing the Medway on to the Downs and Boxley.'

'Are the police marching with them?'

'No. Tim said Val offered to keep in touch daily and to be responsible for keeping the group together. There are plenty of mobile numbers they can ring if Will Whitton wants to speak to any of them. Anyone leaving the group has to be reported.'

'Soon they'll be reaching Mike's area,' Peter said reflectively.

Georgia realized with resignation that Peter would be planning close cooperation with him. Fortunately, Mike had his own ways of saying 'no'.

'How's Tim feeling?' she asked Luke. 'Better?'

'Worse. Can you imagine ploughing along the Old Road wondering whether there's a murderer marching behind you?'

'Murder isn't unknown, even on the Old Road,' she pointed out. 'There was Hugh Wayncroft.'

'There's also the play. I know it seems a minor matter to worry about in comparison with Anne's death, but it means Tim's whole future, and Simon's too, so there's plenty for them to be worried about.'

'But if this daughter inherits her estate and is as thought to be a chip off the old block, couldn't that be a good thing?'

Luke looked blank. 'How? She won't want to open up the ruins either.'

Peter saw what she was implying, however. 'You mean if the daughter takes the same position as her mother, the Becket ruins can't have been the motive for her killing. So unless someone present last night had more personal reasons for killing Anne, the group in the pub might be off the hook.'

'Yes.'

'Wrong,' he pointed out. 'That would depend on who the murderer *thought* would inherit the land.'

'No, I'm *right*,' Georgia argued. 'It was generally known that Anne had a daughter, so she would be the obvious person to inherit them.'

Peter glared. 'Perhaps. But –' a last ditch attempt – 'it all depends what was in her will, if she made one, *and* in Robert Wayncroft's. *And* if it's true about its being generally known. If not, she could well have left everything to the church, which is a much easier target for the pro-development side.'

'Call it a draw,' Luke said before Georgia could reply. 'Supper's ready. Incidentally, do Georgia and I have to regard ourselves as suspects?'

'No, assuming Whitton doesn't find trace evidence that implicates you, and it's hard to see how he could,' Peter said almost grudgingly. He was in a really bad mood, Georgia realized. 'You didn't kiss her goodnight, did you, Luke?' Peter shot at him.

'No, and nor did Georgia. Neither of us was on kissing terms with her.'

'Good. Now about *our* case, Georgia.'

Back to square one. 'Do you think Anne's death is linked to it?' she asked. What did she hope the reply would be? Yes or no? She couldn't decide, and nor could Peter from his answer.

'I don't know. I usually have a good nose for such things, but in this case I don't. The only link I can see is Thomas Becket, and for the life of me I can't see that Anne's death is going to affect that much, if the daughter and half the village are still opposed to it. Including the Moons.'

*   *   *

Georgia had to force herself to visit Chillingham again. It was only five days since Anne's murder, and she still felt raw inside about it. The pilgrims, so Tim told Luke last evening, had reached Boxley and were doing the short seven mile haul to Hollingbourne today, Thursday. He had said that Simon was planning on returning to Chillingham, which meant he might even be back by now.

The publicity for the pilgrimage was ironically all Tim could have longed for when they'd first set out. Now it was unwelcome as the murder dominated every interview, and the play and its longer term objectives had slipped into second place even amongst the cast.

She could not bear to park by Chillingham church with its memories of Anne, and so she drove on to the Three Peacocks – only to find the car park full again. Good news for Simon, although she doubted if his present customers would be gastro diners, and even more whether they would be regular customers. She found a spot to park on the street and went into the bar, which was also packed. Some were obviously from the media, but many seemed to be curious sightseers. Chillingham as well as Wrotham had been much photographed and filmed in the press and on TV.

Derek was behind the bar, and she could glimpse Simon in the kitchen, but there seemed no sign of Lisa. Then she spotted her sitting at a corner table with a smartly dressed woman in her early thirties, with long blonde hair and sharp features. She set her down as an interviewer and was surprised that Lisa was cooperating.

Even more to her surprise, Lisa beckoned to her to join them. There seemed no trace of the hostility or defensiveness that Lisa had shown her earlier. It was as if she had relaxed her guard, and from her face and body language, Georgia could at last see why Simon referred to her as a gentle soul. What had made the difference – the news of Anne's death?

'Georgia, this is Stella Hales, Mrs Fanshawe's daughter,' Lisa introduced her. 'I've been telling her about you and how you're interested in the village history.'

Point noted. How, Georgia wondered, had the subject arisen? She was aware that as she greeted Stella alert eyes were summing her up. This, she decided, was one high-powered

lady. She could easily believe that she was a chip off the old
block, perhaps more to be feared than Anne herself.

Stella rose to greet her. 'Do join us,' she said. 'Simon told
us that you were talking a great deal to my mother the day
she died. I'd like to hear about it.'

Georgia began to think she'd judged too hastily. There was
a humanity in Stella's face as there had been in Anne's, and
she told her as much as she could about her talks with her
mother. Excluding that final row she had overheard. 'I liked
Anne very much. I wish I'd known her better,' she finished.

'So do I. Isn't that what daughters always think when they
lose their mothers? That they never really knew her as a person,
only as a mother?'

Georgia thought of her own mother, Elena, happily not
dead, but living in France with her second husband. Georgia
had been on strained terms with her after she had walked out
on Peter, but they had been reconciled over the discovery of
what had happened to Rick. Elena had listened to the explanation and accepted it. Georgia was relieved at that, but an
unexpected ache persisted. It was almost as if, with that settled,
Elena had broken the last tie not only between herself and
Peter, but with her daughter too. She lived in another country,
and had another life. Georgia was sure that if she visited her
there, Elena would be delighted to see her; if she needed help,
Elena would give it as far as possible, but the tie had been
broken. If she had a grandchild . . . Georgia stopped herself.
She must face the probability that she would not. She and
Luke had agreed that if IVF did not work, they would share
their lives, they would love, they would move on. But would
it work like that? Perhaps just one more session . . . With great
effort Georgia pushed it from her mind. Stella had just lost
Anne, and that was what mattered now.

'You must have a lot to do here,' Georgia said. 'Do you
need help?'

'There's no date for the funeral yet. I'm still waiting to hear
when that can take place, and so no, there isn't, thanks. The
house belongs to the church, and Mum owned the house in
Blackheath that I'd been renting. So it's only the personal posses-
sions, the car and so forth to be sorted, and then I can go.'

'But the land—' Georgia said without thinking.

'What land?'

Lisa was unperturbed. 'Georgia will be talking about St Thomas, his land, his well and his chapel. She doesn't know, you see.'

'Nor did I until the solicitor told me, but I thought the whole world knew by now,' Stella apologized. 'News usually travels fast.'

'Knew what?'

'My mother bequeathed them back to the Wayncrofts.'

SEVEN

Georgia was doubtful about joining Stella and Lisa at the table, but Stella insisted. She had to struggle to make sensible conversation, however, probably because she was still reeling from the astonishing news of Anne's legacy to the Wayncrofts. They opposed everything that Anne and Robert had believed in. Could it have come about because Robert had asked Anne to will the ruins back? If so, why leave them to Anne in the first place? Stella would probably not have an answer to that, and nor would Lisa, even though she was looking sympathetically at Georgia.

The situation became even more awkward. 'Mrs Moon tells me,' Stella said, 'that you and your father write books about the crimes you investigate.'

Subtext: she doesn't read them, Georgia thought. There had been a disdainful note in Stella's voice. Hardly surprising, considering her mother's murder, Georgia supposed, and the fact that the whole pub must be buzzing with the story. A large part of its clientele must be here for just that reason, and Stella was lucky that her identity had apparently not yet been disclosed to them.

'We do,' Georgia answered, 'although—'

'Crimes such as my mother's death?' Stella's voice was cool as she interrupted.

'It's Hugh Wayncroft's death forty years ago in which my father and I are interested.'

'But now you have another more recent one handed to you on a plate, you can broaden your scope.'

'Unless it's linked to Hugh Wayncroft, there's no way your mother's death would concern us.' Georgia did her best to sound neutral. 'The police would not take kindly to our poking our noses into their area of responsibility.'

'But the past is fair game, open to all.' Stella wasn't going to give up.

'That's one way of looking at it; the other is that just because

something happened in the past there is no reason that it should
be forgotten or remain unsolved.'

'Provided the living don't suffer,' Lisa murmured.

'With the exception of Hugh Wayncroft's murderer, if he's
still alive,' Georgia amended. 'Otherwise, I agree with you.'

Lisa looked at her thoughtfully – and, Georgia decided,
more kindly. 'Isn't that God's business?'

'Not if the living are still suffering because of what happened.'
Where did that come from? Georgia had surprised herself. She
hadn't consciously considered that might be happening in
Chillingham because of Hugh Wayncroft's death. Her response
seemed to have satisfied Lisa, because she said no more.

Stella's belligerence must have also softened, because she
leaned spontaneously towards Georgia. 'The police won't tell
me anything, which I suppose is to be expected, so, tell me,
do you think there really could be a link between Mum's death
and this other one you're investigating? I remember she told
me once she was pally with this Hugh's brother Robert.
Or are you putting two and two together just because the
circumstances are so much the same?' She seemed genuinely
concerned, and Georgia sought for the right answer.

'Your mother was a brave woman *and* in holy orders. She
could have been carrying secrets that she could not share.'

'Did you get any hint of that? Was she worried when you
saw her on Saturday? What did she say?' The questions were
tumbling out now, and Georgia did her best to answer them.
The first was the most difficult and so she left it until last.

'As for secrets,' she finished, 'yes, I did think your mother
was holding back on me.'

'About those ruins?'

'I can't be as precise as that. She talked a little about them.'

Lisa promptly took her up on this. 'She don't seem to have
told you she was leaving them to the Wayncrofts.' Her voice
had a hard edge to it.

'Did you know about it, Lisa? It must have been a shock,'
Georgia said, 'especially coming at such a time.'

Lisa was caught off guard. 'No, I never knew,' she said
woodenly. 'I dare say she had her reasons.'

Stella turned down Georgia's renewed offer of help as she
departed after lunch for the vicarage. Good relations had been

restored, although Georgia sensed this might be because Stella
needed allies not enemies. Some day, she decided, she would
talk to Stella about her mother, when emotions were less
fragile and when she would not be preoccupied with work for
Marsh & Daughter.

Lisa returned to the kitchen after bidding Georgia goodbye,
but then changed her mind and came back to the table again.
'I'll be free in thirty minutes or so, Georgia. Like to see a bit
more of Chillingham?'

This was an olive branch she could not refuse. Whatever
Lisa had in mind it could hardly be a simple sightseeing
tour, and so Georgia accepted. If the apparent head of the
Moon clan was extending such a hand of welcome it could
be significant.

The waiting period provided a good opportunity to ring
Peter with the mind-boggling news about the Becket ruins.
Stella was definitely the horse's mouth as regards its accur-
acy, and the legacy could have a significance that she herself
had not spotted. So far the Marsh & Daughter case was stalled,
and Anne's death conjured up sombre possibilities.

The noise level in the pub was still high, and so she went
outside to make the call. A long sigh of satisfaction greeted
her news.

'Ah,' was Peter's illuminating reaction. 'This could change
everything, both for the police case *and* for us.'

He didn't need to spell it out. It was obvious that if Julian
and Val had learned of the bequest in advance, then a motive
for Anne's death immediately sprang up. It could even have
been Anne who had told them about it. It put Julian, Val and
anyone else who felt strongly on the development issue in
the spotlight – even, though she hated to think of it, Simon
and Tim.

The same motive must have existed for Hugh's murder. His
rigorous opposition to development gave all those who
supported it, including Val Harper, Jessica, Clive Moon and
Fred Miller, a motive. In Jessica and Val's case they would
have been cutting off their noses to spite their faces however,
as the property they wanted to control reverted to Robert.
Nevertheless, Val's presence was a factor common to both
pilgrimages.

When Lisa appeared, right at the promised time, Simon was

with her. 'You must be pleased about the news on the St Thomas ruins,' Georgia said, uncomfortably aware that it was hardly good news for Lisa.

'Yes, but it's hard to deal with at the moment.' Simon, too, glanced at Lisa.

Most of the customers had left now, but a group of press were still clustering in the car park. 'Quaint old village shocked by vicar's murder,' he added wryly.

'We'll need to be getting used to crowds, Simon,' Lisa observed.

'Thomas Becket is one thing, this is quite another,' he replied. 'I'm proud of my cooking, but I doubt if the crowds we're getting at present even notice what they're eating. Tim says the pilgrim band is swelling hourly too. When they reached Boxley yesterday, the cameras were waiting for them, and today the more determined sightseers have donned their walking boots.'

'How is the cast taking it?' Georgia asked.

'They're split. Some of them want to come back home, either because of the press or because they think it's not respectful to Anne for the play to go on. The rest want to continue as if nothing had happened. A lot didn't know Anne well at all, so I suppose it's understandable. Val, Julian and Aletta are all for going on. All grist to their publicity mill.'

'You and Tim changed sides then, Simon?' Lisa asked caustically.

He gave her a hug. 'Nothing is ever as clear cut as that. I'm still in favour of publicity, but not through Anne's death. Tim feels torn in two, and I'm much the same. Whatever the reason, I can't ignore the fact that we did ninety covers at lunch, and we're fully booked this evening. So is Molly Jones.'

'Who's she?' Georgia asked.

'One of the Painters.'

'Artists?'

'No,' Simon answered and too late she remembered the name from her walk around the churchyard. 'The Painters are like the Moons,' he continued. Another affectionate hug for Lisa. 'They're built into the Chillingham fabric. Molly's husband Bill Jones is regarded as an incomer like Tim and me, the difference being he's been living here forty years and is *still* seen as an outsider.'

'Molly's dad was John Painter,' Lisa explained. 'He were one of the gardeners on the estate, but he was a canny chap,' Lisa told her. 'He bought the house off the estate when he was getting older, with Mr Robert's help, and began the bed and breakfast business in it when the North Downs Way was set up. That would be in the late seventies. Molly and Bill ran it for him, together with Vic Painter, Molly's brother. He lives in the lodge by the entrance to Chillingham Place.'

An incomer after forty years. By that reckoning Georgia thought Peter would still be regarded as an incomer to Haden Shaw. As for Luke, he was so new to the area he was not even in the reckoning yet. He was probably still considered a tourist.

'I'll show you Becket House,' Lisa offered. 'That's their place.'

Becket House? No need to ask which side the Joneses were on, Georgia thought.

'Before you think this is more village politics –' Simon laughed, echoing her thoughts – 'it was always called Becket House, even when it was part of the estate. Before John worked for the Wayncrofts I gather he had a job in Canterbury Cathedral grounds, so he was dead set on local history. He only died a year or two back, so I knew him reasonably well.'

Simon made his way back to the kitchen as Lisa and Georgia left for their tour. Georgia had assumed that all she had wanted was a quiet chat, but as soon as they set out, Lisa began to talk knowledgeably about the origins of the village in Saxon times as a farming community bordering the Old Road, and how it had developed in Norman times. Georgia was some-what puzzled. Why was this seemingly prototype silver-haired lady equipped with sensible walking shoes choosing to give her a historical tour of Chillingham now? After all, she must have been close to Anne, and the aftermath of her murder seemed an odd time for mere goodwill cooperation and history tours. Could it be that this was Lisa's way of hinting that the answer to Anne's murder lay here in Chillingham itself? She waited patiently for a clue.

'Where do you live, Georgia? A villager, are you?'

'Not quite. Luke and I live quite close in fact, in a hamlet outside Old Wives Lees. I was brought up in Haden Shaw.'

'I know Haden. Clive's sister used to live there. Hasn't got Chillingham's history, has it?'

'Chillingham is more of a community,' Georgia agreed.

'Bit too much of a community sometimes,' Lisa grunted. 'Mind you, the village shop is all we've got left here. Alison – she's my daughter-in-law, Matt's wife – she'll tell you. They're going to take away her post office, so she and Matt have to start running a posting service down to Chartham. Government doesn't even know we're here, let alone care. If you ask me they're cutting us off in the hope we oldies will die off without a fuss.'

Georgia duly laughed, as she was meant to, but she could tell how intense the feeling was behind Lisa's words.

'We're a community though,' Lisa continued. 'I agree with you there. Have to be. We depend on each other; we mostly know everyone else here. You see this building?' She pointed to a large ragstone house on one side of the road. 'The old church school house, that is. It's over a hundred and fifty years old, and that's still reckoned new round here. The almshouses are seventeenth century, and Becket House, where we're going, I reckon it was here when old Thomas himself came galloping along the Old Road. If not, then it started life as a pilgrim hostel.'

'Do you think Becket really know Chillingham well?'

'Dunno, reckon so. After all, he liked that old manor at Otford, where he told the nightingales off good and proper. He might have liked it here in Chillingham because of the peacocks. Rather have the nightingales, myself.'

'He left a well too.'

'So they say.'

They were skirting around the central issue, Georgia thought, and it was time to call a halt. 'Why did you suggest this walk, Lisa?' she asked forthrightly. 'Is it something to do with Anne's murder?'

She didn't think Lisa would answer, and indeed she took her time. 'If you're going to find out about Hugh Wayncroft, you have to understand how Chillingham came to be. Can't write about it as an outsider.'

'Don't you think that it might need an outsider's eye?'

'That eye only gets so far,' Lisa answered drily. 'You can look at these buildings all you like, but they're like a painting.

It depends on what you see. You need to know how it got this way before you can begin to understand it.'

'Beginning with the Wayncrofts, I suppose. They must have first owned, then dominated, the village for centuries. Most villagers must have worked for them in one way or another. But now it's different.'

'Not really. It's like my kids,' Lisa replied. 'They lead their own lives, but I'm still their mother. They can't change that. I just take a different place in their lives. It's like that with the Wayncrofts and the village, I reckon. Mrs Jessica still totters down to the service most Sundays and does what else she can. Mr Julian does a lot; so does Mr Val now he's back.'

'And Sebastian?'

'Him as well. But he's young.' The expression on Lisa's face read 'don't go there', Georgia noticed. All the more reason to push ahead.

'He seems very fond of your granddaughter.'

'That's as maybe. She'll be leaving the village soon, though, and going to uni.' Lisa was brisk.

So why didn't Sebastian endear himself to Lisa? A touch of Tess needing to 'know her place' perhaps? Lisa seemed too sensible for that. It must be that Lisa considered that as Tess was a Moon, she should be opposed to development, even though Seb was all for it. Strong feelings indeed.

'If the village looks to Chillingham Place and the Wayncrofts, why is there so much opposition to their views over the chapel?' Georgia tried to avoid singling Lisa herself out, but Lisa was not fooled.

Nor, it seemed, was she upset. 'I'm a Roman Catholic, m'dear. That's why.'

'So were the Wayncrofts,' Georgia said reasonably. 'And the Roman Catholic Church exploited gullible pilgrims too in medieval times, just as I'm sure the Anglican church would have done in the same circumstances. There was the Rood of Boxley—'

'That's as maybe,' Lisa cut her off. 'There's dark and there's light to everything. And there's darkness in Chillingham Place just the same as there was in the inn.'

Georgia didn't follow this. 'In the Three Peacocks?'

'The inn that turned Mary and Joseph out into the stable,' Lisa said.

Was this matter of fact statement as straight as it seemed, or was Lisa trying to direct her attention away from Chillingham? The going was getting heavier.

'I heard your husband supported the Wayncrofts over village development.' She waited to see if Lisa would take offence, but again she did not.

'Everyone's entitled to their own view,' she answered. 'And my Clive had his. If that meant supporting Mrs Wayncroft and young Mr Harper he would do it, he said. He believed in progress, but I takes it with a pinch of salt. One step forward, two steps back if you're not careful. Clive wasn't a Catholic like me, but we brought our children up in the true religion.'

'You've two sons? A daughter too?'

She shook her head. 'Just Matthew and Derek.' She stopped by a row of cottages set back from the road and explained their history at such a length that Georgia was sure she was deliberately changing the subject. But again Lisa surprised her by briskly returning to her sons.

'Everyone likes Matt and Derek. Derek's a chip off Clive's old block, but Matt takes after me.'

'They could only have been toddlers in 1967, and you would have had other things on your mind than village politics, but can you remember how you felt about the development project then?'

She thought Lisa was not going to answer, but she did after a moment. 'Just the same, but I wasn't so bothered. I was a mum with a small child of three. Derek didn't come along until 'sixty-nine. I look at things differently now. The Wayncrofts want to change the village for good, with theatres and visitor centres and what have you. They say the shops, pubs and bed and breakfasts will flourish, but what about the cost of houses, eh? That will go up, planning permissions will turn the place into a building site, and then where will we be? And, what's more important, where will St Thomas be, you tell me that,' she added amiably. 'Lost in the middle of a pile of money.'

'But he's nowhere now,' Georgia pointed out as gently as she could. 'There are only ruins left.'

'If you think that, then you're not the lady I took you for. If you were standing by those ruins with a bus-load of tourists I'd agree. St Thomas won't bother to pop in. But you try standing there alone by them, as I do, with the Old Road running close by, and the green grass as green as ever it was, and in the silence he'll come. He always does. It's his chapel, his well.'

Georgia felt humbled, but she had to go on. 'To the ruins, maybe. But what about the village? It has to survive or it will just be a dormitory for Canterbury.'

'St Thomas is here in the village too. Don't you feel him?' Lisa could have been discussing the shopping list for all the passion in her voice, Georgia thought. Thomas Becket was clearly an everyday presence for Lisa, however, so Georgia did not doubt her sincerity. For her he was a living entity. 'He's here all right,' Lisa continued, 'but he's not going to stroll around a blinking visitor centre with a load of gawpers or sell ice creams to overstuffed playgoers.' Lisa laughed. 'You think I'm barmy, don't you?'

Georgia grinned. 'No. I think you have a valid viewpoint, but a personal one. All villages change over time; even Chillingham has changed. Look at these Victorian cottages here, and the church. That's only Tudor-built. People must have grumbled about all these new buildings when they came around.'

'They came gradual like, with Thomas leading the way. But the Wayncrofts will manage to kick him out. He's here, I tell you. You just follow me.'

She turned and walked across the road to a row of cottages set at right angles to the main street and facing a stretch of grass. They looked eighteenth-century to Georgia, but it was hard to tell – for the bricks were patched where, over the years, doors and windows had varied their place or size.

'Here's where we Moons live. I'm here, next to the road. Derek's in the middle with his wife, Joannie. His kids are still living here. Matt is at the end of the row with Alison, Tess and Will. That's where I'm taking you. They won't mind. Well, we won't go to his house, but the workshop at the end.'

When they reached it, Georgia saw a building completely different in style to the red-brick cottages. This had once been a ragstone barn; it had now been converted to have windows, and the roof was ancient corrugated iron. It looked solid and workmanlike, but hardly state of the art, so Georgia wondered why Lisa had been anxious for her to see it.

As soon as Lisa unlocked the door and ushered her in, the smell hit her.

'Wood,' she exclaimed.

Lisa nodded. 'Special, that is.'

There was wood everywhere: on the long middle table running the length of the barn, on the shelving, in piles under the side work bench that had lathes and equipment on it.

'I want to show you something,' Lisa continued.

Georgia watched as Lisa bent down to open a cupboard and brought something out. She half expected to see a wooden statue of St Thomas, but this was not so intricate. It was a simple box, maybe a foot square, with an arched lid and old-fashioned lock. It gleamed golden brown, the polish bringing out the varying shades of colour, and it seemed almost to be crying out for her to touch it.

As if reading her mind, Lisa said softly, 'The living wood. You can see it. Run your hand over it. It likes being touched. Matthew's good with wood. This is his special favourite.'

As Georgia put her hand on the rounded lid, it did indeed feel not only smooth, but also warm, and most of all alive, as if it were bonding her to it. Would she have felt that way if the room were full of people? She doubted it. This was a personal experience, and she saw what Lisa had meant by being alone with the Becket ruins.

Lisa was watching her carefully. 'See what I mean? Not like stone, is it? Stone's death to my mind, but it's easy to believe St Thomas lives on here, isn't it? Maybe you're right, and he doesn't, but if you feel he does, that's what counts, isn't it? The Moons and the Painters, you might be told we're the living village, but it's not us. It's old Thomas. He wants us to carry on.'

'But Lisa,' Georgia began hesitantly,' there was a murder in 1967. And another one only two days ago. What if they were committed in St Thomas's name?'

For the first time she saw Lisa's calm confidence shaken, and she shook her head violently. 'Mrs Fanshawe killed because of that? That would be real wickedness, that would.'

'St Thomas was murdered too,' Georgia said. 'Good has to fight evil.'

'Wickedness,' Lisa repeated, her eyes on Georgia's hand,

which was still caressing the wood. Then, abruptly: 'You'd best go on with that book of yours.'

The official sanction? Georgia could hardly believe it, but she had to be sure. 'If Peter and I do go ahead, it would not be Anne Fanshawe's murder that we investigated, but the 1967 death.'

'My golden year,' Lisa murmured. 'When I played Rosamund, and look what happened.' A pause, then she looked straight at Georgia. 'You go ahead. The time's come. I know it.'

Time for what? Lisa seemed to be in a place Georgia could not reach. Time that the truth was known? That Hugh Wayncroft received justice at last? Had the Moons been implicated? Had Clive been Hugh's murderer? Reluctantly, Georgia withdrew her hand from Matthew's box, and Lisa returned it to the cupboard as a signal it was time to leave, to begin the quest – presumably – that she had now sanctioned. Georgia knew she was right. She'd been given the open sesame to Chillingham.

'You'd best meet the Painters first,' Lisa said briskly, and she led Georgia back the way they had come – across the road, past the church and along the lane that she had driven along before. First came the entrance to Chillingham Place, with the lodge on its corner. 'That's Vic's place,' Lisa said, 'but it's his sister Molly you need to know first if you're going to stay here.'

Stay here? What was this?

Already, a formidable picture was beginning to build up in Georgia's mind as they walked into the forecourt of Becket House. What would this Molly be like? A Mrs Danvers as in *Rebecca*? The forecourt was full of cars, suggesting that the press were encamped here too. It was noisy as several cars were about to leave; with laughing, slamming of doors and engines roaring, it hardly seemed a quiet backwater. She had assumed that the Painters, like the Moons, were against development, but their business and the name of this house suggested otherwise.

Lisa led her round to the back of the house, opened the kitchen door and called out: 'Client for you, Molly.'

It wasn't Molly, but a man, a surly-looking one in his sixties. Would this be Bill Jones or Vic Painter, she wondered, aware that she was being summed up by the man's unexpectedly piercing blue eyes. He merely grunted an acknowledgement as Lisa introduced her, before disappearing back inside and muttering that he'd call Molly.

'Don't take no notice of Vic,' Lisa told her. 'He's a caution, that one. Comes in to help out when Bill can't. He works part-time in Canterbury.'

Molly, when she arrived, also looked in her early sixties, and was no Mrs Danvers, to Georgia's relief. She was a pleasant looking woman, with a contented face, the sort that would be unfazed by anything less than an earthquake. 'Full up,' she announced. 'Couldn't squeeze a lemon in here. What a shame.'

She said it not with the usual triumph at being able to turn people away, an attitude all too common, but apparently with genuine regret. It was just as well, if the idea of her staying here took root. Georgia began to feel she was being manipulated, but had no objection. If Lisa wanted her closer to Chillingham, she must have a reason for doing so.

'It wouldn't be for today,' Georgia explained, 'but maybe soon.'

'She's writing a book, Molly.' A familiar female voice sang out from the kitchen table, its owner obscured from Georgia's view. But she knew that voice.

'Her Ladyship's here,' muttered Lisa.

Georgia could now see Her Ladyship, Jessica Wayncroft, clad today in bright magenta and sitting regally at the table. She could also see what Lisa meant by her still keeping an eye on things.

'I hear,' Jessica remarked, 'that you were on that walk on Saturday when the poor vicar died.' Then came an artificial start of surprise. 'Oh, Lisa, how delightful to see you. I didn't notice you at first.'

'Sentiment not returned,' Lisa replied.

For a moment Georgia thought she had misheard, but from the atmosphere it was clear that she had not. Fortunately, Jessica seemed to think this a great joke. 'Come, Lisa, not in front of guests to our village.'

'Don't see why not.' Her voice still cool, Lisa advanced into the kitchen and Jessica switched subjects.

'I'm told you were talking to Mrs Fanshawe on Saturday,

Georgia. Julian is very upset, and so are Aletta and Val. I haven't quite taken it in yet; it seems so extraordinary to think it happened on a pilgrimage just like the one during which my poor Hugh died. But then you weren't there this time, were you, Lisa?'

'I wasn't, Mrs Wayncroft. Not like Mr Valentine.'

The darts flew to and fro with a vengeance that startled Georgia. What on earth was going on?

Jessica ignored the mention of her son. 'Dear Tessa is playing Rosamund this time, isn't she? The casting isn't quite so convenient as last time.'

Lisa said nothing, and Georgia was torn between hope that the cat fight was over and longing for it to continue. It wasn't over, as Lisa said very deliberately:

'I remember that. You being Queen Eleanor out to poison me.'

'Quite right too,' Jessica said blithely. 'Fair Rosamund was the King's paramour.' A pause. 'However, I was more concerned with your relationship with your protector and saviour, Becket. I'm sure Lisa has explained to you, Georgia, that she was my Hugh's dearly beloved mistress?'

EIGHT

'Hugh was gentle. Kind too. I'd never met anyone like him before,' Lisa said at last as Georgia walked back along the lane with her. 'Never since, either. He'd look at you in a way that made you want to be as good as him, not reproving like, or holier-than-thou. Hugh didn't need to prove he was a good man. He *was* good. And before you say, how does that fit with him having a bit on the side, it doesn't. Maybe outsiders wouldn't agree, but Chillingham still looked on him as good. And that includes me.' A pause. 'So how about coming in for a cup of tea.'

Georgia willingly accepted. Far from being thrown by Jessica's outburst, Lisa seemed to be taking it in her stride. She had behaved so matter-of-factly as they left Becket House that Georgia assumed Jessica's accusation must be general knowledge in the village. Georgia was an outsider, however, so today could have been a declaration of war on Jessica's part – but against Lisa or herself? It explained a lot, but whether it affected Hugh's death remained to be seen.

'I'll get the tea,' Lisa said, once they were back at her cottage. She disappeared into the kitchen, leaving Georgia in the cosy living room. There was still an open fireplace, which suggested that in winter time it would be even cosier. There were photographs displayed of Matt and Derek as children, a portrait of Clive in perhaps his thirties, which Georgia studied, and a wedding photo of them both. Fair Rosamund indeed, Georgia thought as she studied it. This girl with the dancing eyes and long flowing blonde hair was hard to see in the Lisa of today. Her beautiful face shone out with hope and expectations of life and love. The bridegroom was good-looking, earnest and proud. By the time the later portrait of him had been taken he had lost that look. He was still handsome, but maturity had given him a wary, almost sly appearance. Georgia knew it was unfair to judge by photos, but nevertheless she decided she would not have liked Clive Moon, and she wondered how happy a marriage it had been. Presumably he had known about the affair with Hugh, especially if it had continued after their marriage. They'd married, according to the photo, in 1963. Had the affair still been going on at the time of Hugh's death?

Lisa reappeared first with a tray, then a teapot, then a cake – of course Lisa would be a cake-maker, Georgia thought enviously. And it would be delicious.

'Now you'll be wondering whether Mrs Wayncroft was right about Hugh and me,' Lisa said comfortably as she cut a slice of cake for Georgia.

'Yes, I was. Jessica's quite what one might call an attention-seeking lady,' she added.

'Always was.'

'Was her marriage to Hugh unhappy then?'

'Never asked,' Lisa said. 'You'd think it was, seeing that Hugh fell for me, but you can never tell. He was a simple sort of fellow, and Jessica, well, you can see, she stirred him up, got things going. To my mind, looking back, he loved us both.'

A remarkably objective summary, Georgia thought. 'She didn't get her way over the Thomas Becket remains.'

'No.' Lisa grinned. 'Hugh could be real obstinate, and over that he was. Surprised me. I was all for a bit of excitement in Chillingham at first, and so was Clive. He thought the Becket well a hoot and was all for milking it dry – if you can say that of a well. Being young, we thought the village needed to wake up a bit. But then Hugh talked to me as no one had before. He told me all about St Thomas and the Old Road, and even risked taking me to the pictures to see that film *A Canterbury Tale*. It was made near the end of the war to get folks worked up about D-Day, but it was sometimes put on in Canterbury for years after that. I didn't think much of it at first, wasn't like the Hollywood stuff I was keen on. This was the time of the Beatles and brave new worlds opening up, so a film about an old country road and war didn't hit the right buttons. Then Hugh explained to me about the pilgrimages along the Road in the old days and how we were all here not just for ourselves but as guardians of what was to come. Just look at us now, eh? Acting as though there were no tomorrow for the poor old world.'

'Did you love Hugh, or were you just bowled over by him?'

Perhaps this was a step too far, but she felt sure that Lisa was well able to field anything she didn't feel like answering. But this question she did.

'No doubt about it. I loved him. Clive had been courting me for a year or two, but I wasn't too sure about him. Then I met Hugh, and it all began. I didn't have no stars in my eyes. He won't leave Mrs Wayncroft for you, my girl, my mum said, and I knew that. So after a while I married Clive, had Matthew and later Derek. I didn't see so much of Hugh for a while, but the play brought it all back. On stage as Becket with his arm round me, saving me from that she-wolf, murmuring, "Come with me," I could feel him trembling. Everyone knew about him and me, but no one much cared, not even Mrs Wayncroft.'

'Are you sure about that?' Unusual, to say the least, and with anyone but Lisa Georgia would have dismissed this out of hand.

'I should be. She came to tell me herself. I was married by that time and had Matthew, and she could see I wasn't much of a threat. She came steaming round to size me up, told me she was pregnant at long last and having a hard time carrying the kid. She said if I didn't cause any trouble, and didn't flaunt around, she'd live with it. She didn't want no upset, probably thought I was just a passing fancy because she was pregnant and out of action.'

'And was she right about that?'

'No. But I didn't tell her that. Hugh wouldn't go mistreating her though. He loved her in his way.'

'So the affair went on for some years.'

'Off and on. That's the way it can go in a village. If you make a fuss about it, it's high drama, but if you don't shout it from the housetops, everyone knows, but no one talks about it. That way no one's hurt.'

'Mrs Wayncroft was shouting from the housetops today.'

'Yes. Odd that.' Lisa frowned. 'Not Her Ladyship's style. But then –' she looked hard at Georgia – 'you're writing about what happened in the 1960s, aren't you?'

'We hope to. It's Hugh's death that interests us from the professional point of view; the vicar's would only come into it if it links back to Hugh's. Could it?'

Lisa sighed. 'I don't know, m'dear, and that's the truth. I

don't know who killed my Hugh, and I don't know who killed
the poor vicar. I get along by steering my way through the
shallows; deep water needs more than I can manage.'

'And yet you're talking to me.'

The sharp eyes fixed on her. 'Think I like it, do you? Well,
I don't, but it's time someone found out who took Hugh away
from me. You're clever, you and your father. Before long
you'd have found out about Hugh and me and be off on the
wrong track. Clive, Mrs Wayncroft, Hugh and me – we're
the wrong track for you. We'd sorted out where we all stood
long before. If there was any high drama to be made of it,
it would have happened much earlier than 1967. There weren't
no question of me leaving Clive for Hugh or for Hugh leaving
his wife for me. It was all sorted.'

'I'm sorry, but I have to ask this. Did Clive mind about
Hugh?'

''Course he minded,' Lisa said. 'We had a few rough
patches, but it sorted itself out.'

Before or after Hugh's death, Georgia wondered, but Lisa
had clearly decided she had said enough on that point because
she continued, 'There were plenty of walkers on the path,
even in those days, and some odd characters all right. The
police questioned one or two of them and ruled them out.
The village went quiet after that, numb you might say, and
the case was closed. But someone knows more than they
said. Must do.'

'Were there fireworks on the pilgrimage, or at the play?'

'I wondered when you'd ask me that,' Lisa said with satisfaction. 'Answer's yes. We had everything from damp squibs
to rockets in the way of temper tantrums, together with a few
fancy Catherine wheels in-between. It started off all hunky
dory. We took our summer holidays so we could do the
pilgrimage, and those who could walked it, just as they're
doing now. I had Matthew though, and Mrs Wayncroft had
Julian, so neither of us did the whole lot. I joined in for the
last twenty miles or so while my mum looked after Matthew,
and Mrs Wayncroft got Hugh's mum to do the same. By that
time things were getting edgy on the Old Road. I could tell
that. I remember waiting for them at the Hollingbourne stop.
The old vicar was with me. Funny old chap, but we felt the
same about St Thomas. Mr Riding did the whole stretch, but

not little Anne. His wife brought her along on the last stretch from here to Canterbury. So excited she was at the thought of the play and walking with the grown-ups. Fred Miller did the same – never liked him much. He and his wife owned the Three Peacocks and were always arguing. She ran off with a soldier in the 1980s, and after that he didn't make such a song and dance of what a great chap he was. Nasty piece of work was Fred. He was always at loggerheads with Hugh over the St Thomas chapel. He and Mr Valentine were the worst for that. Never saw anyone's point of view but their own.'

'What was your husband like? In the photos he looks quite dashing.'

'Clive was a funny old cuss. Loved wood, like Matt and Derek. He was the temperamental sort, emotional. Sometimes he'd retreat into himself, and I couldn't get a word out of him for days. He'd stomp off into his workroom and carve away endlessly. Liked his football, though. He'd come out for that. Look I'll show you something.' Lisa fetched a photo album from a bookshelf and rummaged through it until she found the one she wanted. 'The happy band of pilgrims, look at them.'

Georgia studied the snapshot. The party had been photo-graphed in a field presumably on the Pilgrims' Way; they were in a group yet somehow didn't look united. She managed to pick out a much younger Val Harper and Lisa herself.

'There's my Hugh,' Lisa said, pointing to a tall slender man with light coloured hair who stood to one side of the group as if to declare he was indeed merely one of the gang. Julian, Georgia thought, would automatically have taken centre stage.

'Which side were the Painters on in the St Thomas argu-ment?' Georgia asked her.

'Funny you should ask that. You'd expect them to be all for development, given what their livelihood is, but they're not. They want St Thomas to lie in peace. John now, Molly and Vic's dad, sided with Mrs Wayncroft way back, but when he bought Becket House blow me if he didn't change his mind, even though he needed the trade. He was an odd chap. Only died in 2004, spent the war in Canterbury because of a bit of a limp, no good for the forces. He was a cathedral fire-guard on the night of the big air raid in 1942 and said he felt he'd done his bit overall. But it rankled. Vic and Molly have always stayed on our side, against tourism for the sake of it. He don't mind chatting to outsiders who are generally interested though. Bit of a historian is Vic.'

'One could argue that pilgrimages were merely the medieval form of tourism.'

'They were God-fearing folk,' Lisa said firmly. 'Not like today's gawpers.'

Time to change direction, Georgia thought. 'So what happened on the 1967 pilgrimage?'

Lisa was willing enough to talk about it. 'There was a funny atmosphere, and I began to get worried the nearer we got to Canterbury. The group was beginning to divide up, and that didn't seem right to me. It was the same in the evenings. Different groups, different rounds of drinks.'

'And what happened when you reached Canterbury?'

'The play? We gave a rattling good performance, but the cast divided into two sides, just like the pro-Beckets and the anti-Beckets in the play. Hugh was the perfect Becket – he was a wonderful actor. He'd blossom on stage. You'd not look twice at him if you passed him in the street but on the stage he'd come out like a king. Mr Val was good – he was Fitzurse, the chief murderer, and Clive Moon was the king. He was all bluster, no finesse, not like Hugh. I hated it when Clive kissed me. Had to pretend it was Hugh. Bill Riding was directing the play, and Fred Miller was one of the other murderers.' She paused. 'You'll want to know about the last night. Well, I'll never forget the look Hugh gave me in the last scene when they murdered him. I was doing my Rosamund act sobbing in the background, and Hugh seemed to be looking at me as though it really were the last time.'

'Were there any fireworks after that?' Georgia remembered Jessica's story of the glass of wine and was intrigued to know what Lisa's version would be.

'Oh yes. At the after-show party. That's the usual place to let off steam. We had a party on stage in the theatre, when we were still on a high. Clive was full of his own importance and booze, and I suppose we were all pretty tanked up. It was a little thing that began it. Bill Riding said something about it being a pity the play couldn't have a longer run, and Mr Val said quick as a flash, "Let's put it on in Chillingham, outside St Thomas's own chapel." In a minute it all seemed settled. Hugh went very white and stayed out of the discussion though, until someone – can't remember who – thought to ask him if it was OK by him. Hugh just said no, it wasn't. Even I was a bit surprised, as it would only have been a one-off event, but it triggered off a row. His wife was laying into him, until she saw he was really upset and changed sides. Hugh said he might think about it, which was a mistake, because everyone took that as a yes and immediately there were big plans for opening up the ruins for cash – at which Mrs Wayncroft changed sides again. It was Hugh, me, the vicar and Bill Riding against everyone else. The result was that Hugh refused point blank to let the ruins be used, and the atmosphere got very nasty. Mrs Wayncroft threw a glass of wine over me and accused me of being his whore. Poor old Hugh. Doubt if he knew what the word meant. It quietened down, but that was almost worse. The clearing up next day was done in silence, and we were all pretty miserable on the walk back. We couldn't get back home quickly enough.'

'But you celebrated in the pub when you arrived.'

'Only because it had been prearranged. No one had the heart for it, and that's the reason we didn't hunt earlier for Hugh. We all thought he'd gone straight home to avoid more conflicts.'

'When did you last see him on the walk back?'

'Hugh and I tried to keep apart, so I don't remember talking to him there. We had a quick kiss at the clearing up. He looked so apologetic, as though it was his fault; he explained he had to take that position because it was the Wayncroft heritage. That was the last time I saw him properly – only glimpses after that, if I turned round. I know he was at the back of the column during the walk home, but I tried not to look at him. Clive was behind me, and he'd have had his eye on me, you can count on that. I saw Hugh with his wife at one point before she stalked off. She must have been nagging him about the ruins, because as she passed Clive and me she had a face like a thundercloud. She said, "He still won't budge. Says Robert wouldn't like it." Then she went up to join Val. I looked back and saw poor Hugh all alone and wanted to go back but thought I'd better not. Clive was still watching me. Then we paused a bit and might have got into a different order. I don't know what happened then. As we went round the corner of Peacock Wood, we were too busy picking our way along the path – not so well kept as it is now, and so we spread out a bit. The word went back that we were going to have a ceremonial entrance on to the road, with the band at the front and the main characters at the front and rear. And that was about it. I didn't see him again, just thought he was so fed up that he'd gone home.'

'What did Jessica mean by Robert not liking it? What was *it*?'

'The whole idea of opening up the ruins for cash. I don't know why. Hugh never talked about Robert much, but sometimes it felt like he thought Robert was still owner of the house, so whatever he said went.'

'The discovery of the body must have been terrible for you.'

Lisa looked back over the years and grief filled her face. 'One of those nightmares you don't revisit,' she said steadily. 'It was beginning to rain and so we were all hurrying to get home through the wood and weren't so much in the column. I couldn't see Hugh, but the path or paths at that point kept twisting.'

'Did you go straight to the pub? Did you look for Hugh?'

'No. I nipped back to check on Matthew, so when I got to the pub and saw Hugh wasn't there, but Jessica was, I assumed he might be doing the same as me and checking on his baby Julian. Although in his case it would have been an excuse to avoid the row breaking out again. Then Jessica and Val came back from the manor and said Hugh wasn't there after all. I began to feel scared then. Nothing seemed right.'

'Did you go on the search party?'

'Yes, but I hung back. I was scared by then, really scared. Mrs Wayncroft was leading it; Vic Painter was there, and Mr Val of course. They'd both have been about twenty and full of the joys of spring. Not that day, though, even though Mr Val was just as keen on developing the place then as he is now. He never got on well with his stepfather, and least of all over that.'

'It must have caused a terrific uproar in the village.' Georgia tried to imagine the horror of it. 'It's still surprising to me that the talk seems to have died down so quickly after Hugh's death. You'd think that it would go on being discussed for decades, but it doesn't seem to have been.'

Lisa's mouth took on the set look with which Georgia was becoming familiar. 'Don't see why. We were all shocked, no matter which side we were on – and some of us had seen Hugh's dead body. So we never talked about it much.' Georgia saw her swallow. 'Have another slice of cake.'

The subject of the Wayncrofts was closed.

When Georgia returned to the Marsh & Daughter office at Haden Shaw, she found Peter in a familiar position, peering at his computer screen. Nothing new about that, nor about his opening grumpy comment as he swivelled round to greet her.

'What kept you?'

'Lisa Moon.'

'To good effect?'

'I think so.' Georgia had a moment's doubt. Had Lisa's story sounded just too good to be true? She proceeded to recount all she had been told – often a good policy. Peter could make his own decisions about whether it added up. His reaction this time was predictable.

'As full of holes as a sieve.'

'Don't exaggerate.'

'Some holes,' he amended. 'Time for Suspects Anonymous.'

This software, created by her cousin Charlie to keep track of Marsh & Daughter evidence and theories, was Peter's pride and joy. Sometimes, Georgia grudgingly admitted, it could be helpful, but for her it was a distraction that often misdirected them. Peter would hear no ill of his favourite toy, however.

'I didn't know you'd begun a file for Hugh Wayncroft,' she said.

'Indeed I have, and most interesting it is. All the witnesses' stories run in more or less parallel lines, but occasionally one makes a dash for the victim.'

'What happens then?'

'So far, he or she gets back in line and the victim goes merrily on in good health.'

'Not helpful. Anything else?'

'Oh yes. A flag of omission waving in the evidence.'

'Sparked off by what?'

'Lack of trace evidence. Lack of dovetailing statements for that pilgrimage.'

'Who does Suspects Anonymous fancy?' she asked.

'Hardly surprisingly, Val Harper. He'd clashed with his step-father over the Becket ruins, only to find out after his death that the estate reverted to Robert, on whose charity he, Julian and his mother became dependent.'

'We don't know that Val and Jessica Wayncroft were igno-rant of the arrangement. If they knew it, that does away with their motive, but I wouldn't mind betting they didn't. At Hugh's age, and being younger than Robert, it would hardly have seemed a pressing problem as regards his family's future. Far more interesting is why Anne Fanshawe bequeathed the ruins back to the Wayncrofts, whose plans for development she was strongly resisting. And then, of course, there's Aletta.'

'She wasn't around in 1967.'

'But she is now. And so is Val.'

There was no sign of Luke when Georgia at last reached Medlars, although it was getting on for eight o'clock. He must still be working in the oasthouse office, Georgia thought, but she decided to break unwritten rules and dig him out of his cocoon. She found him still feverishly working at the computer, with hard-copy proofs to one side and the screen version in front.

'You can't blame me,' he said in self defence as she appeared through the door. 'Tim was on the phone for hours. I couldn't get him off the line, and I need to pass these proofs tonight.'

'No printers work through the night any more,' she said firmly. 'So pass the proofs early tomorrow. What's up with Tim?'

'Desperate over his play. The whole thing's falling to pieces, with the press pursuing them about the murder. So much for the unity he hoped the pilgrimage would generate. The two camps have split wide open, with that poor woman's death as the trigger.'

'I hate to be cynical, but they wanted publicity and they've got it.'

'Not the kind they wanted.'

Georgia sighed. 'There's nothing they can do about that. Nor do I think they should. Chillingham smoothed over murder once before.'

'That's hard of you.'

'Maybe. I can see Tim's viewpoint, but in the wider scale of things, plays can be put on again. Anne's death has to predominate. What does Tim want of you? Just a shoulder to cry on?'

'Moral support from us, and from Peter.'

'Surely we're the wrong side. We represent finding out what happened in the past.'

'I know that. Maybe that's why he wants us. An impartial but friendly voice. And one that has links with the police.'

'When are we supposed to show this support?'

'Easy one to answer. Tomorrow night they're booked in at Charing. On Saturday morning he proposes they should all take the coach back here to Chillingham to have a crisis meeting at the Three Peacocks.'

'But what's the crisis?'

'Whether the play should be cancelled.'

NINE

In the morning sun the Three Peacocks looked a peaceful place, with the green Downs as its background and the village clustered around it, but Georgia shuddered to think of the drama that must be heaving away inside it. Compared with Anne's death, however, the play had to be a side issue, although perhaps that should not be the way to look at it. The question of whether the play should go ahead was a battle in itself, and it still had to be fought, even though death overrode all.

It overrode Luke's and her private problems, but that didn't stop her worrying about them. Just one more IVF course would surely settle the issue. If it didn't work then she would call a halt to it. Yes. Luke would surely agree that was reasonable, and yet the last time she had brought it up he had clearly been against it. Only if *she* wanted it, he had said. She had changed the subject to that of Mark, asking if he had heard anything from his son in response to some information he had sent about Otford. Luke had been keen enough to talk about that last night, to her secret frustration, even though the answer had been no.

This morning was a new day, however. Georgia could see Peter's car in the pub parking area, so no doubt he was already embroiled in the battle. Luke had been torn between his personal loyalty to Tim and the mounting stack of publishing work facing him, but had realized he had no choice. Even so, Georgia could tell by his face that he wished that all they had to do was to put on their walking gear and set off for a stroll along the Old Road, preferably in the opposite direction to Canterbury. She would be all for it. She had no wish to pass Peacock Wood again. The spectre of Hugh Wayncroft needed no reminders.

'Advance or escape?' Luke asked.

'Duty calls.'

She, Peter and Luke had agreed that, as outsiders, their presence should not be too obtrusive, and so it might be as well not to arrive until the meeting was under way. How long had Peter been here? Already she could hear raised voices inside, and she and Luke quickened their step.

'Into the cauldron,' Luke said. 'Sounds as if there's a good stew bubbling.'

When they entered, however, the bar itself proved empty, save for Peter sitting in state at a table by the door that gave access to the Peacock Room from which the noise was coming. That was where such events were obviously usually held, but so far Georgia had not seen it in use. Today it was coming into its own, and behind the bar Derek Moon grinned at them in sympathy.

Peter beckoned her over as Luke hurried to the bar to order coffee. Simultaneously, the door to the Peacock Room opened and Simon emerged. Through the open door, Georgia could glimpse Val inside with a microphone, but Simon then shut the door firmly behind him.

'Is the temperature as high as it sounds?' Peter asked.

Simon grimaced. 'Tim's winning so far,' he said, 'but it's not in the bag yet. Julian and Val want to go on, of course. Julian banged on about the need for unity and the village sticking together in times of trouble such as this, and Val's taking the line that as Anne had supported the play and the pilgrimage, cancelling it as a mark of respect must surely be daft.'

'How strong's the opposition?' Luke asked.

'Tenacious. Of all things, Seb Wayncroft's just come out in favour of cancelling, which has swayed all the youngsters. He took the moral high ground and had the nerve to point out that those with large parts in the play seemed the keenest to continue.'

'Not calculated to improve family harmony.' Georgia was puzzled. 'Weird. I thought he was firmly in the Carry-On Brigade.'

'It can't have been Tess's idea,' Simon said gloomily. 'She's got a leading part in the play. Seb hasn't.'

Strange, Georgia thought. She would have expected Seb to be gallantly standing by his sweetheart. 'Is Lisa in there?' Georgia asked.

Simon looked more cheerful. 'She is. But, guess what, she's come out in favour of going on, bless her. Tim thought the battle was won then, until Seb started up in a big way.'

At first Lisa's attitude did not seem to make sense, but
then Georgia saw the reasoning behind it. If the play was
cancelled, the pilgrimage petered out and those involved
retreated behind their own front doors, there might be another
festering sore in Chillingham's history. Anne's murder could
remain unsolved, as had Hugh Wayncroft's. If the play went
ahead, then there was a chance that light might be thrown
on both deaths.

'Let's go in,' Peter said firmly as Derek brought coffee
over. 'We won't be booed as outsiders, will we?'

'No way,' Simon said. 'Everyone's so intent on the right-
ness of their cause, they wouldn't notice if the Queen slipped
in to listen.'

He was right. The room was a large one, with a raised area
at one end where Aletta, smartly dressed in black jacket and
trousers, was currently holding the mike. Whether out of
deference to her sex or because she was a Wayncroft, the forty
or fifty people in the room were allowing her time unbar-
racked. Attention quickly returned to her after Peter had led
the way to the back of the room. It was standing room only
now, and Georgia found herself next to Stella, who greeted
her with a whispered hello.

Aletta had probably been summoned onstage by Tim to
counter Seb's bombshell, Georgia thought. She listened as
Aletta's dispassionate voice dispelled all the opposition's
arguments one by one. A Queen Eleanor indeed, politically
ruthless, a role in which Aletta would excel. It might even
have been a 'political' marriage between herself and Julian—
Georgia firmly stopped her roving mind. That was mere spec-
ulation, theory without facts, save that Val seemed to have
left the village in the eighties and Julian had married Aletta.
Queen Eleanor – in the play, at least – had also been a would-
be murderer. Georgia remembered Will Whitton saying it was
possible that Anne Fanshawe's killer had been a woman, but
could she see Aletta in that role? No, she admitted, and at the
time of Hugh's death Aletta, like Julian, would have been a
baby. A step too far, Georgia told herself. Imagination was
roaming out of control.

'We are playing *Becket* to commemorate a great saint on his
Jubilee anniversary,' Aletta was saying earnestly. 'If we
cancelled now, it would not be taken by the media or anyone

else as a sign of respect. It's far more probably that conclusions would be drawn that we had something to hide over our vicar's murder. That one of us was guilty.'

'One of us probably was, Ma,' Seb yelled out.

Aletta seemed to have won her point, however, judging by the general murmuring of her listeners as she ignored him and stepped down. Seb said no more, but Georgia's relief on Tim's behalf proved premature, as someone else took the microphone.

'Who is *that*?' Stella turned to Georgia in astonishment. 'I haven't seen that one before.'

Today 'that one' was clad in a glimmering bright scarlet shirt over blue trousers, against which her white hair made a startlingly effective contrast. 'That,' Georgia answered with foreboding, 'is Mrs Jessica Wayncroft, no doubt intending to weigh in on the side of the Wayncroft battalions, excluding the rebel grandson Seb.'

'So what are you looking worried about?' Luke asked. 'All good news for Tim, surely.'

'Jessica's unpredictable.'

How right she was. Jessica made a brave picture as well as a striking one, but as soon as she began to speak, Georgia feared the worst. Jessica looked out at her audience with a look of tremulous appeal that, given Jessica's strong will, was surely as good as the act she must once have put on as Queen Eleanor.

'I do believe that developing the St Thomas ruins is right for Chillingham, and I am so very pleased to know that it will now go ahead thanks to our dear late vicar's foresight. But somehow – I can't feel it's right that the rest of the pilgrimage and play should take place. The next stage of the walk will take it past Peacock Wood where my own dear Hugh was found dead so many years ago, and—' She faltered, braced herself and began again. 'In the light of Mrs Fanshawe's death it seems very wrong just to walk past that point, and then put on the same play in which my husband so brilliantly played Becket. I shall weep. I know I shall.' She looked very distressed, and even Georgia was swayed. That was surely no act.

'Mother!' Julian rushed up to her, looking shell-shocked, as well he might.

'I know you're disappointed, darling, and dear Tim too.'

Jessica stretched out a hand in appeal towards Tim, who looked about to faint. 'But perhaps next year we could put the play on ourselves, presented in front of St Thomas's very own ruins. Val,' she called, 'we could do that, could we not?'

Oh, what a politician we have here. Georgia was impressed. Simon was already at Tim's side however, and Luke made his way to join them. It was Val, shattered out of his usual suavity, who lost control as he rushed up to the stage. 'No. It won't be ready,' he shouted. 'Not then. No way. It will take years, won't it Ally? It has to be this year.'

Even Aletta looked shaken as she went up on the stage to talk to Jessica and Val. Jessica looked stricken at Val's outburst – and, for once, old and tired. 'Have I said something to upset you, darling?' she faltered very audibly.

'I wouldn't have missed this play for worlds,' Peter whispered.

He was loving every minute of it, Georgia thought, perhaps unfairly. It was his – their – job to analyse, not take sides, but oh how hard that could sometimes be. The general murmur of support for Jessica was growing louder, and she was going unchallenged. The battle was lost, Georgia feared, wondering what Stella was making of this. Even as the thought went through her mind, she saw Tim taking the mike, presumably to announce reluctant surrender.

He was forestalled, however. Matthew Moon had followed him up and was taking the mike from him. Unfortunately, whatever it was he wanted to say, he couldn't have a chance in hell against Jessica's performance, Georgia thought.

When Matthew began to speak, however, there was an instant hush as his soft voice held his audience. It had a remarkable power in it. 'Mrs Wayncroft's right on one thing. There's grieving to be done in Chillingham, so we'll do it. If there's penance to be done, we'll do that too. While we finish this pilgrimage and put on the play, we'll be remembering St Thomas, riding along the Old Road into Canterbury, and I reckon Mr Wayncroft and Mrs Fanshawe will be walking right along with us in spirit as we do so. They'll be there at the theatre too, so we'll say a few words about them before the curtain goes up and as it falls.'

That was all. There was a dead silence, broken only by a

whispered, 'Oh yes,' from Stella as she pushed past Georgia and made her way to the stage.

'No one's asked me what I think yet, although I'm Anne Fanshawe's daughter. But I'm going to tell you what I know. My mother would have wanted this play to go ahead. She loved acting, she walked part of the pilgrimage with you, and she wasn't one to give up anything she believed in halfway. Tennyson's *Becket* is about murder for political reasons in the interests of power-holding. Anyone disagree with that?'

Silence.

'And,' she continued, 'it's a play in which the victim wins. A victim who's more memorable than the villain. I want my mother to *win*. Next week, at the Stour Theatre.'

'And that,' Georgia whispered to Luke, 'is surely *that*.'

Peter had been determined to come, despite the bumpy ground. When Stella had suggested at the Three Peacocks meeting that anyone who was interested in the Becket ruins could walk over to look at them now, some people had preferred to return to their homes to regroup for the final stage of the pilgrimage the next day, but quite a few accepted Stella's offer with eagerness. Including Peter, who wasn't going to be left out, no matter what the difficulties.

In the event, Luke was having to help Peter negotiate his way across the field, and so Georgia seized an opportunity to talk to Julian. It was difficult to know whether to congratulate him or not, in view of the fact it had been his mother and son who had tried to throw a spanner in the works over the play. Should she tread carefully, or barge in? The latter.

'You must be delighted that this land is coming back to your estate.'

'Why?' Julian asked coldly. 'These ruins have always belonged to the Wayncrofts. They're part of its heritage, and Anne knew this was the best answer.'

Julian might look and sound the prototype country squire, but he was an actor too. Georgia decided to push further. 'Yet your uncle left them to her, presumably because she was opposed to their development whereas your family is in favour of it.'

She'd typecast Julian as a large, rather bad-tempered bear-like sort of man, who would ultimately be amenable to meekly

following Val's plans. Bears have large claws, however, and
the look on Julian's face definitely suggested they were being
sharpened. 'It hardly matters why Uncle Robert acted as he
did, because I had understood that you were interested in my
father's death, not that of Mrs Fanshawe. Or have the police
hired you as a civilian investigator?'

'These ruins might have relevance both to Anne's death
and to your father's. As Stella pointed out, *Becket* is about
murder for political reasons.'

'Obviously, you have not read the play,' he rejoined.
'Certainly, that factor comes into it. So do betrayal, passion,
and human relationships. Tim is always asking us to remember
that. I suggest you do too.'

The bear was getting agitated. Time to switch tack. Georgia
asked him a few neutral questions about the ruins, and then
slid in gently, 'You spoke of the Wayncroft heritage and the
ruins being part of it. What's the other part?'

'You misunderstood,' he said instantly. 'The heritage is
the Becket connections, of which the ruins are a part. The
Wayncrofts kept to their Catholic faith during the Reformation,
and when Queen Mary came to the throne she paid special
favour to us. That's why we are entrusted to look after the
ruins.'

'And what might lie in them, Julian,' Val said softly as he
and Aletta joined them. 'Don't forget those *bones*.'

Julian turned furiously on him. 'You're wrong, Val, and
you know it all too well, don't you?'

'The boot is on the other foot, brother mine,' Val shot back
at him.

No pretence at cordiality between them now. Even Aletta
looked thrown by the suddenness of the outburst. 'If the bones
are here,' she said coolly, 'one day they'll be found.' Both
men turned to her, as if she were calling time on the battle.

Georgia fumed at this intervention just as she might have
been getting somewhere. Now she had to resurrect the subject.
'Do you really think there's a chance they're buried here?'

Julian made an effort to be civil. 'According to Uncle
Robert, yes. Every time he paid us a visit he impressed that
on me.'

'The poor chap was going gaga in his last few years,' Val
added calmly. 'That's why he left the ruins to Anne by mistake.

He was pretty old by then so he probably never noticed. Anyway, Anne realized what had happened, and so we've now got them back.'

'We?' Julian asked acidly.

'Sorry, Jules. Just identifying myself with your interests. Where do you think they'd be hidden?'

Julian eyed him coolly. 'In Chillingham Place *somewhere*. Not necessarily in these ruins.' He turned to Aletta. 'Stella wanted a word with us. Shall we go?'

Both she and Val were clearly persona non grata. No problem, Georgia thought. She would take a look at the ruins herself. Val ostentatiously left her to it and strolled away, leaving her to walk round the ruins.

'Bloody snoopers.'

Georgia turned round at the unfamiliar voice. She knew the weather-beaten face though, and the piercing blue eyes. It was Vic Painter.

'Miss Marsh, ain't it?' he asked. 'Been talking to your dad, I have.'

'And you're the village historian,' Georgia replied, 'who helps Molly Jones at Becket House.'

'Historian's a big word.' He grinned. 'All stored up in my head, it is. Don't have the skills to put it on paper like I should. It all came from my dad, see?'

'John Painter. Was he another Bill Riding where history was concerned?'

'Bill was a real historian, a teacher and all that. Dad just liked the local stuff.'

'Such as Thomas Becket?'

'Yeah. He did guide work in the cathedral at Canterbury in his later years. He was on fireguard duty during the big raid in 1942 and reckons he owes St Thomas because he weren't hit himself. Parts of the cathedral were knocked to smithereens, but the main part of it came through. Ever thought it's interesting how Canterbury Cathedral came through it all, like St Paul's?'

'Coventry Cathedral didn't.'

'Yeah. Reckon Lady Luck was asleep that night. 'Course, it was two years later when Canterbury copped it. St George's went for a burton, and so did Rose Lane and a lot more of the town, but not so bad as it might have been. We had our own system of air-raid warnings.'

'You're not tempted to be a cathedral guide yourself?'

'Nah. Too much on at Molly's place. Besides, too much like hard work nowadays. I'd have to go on courses and that. I'd rather be at the pub.'

'Did your father believe that Becket's bones are buried here?'

'No, bless you. Reckon he thought it all a legend, but then legends are sometimes based on some kind of fact, whether it's twisted or not. Mind you, he was Becket-mad, was Dad. Makes me laugh all the stuff about not wanting tourists here on the one hand, and on the other telling me all about the pilgrims at the Becket shrine in the Cathedral before it got destroyed by that there Henry VIII. A real guided tour was laid on for them, just as grand as Mr Val's got in mind for this place. First they saw where the poor chap was killed, then it was up the steps to the next station, and the next and so forth. At each one they were shown something special: the sword that killed him, the bashed-up skull, bits of this that and the other, and finally the golden shrine itself.

'Those crafty old monks had an eye for showmanship, so they'd fixed a sort of lid on ropes over the casket with the bones so that when they'd got everyone's attention they could pull up the lid and show the golden shrine to gasps all round. Covered in precious stones every colour of the rainbow, some bigger than eggs, so it's said. Then the guides gave their sales pitch, hoping the pilgrims would put their hands in their pockets. The best jewel was the one from the King of France, the Regale ruby, which gleamed out ruby red even in the dark. That had them gasping all right. After that they couldn't wait to get their badges and bits and bobs. And then what happened? You know what they did in 1538?'

Georgia did, but wanted to keep Vic talking. 'Not in detail.'

'Henry VIII's thugs smashed the shrine to bits and carted off the valuable stuff. What happened to the bones, we'll never know. The old Regale ruby was made into a ring from Henry, and after that his daughter hung it round her neck. Never seen again after that, nor the bones. Plenty of theories though.'

'In that case the bones could indeed be here in Chillingham. The Wayncrofts kept to the old faith, so the monks could well have brought the bones to them for safe keeping.'

Vic's eyes weren't meeting hers, she noticed. 'Why come all the way here,' he said, 'when they could have buried them down in the Cathedral crypt, or in its graveyard amongst the other bodies?'

'Perhaps,' she acknowledged, 'but Robert Wayncroft seems to have believed they are here. Did Hugh too?'

'I was only twenty or so when he died. Didn't have time for no long chats about bones,' Vic said carefully. 'Dad was real upset when the squire died, though. I remember that, and he was that happy when the land all went back to Mr Robert. Mr Julian being a baby then, Dad was afraid Mr Val might take it over for all he was only a stepson, because Mrs Jessica thought the world of Mr Valentine. Still does. With Mr Robert, though, the land was in safe hands.'

'And your father came to agree with him. And you too.' There was something here that Georgia was not getting, and Vic was still looking evasive.

'Tourism's the thing, ain't it, and with Molly living in a house with some of the stones from the old chapel in it, you'd think it a natural. But Dad was dead against development. The older he got, the more obstinate, and we're the same, Molly and me. When Mr Robert came back here to live in 2002 Dad got real pally with him again.'

Georgia fastened on this new piece of information. 'Stones from the chapel? But Becket House looks as if it was built in the eighteenth century.'

'So it was mostly, but if you look round the back you can see some ragstone: a few stones in the house itself, and one of the outhouses. Once the new church was built I reckon the old chapel was up for grabs and whoever wanted a few of its stones just helped themselves. A lot must have been used in whatever house was here before Molly and Bill's, and when theirs came to be built the builders economized where it wouldn't be noticed too much. You go and have a look, stay a night or two as you're so keen on St Thomas.'

'Good idea,' Peter said when she related this to him the next morning. Luke had retreated into his office and she had driven over to Haden Shaw. The Fernbourne Museum was open on Sundays, and so it was unlikely she would be usurping Janie's place. 'I'll come too if they can manage this thing.' He patted the wheelchair.

Georgia began to warm to the idea. If they could fit her in for a day or two it would – apart from anything else – give her space to think about her own problems, as well as giving Luke a breathing space to catch up with his own work.

Peter, evidently already presuming the matter settled, moved on to the next item on his agenda. 'Mike's coming to see me today or tomorrow, but I presume that Hugh Wayncroft's death isn't top of his list, although it's possibly a relevant factor.'

'Only if the same person committed both murders.'

'Val Harper couldn't have killed Hugh unless his mother was lying when she told the police she was with him, but witnesses confirm they were together in the front of the column.' A pause. 'He could have committed Anne's murder, however.'

'Police territory,' she warned him.

'Nonsense,' Peter declared. 'It's ours too, as Mike is coming here. Tell me again about that evening in the pub and the row you overheard.'

'Anne had had some kind of set-to with Val earlier in the day so it was hardly surprising it broke out again.' Georgia did her best to remember both that and the evening quarrel word for word, but with Peter best was never enough.

'Was Anne still at that table when you and Luke got up to go? Had she gone to the Ladies? Was she at the bar? Getting her coat?'

Georgia concentrated on her images of that evening, but had to give up. 'I don't remember, and since I saw her in the car park it can't be that relevant. There was one interesting thing about the row, however.'

'What is it?' Peter asked sharply.

'It stopped. That's what was odd. There's usually a grim silence at the very least after a row such as that, or people leave the table. But, in this case, Anne stayed there, and so did Aletta, Julian and Val. Seb joined them, in fact, and they were all *talking*.'

'How talking? In surrender, would you say?'

'Anne wasn't the sort to surrender over such an issue, and the others couldn't afford to do so.'

'How long did this possible reconciliation last?'

Georgia considered. 'I can't be sure, but Anne must have left the pub very shortly after Luke and me because we were only unlocking the car as she passed us by. And, since you asked, I don't remember seeing her wearing a coat, and Will Whitton said she wasn't wearing one. Most of the coats were hung in the corridor by the toilets off to one side of the main bar.'

'What about an overnight bag?'

'Anne checked in at the B and B before she came to the pub. She had an anorak on during the day, so that could have been left in the B and B.'

'I'll ask Mike. Could it be that Anne saw you leave, wanted to say something to you, paid her farewells to the others and tried to catch you up?'

'No. If she'd wanted to talk to us, she'd have done so in the car park. She didn't, and you'll remember she turned down our offer of a lift to drive her back.' That still stung – shouldn't she have tried harder to persuade her? Georgia replayed the scene in her mind. She remembered Luke fiddling with the key to get it into the lock. 'It was pretty dark by then, even in the car park. I was watching Luke, and then I saw Anne passing us, which must have been perhaps three or four minutes after we came out.'

'Enough time for someone to see Anne leaving and either decide to leave himself or make an excuse such as going to the toilets or to the bar.'

'Yes.' Georgia began to warm to the theme. 'The pub's layout would help. There was a side door, which opened into the corridor with the toilets and coats. The corridor had an outside door and went past the bars and the stairs to the first floor for overnight guests.'

'And presumably residents could use the door to the outside with a key if the main pub was shut?'

'Probably, although the pub was still open at that point, so that door, too, might have been open.'

'Good. So our chum might have escaped notice.'

'Yes.' Georgia thought this through. 'Anyone staying overnight in the pub wouldn't be noticed if they disappeared for a while. It would be assumed they'd retired for the night. Of course, if her killer hurried out to catch Anne up, he'd have been gone for some time, because she was a fair way along by the time we left. If he had a room in the hotel, though, that wouldn't matter so much.'

Peter ruminated. 'He'd need a torch, which would suggest a degree of planning. Who was staying there? Valentine Harper . . .'

'Julian and family, Tim and Simon, Matthew and a few more. It was more the youngsters who were camping. However,' Georgia added firmly, 'could I remind you that this takes us no further forward on Hugh Wayncroft?'

'But how tempting to think it *might*,' Peter said gently.

TEN

Georgia groaned. 'Ever decreasing circles, Peter. The most likely link is that legacy of the ruins. Or *seems* to be. But there's no evidence that the Wayncrofts knew about Anne's will. It doesn't add up that Anne should have been so adamant at the Dog and Duck about not opening the ruins up for development now, if the Wayncrofts knew perfectly well that they'd inherit sooner or later. A row yes, if she refused to open them immediately, but not on the scale I remember.'

'In that case we're back to why Robert left them to Anne in the first place. If Anne was willing to bequeath them to the Wayncrofts, and presumably assumed she wouldn't die for another thirty or forty years, what would be so different about the Wayncroft family by then?'

'Because Julian might by then also have died?' she ventured. 'Did she or Robert not want to leave them to Julian, but wouldn't mind their going to Seb? No, that doesn't make sense. Anyway, there's a snag,' she pointed out. 'Sebastian was already growing up fast when Robert came back to Kent. He'd have consulted him.'

'Seb's as much in favour of development as his father. It was putting on the play that he got hot under the collar about.'

'It might have been a gamble that Robert thought worth taking. Exclude Julian because he didn't share his views on what should be done with the ruins and hope that Seb would see things differently as the years went by. And yet it was the Wayncroft heritage, so he . . .' Peter broke off. 'Why does that word bother me?'

'It bothers me too. It's like a bolt across a door. It tries to forbid open discussion. A sort of: "Oh, it's the heritage, that's that, then." Anyway,' Georgia continued, 'there's a flaw in our argument. The development issue didn't rear its ugly head again until after Robert died – obviously, but also after Val came back to Kent. We can't be sure of Julian's views before that.'

'Unfortunate that the two brothers don't get on personally, but see their futures tied up together,' Peter speculated. 'That word heritage, though. Didn't you say Hugh used it at the after-show party in 1967 or after it?'

Georgia patiently flipped back to the notes she had recorded after meeting Lisa. 'Yes. Hugh told her that he had to take a stand over the ruins. It was the Wayncroft heritage, he said. Julian himself used the same word to me.'

'But what does it *mean*?'

'That's what I asked him. He said it was the Becket connections, of which the ruins are a part. Including the bones, if any. But Lisa,' Georgia said, remembering, 'took it to mean that the manor and the ruins of St Thomas passed down the line via the eldest son, in Hugh's case baby Julian.'

'But that must have been obvious, even to Lisa. Why should Hugh bother to point that out to her? He said "it" was the heritage, if Lisa remembered it correctly. "It" wouldn't apply either to the ruins or to Becket.'

'Perhaps he was really trying to explain why he couldn't leave his wife and marry her?'

'Good shot,' Peter said patronizingly, 'but Lisa claims he loved his wife just as he loved her. She would hardly admit to such a thing unless she believed it. Unless –' he quickly caught himself before Georgia could say it for him – 'Lisa was anxious to make a case out to you that she was innocent. I take it you *don't* think Lisa killed Hugh?'

'I don't, but it was forty years ago, so how sure can I be?'

'I don't either, although I'm with you – it could have happened. So we come back to Hugh, heritage and *it*, bearing in mind that everything reverted to Robert after the murder.'

'You've missed a shot,' Georgia said triumphantly. 'Hugh didn't *know* he was going to die long before Robert did.'

Peter looked appalled and clutched his head in his hands. 'Do you know, Georgia, you're right. I'm slipping. Is this old age rearing its head?' He looked at her hopefully.

'No,' she replied. 'You've just got too much on your mind.' She nerved herself to speak out. 'You're still thinking about Rick, aren't you?'

Peter looked mutinous. 'All right. Rick, then. I suppose it was that word "heritage" set me off. What heritage do *I* have if he doesn't return?'

Georgia froze. She had to step very carefully indeed. She might wade through the endless shallows into the deep mud all too easily and become embroiled in Peter's nightmares, whereas she had one of her own to cope with.

'Rick *isn't* your heritage, Peter. Nor mine. Heritage is not only human succession, it's what you've achieved; what you contribute for others to build on.'

'And what might that be?' Peter waved a disparaging hand over the bookshelves in front of him that held the file copies of Marsh & Daughter works. 'Only books that no one will read in twenty years' time.'

'Plenty of people have read them now. We can't know how what we've written affects them – those that might have been involved in the cases, those who care whether the right answer is recorded where there was only a question mark before. Even if it affects them just a little, it could change lives.' Georgia stopped. 'Am I making sense?' she asked awkwardly.

'Yes, but you're being highly sanctimonious,' Peter said savagely. 'How does this "just a little" compare with having Rick back? Tell me that.'

Tackle this head on, she thought. If she could. 'I'm sorry Austria didn't do the trick for you. It has for me.'

'No, it didn't. And what *trick*? Tell me that. It's a question of whether he's alive or not. How can I believe—'

'That Rick's dead? Well, I'll tell you how.' Georgia was beginning to fume, but tried to stay cool. 'By looking at the facts, just as you do in our work. Including this case.'

'I *am* looking at facts. The records of that bloody watch – it wasn't Rick's.'

'How do you know that?'

'I *know*.'

She was in too far to retreat now. 'How often have you refused, rightly, to accept those words from witnesses? True views, honestly held, but which turn out to be false memories. Look at all those miracles St Thomas was supposed to have performed. They were believed to be fact at the time. Fact expands and changes like a plume of smoke and can settle down into mere fantasy. What were facts of St Thomas's miracles are now legend for most people.'

His jaw jutted out in fury. 'Are you saying I'm wrong, Georgia? Just look at this.' He pulled open a drawer at his

side and took out what looked like an old bill. It must be no
coincidence that he kept whatever it was so near at hand. Peter
had been brooding more deeply than she realized. The worst
had happened, and Peter's nightmares could return in full
force.

She stared at the bill. It was for an Omega De Ville watch,
dated a month before Rick had disappeared.

'*That* was Rick's watch, not the model they had recorded.'

She thought frantically. Where could she go now to convince
him? 'In that case,' she said steadily, 'you must be right. But,
Peter, if he were still alive, where is he? The fact that the
watch might not have been his, doesn't make Rick alive. It
just means they ascribed the wrong model or artefact to him
or that he still kept his Seamaster as well as the new watch
and had it with him when he died.'

'Damn it, Georgia, I don't want to *talk* about it.'

'And there lies the problem.'

She returned to Medlars still smarting from the clash. How
dared he, how *dared* Peter say all that stuff about heritage
when he knew full well what she was going through in order
to present him with a grandchild. Didn't she count? Was a
daughter's offspring not as good as a son's? Maybe feudalism
hadn't entirely vanished from the scene. The succession had
to be male to count. How could her own father ignore her
plight just when she needed support?

Stop, she told herself, *stop*. She felt wretched and had
hoped to be on her own for a while to recover when she
reached Medlars, but as luck would have it, Luke had finished
his work and was in the kitchen preparing lunch when she
came in.

He noticed something was wrong straight away. 'Why back
so soon?'

'Didn't feel like staying any longer.'

Luke was immediately on the alert. 'Why not?'

She shrugged as though it were merely an everyday occur-
rence. 'We had a row over Rick.'

'That all?

'*All*? Isn't that enough?'

'Not usually. You take that problem in your stride.' He
looked at her carefully. 'Ah, the word usually. Could there be
something dragging you down? Something to do with us?'

She couldn't meet his eye. 'I want to have that third course of IVF. Shouldn't I?' she added illogically.

'Oh, Georgia.' He took her into his arms, and it felt good. 'How many times do I have to tell you it doesn't *matter*. It's you I love; it's you I want at my side for the rest of our lives. If children come, I'll be happy. If they don't we'll have lost nothing that brought us together in the first place.'

'But do you really *mean* that?' she choked.

'What would convince you? You don't seem to have done a very good job in convincing Peter over Rick's death. Aren't you shutting your own eyes in the same way?'

'*No*. This is something much more basic than that. The need to leave some mark behind.' She grappled with the fact that she had been fighting Peter on that issue, but pushed it away. This was different, and Luke didn't understand. He had a son after all, and she didn't. Didn't he want a shared child? Didn't he *care*? He must. He just wasn't admitting it.

'Life's what you make it, Georgia, not how other people think we should live. Even if we had a child, in less than a hundred years' time we'll just be a photo in an album or tucked away deep inside a computer in a landfill site—'

Just the same argument as Peter had made. She managed an attempt at a grin. 'You mean computers will be no more? Oh, I hope I live that long.'

A pause, then Luke said, 'You're sure the last IVF course has failed?'

'Yes.'

'Let's leave it at that, shall we? Move forward?'

'I don't know, Luke. I'll think about it some more.'

'Say no,' he said gently. 'Begin the healing now.'

'Perhaps one more . . .'

He sighed. 'I can't take this decision for you, or even with you, just as you can't help Peter. He has to take the final step himself.'

It wasn't the same, but she knew Luke was right. It was her decision. 'It's been suggested I book in for a day or two at Becket House. Peter thought it a good idea. Want to come?'

She couldn't bear to see the sadness in his face. 'You know that's impossible,' he answered. 'You do it, if you think it might help. It's the first night of the play on Tuesday, isn't it? I'll stay over that night. I presume you and Peter will be going?'

'Peter would be on the Stour Theatre doorstep every night if it were practical. But I'm plumping for the first night and Saturday, the last night. I'll book in to Becket House for tonight if she's got room.' She wanted to say, '*Please* come with me,' but pride would not let her. She'd be better on her own, she told herself. 'They need the trade,'she ended lightly, then turned away so that she could not see that sadness any more. *Why* the sadness though? For her, as he claimed, or for the children they might never have together? Unless she took that third course.

Becket House, its forecourt now almost empty of cars, looked more imposing than Georgia had remembered. On her earlier visit it had looked unremarkable, but now its red brick and elegant windows shone out far more grandly.

'Come in, m'dear.' Molly's warm welcome gave no hint of the drama Georgia had run into on her first visit. No mention was made of that, or of Jessica Wayncroft, as Molly showed her up to a large double bedroom, plainly but appealingly decorated with obviously home-embroidered cushions and bedpane. The windows were Georgian, too, as was the ceiling, but the bathroom, thankfully, was modern.

'You should have seen it when Dad moved in. I thought it was wonderful,' Molly said. 'The Georgians liked baths, you know. He said the original bath had been about eight foot square, like a sort of swimming pool, and in the basement, and when he moved in there was still a Victorian free-standing bath right in the middle of the room, all claw feet and an interior with a Union Jack and God Save the Queen painted on it. It felt disrespectful at first having a bath in it, but then I loved it. I was really sorry when Dad went all modern and had the bathrooms revamped a year or two later.'

Georgia laughed. 'I wonder what Thomas Becket would have used. The well, I suppose.'

Molly chuckled. 'Maybe he did. Dad always reckoned he could have slept over in Becket House on his way to and fro from Otford to Canterbury.'

'Not this one though.'

'No, but there was a house on this site long before that, just as there was at Chillingham Place.'

'Your brother told me you had some of the old stones at the back of the house and they could have come from the St Thomas chapel.'

'That's right,' Molly said. 'Dad used to feel very personal about them. There was a ruined outhouse he restored and called Becket's Shrine. We kids weren't so reverent. To us it was the Poo-house, till Dad found us mucking around in it one day and walloped us.'

'Why would he mind, if it was just an outhouse?'

'Dad said it was just a ruin when he moved in, but now it was his. It was maybe an outside larder or dairy when this present house was built. Why he bothered to restore it, beats me. Too small to be of much use. He said he'd use it for tools and that, and he did, but we certainly weren't welcome to play in it.'

'What's it used for now?'

'Nothing. Go and have a look if you like. It's not locked.'

'Thanks. Did it have any other connection to Becket?' A sudden thought. 'Your father didn't think Becket's bones were hidden there, by any chance?'

Any growing excitement was quickly dampened, when Molly replied, 'Not that I know of. It's the well and the chapel where they're hidden, if anywhere. I reckon it's only a legend though. Nothing to it. Dad liked making legends up about Becket, after having worked so long at the Cathedral, so I suppose he just wanted one or two of his own. He said once that looking up at all that glory in the nave and hearing those bells could drive a man mad if he didn't tear his eyes and ears away soon enough.'

'What did he mean by that?' To Georgia, Molly, like Lisa, seemed a curious mixture of the practical present and the inescapable past.

'Well, I didn't think at the time, but afterwards I saw what he meant. It sort of hypnotizes you if you go on staring long enough. You get sucked into it, instead of taking its strength and going out into the world and *doing*. There's an atmosphere about this place too – not here in this house, but out by those chapel ruins – that makes you feel the same. They're just a load of old stones, so most people think, but then they haven't really *looked*. It makes you feel weird, thinking of all the pilgrims who tramped up to that well years ago, hoping to get cured of whatever was wrong with them by drinking the holy water and praying in Thomas's chapel. I'm not a Catholic myself, but I can see what it can do for you. Faith, you see, faith. That's why I'm against making Chillingham into a real tourist place. Folk would never stop long enough to get the real message. They'll just look, chatter to their chums, and move on. They'll look, but they'll never *see*.'

Becket House provided only bed and breakfast, and so Georgia made her way to the Three Peacocks that evening for a light meal, still thinking over what Molly had said when she'd echoed Lisa's words about the ruins. There were deeply held views in Chillingham, and only now did Georgia really feel she was drawing closer to the village. Lisa had been right to suggest she stayed here.

Doubts came back once she entered the pub. Again it was all but empty, and tonight it seemed soulless as well. She saw little of Lisa or of Simon, and Derek Moon was uncommunicative. A waitress Georgia did not recognize brought an admittedly delicious warm salad, but nevertheless she was glad to leave, armed with the large flashlight Molly had lent her, as it was well past ten o'clock. She had chosen to walk not drive, so that she could get some air and enjoy the silence of the countryside (and a glass of wine). The village, shrouded in darkness the further she got from the lamp posts, had an air of unreality – a stillness, as if it were waiting for something or someone.

Fanciful, Georgia told herself firmly, but she quickened her step past the vicarage, now in darkness. As she walked along the lane to Becket House, she thought uneasily of Anne Fanshawe setting off along that country road only to meet her death. There was nothing to be heard tonight – not a night bird, no traffic, nor even the sound of her own footsteps – and she found herself glancing over her shoulder every so often as though the murderers of Thomas Becket were dogging her footsteps. Why think of that? she wondered. She supposed it was because in this place it was all too easy to do so; the centuries had made little difference because basically, when the sun disappeared and night fell, everyone was a lone pilgrim in the dark.

Home, woman, home, she told herself. Even if tonight Becket House had to be home, it was a welcome one, and she reached the still unlocked door with something like relief. Tomorrow she would begin again, tomorrow she would look at the Becket Poo-house, or Shrine as John Painter had termed it, and on Tuesday she would join Luke at the play. She'd be going in the hope that the hunt for Hugh's murderer might be advanced. How she did not know, but many quests had ended in Canterbury over the centuries, and this might be one of them.

Feeling lost without Luke, she watched the TV news. Missing him was stupid, because she had often spent nights away from Medlars in the course of work, and yet this seemed different. Probably that was because of the momentous joint decision – she still thought of it as joint – hanging over them. To take or not to take the course. That indeed was the question, despite Luke's claims not to mind.

Her heart sank. Why did she have to start thinking about that, just as she was about to go to bed? Her mind would be whirling all night. Concentrate, think of something else, of the play, of the Wayncrofts, of Thomas Becket. Her mind immediately sprang into life again, and turning the TV off she walked restlessly to the window to look out at Chillingham in the dark. Out there was the Old Road to Canterbury, and on this Sunday evening all was still. Over to her right, she could see the pinpricks of light from the village, but nearer at hand there was nothing but quietness and the sky. No moon, only the dark, dark night.

She was wrong. She could see a pinprick of light, a *moving* light. It must be a car – no, it wasn't far enough away to be coming from the road or from the manor house. She felt herself tensing up as she realized it seemed to be by the ruins. Surely she must be wrong. Who would want to look round Becket's well and chapel at this time of night? They held no attractions either for lovers or homeless wanderers, and it was too far into the fields for someone merely to be taking cover for a call of nature or for a dog-walker to be out. The light was definitely at the ruins, but for what reason? A drugs' handover venue? Unlikely. There would be many more suitable and accessible places in Chillingham than Becket's ruins, and Anne would have seen off any attempt for them to make them a regular meeting place.

Georgia looked at her hotel keys, lying on the dressing table, and was tempted. It wouldn't take long to go over to investigate. Dangerous? Of course it was, but she was cautious and karate-trained. Stupid? Of course it was, but she'd be careful. Even so, when she let herself quietly out of Becket House and walked over to the field, she had qualms. Curiosity was not going to kill this cat, however, and if there was some mystery about those ruins, she needed to know.

Her torch led her stumbling over uneven ground until she found a path in the Becket House garden that led to a gate into the meadow where the ruins lay. The path probably continued as far as Chillingham Place, but halfway across the field it deteriorated, and she began to stumble over tufts of grass. For a moment she thought the light had vanished and its bearer with it, and all seemed silent and dark as she approached the well.

Then there was noise shattering the quiet, an exclamation and the light appeared again wavering up and down. 'Who's there?' The voice was male, sharp and nervous, as Georgia herself was. It was a voice she knew, but couldn't place because of the fright it had given her.

'Georgia Marsh,' she called more steadily than she felt. 'Who are you?'

'What the hell are you doing here?' The light came towards her as the voice rang out again, and this time she recognized it.

Valentine Harper's.

She stood still, waiting for him to reach her.

'I might ask the same of you.' She sounded so cool that she amazed herself. It was all she could do not to turn and run.

The nearer he loomed towards her, a dark shape behind the torchlight, the more she had difficulty in standing her ground. Half of her wanted to turn and run, the other half told her to face it out. That half won, but only just.

'I saw the light from my bedroom window and thought it might be vandals,' she said.

'Well, it's not. It's me. And these grounds belong to my half-brother.'

'Not yet.'

'Don't quibble. They will be soon. So now if you're satisfied that I'm not here to steal the crown jewels, perhaps you'll leave.' Val sounded almost as rattled as she was, and that gave her confidence.

'What *are* you here for?'

'I could explain, but I don't see why I should.' His voice was mild, but it held a note of threat that did not escape her.

'I'd be interested to know.'

'I'm sure you would. Would you be satisfied though? Would it be dramatic enough for you? You're searching for something to pop into that book of yours that we'll never let be written, but I'm afraid I have to disappoint you. I can't produce anything exciting. The reason I'm here is sheer self-interest; the ruins will soon be mine – or –' he caught himself – 'Julian's, which amounts to the same thing where our plans are concerned. I'm already planning and working on ideas – I have to – but I couldn't envisage the ruins clearly enough for my satisfaction. Poor Anne was not overgenerous in allowing access to them, and it was some years since I had seen them close up. Except, of course, when Stella kindly brought us here yesterday, but I could hardly indulge my curiosity too far then. It would not have been seemly. And if you ask why I choose dead of night to come here – well, to come during daylight would hardly be seemly either.'

'That's reasonable,' Georgia conceded.

'Good.'

Was there sarcasm in his voice? Had there been in hers? She didn't care, because she did not believe a word of what he'd said, and so retreat was her only and best course now. She bade him goodnight and strolled – she longed to run – back the way she had come. She imagined his eyes on her every moment as she did so, prickles at the back of her neck mounting. Had Anne had the same sensation? And with the same man? Her murderer?

As if reading her thoughts, she heard Val hurrying after her. She could even hear his deep breathing in the night air. Run or stand? She'd never outrun him, much better to face him. She stopped, and he walked round her, placing himself in front, barring her way.

'Oh Georgia,' he purred, 'just in case you are considering

a high-profile role for me in your book, I should point out that whoever killed Anne Fanshawe, it could not have been me, or indeed Julian. We had no idea that Anne was going to leave the ruins to us. And even if I had known Anne's plans, the inspector in charge of the case –' heavy emphasis – 'knows I am, so to speak, out of the running. I, Aletta and Julian remained at the table for a full ten minutes or so after Anne had left – ample time for her to reach home before my murderous self could catch up with her. So very sorry to disappoint you.'

ELEVEN

On Monday morning, after a restless night, Georgia woke up with a sense of doom. Today the dress rehearsal at the Stour Theatre would be taking place and the pilgrims would be dedicating themselves to the play. It couldn't have helped Tim that the last leg of the pilgrimage must have been completed without Val. By daylight his mission to the ruins last night seemed even more curious.

Breakfast, she decided, came first, after which her brain might condescend to work properly. When she entered the pleasant breakfast room overlooking the terrace at the rear of the house she seemed to be the only customer, but Molly was bustling about as if the room were full. Despite her frequent visits to Georgia's table, with orange juice, tea, toast and requests for anything else she might like, there was little opportunity for opening discussions on Chillingham's problems.

To Georgia's astonishment, however, as the 'full English' was carefully set in front of her, its bearer also planted herself firmly before her. 'There's something needs to be said, Georgia, and it's this. Us Painters and the Wayncrofts go back a long way. So you enjoy your meal, and then you and I can have a talk.'

That suited Georgia admirably, relieved it had proved so straightforward. Molly was as good as her word. Georgia's empty plate was removed (it would not have been diplomatic to leave the mushrooms untouched, although she heartily disliked them), the teacup was replenished and Molly sat down opposite her.

'Are you including Jessica as a Wayncroft?' Georgia asked lightly.

'Take one, you take them all,' Molly replied enigmatically. 'And if you're wondering why she comes a-visiting here, she told you right. She came to talk to Vic. He does odd jobs for her now and then, but he's been busy here this summer. Ain't been up to see her like he said he would, so the mountain popped down to see Mahomet. Only he wasn't here.'

Not totally convincing, Georgia thought. Jessica could have used the telephone to summon Vic.

Molly might have realized that doubt was lingering, however, because she added, 'Got a real interest in local history, has Mrs Wayncroft. She likes talking to Vic about the old days, and listening to his stories.'

This was news to Georgia. She'd had it from the horse's mouth that Jessica couldn't stand history, at least not Wayncroft history. 'About the Becket ruins?'

'Anything to do with St Thomas. Even had a look at the old Poo-House the other day. She brought Mr Val too. He had a good nose round.'

Did he, indeed? All the more reason, Georgia thought, for her to look at it herself as speedily as possible.

'Anyway, what I wanted to tell you about,' Molly continued firmly, 'is this. It's about Mr Robert. Dad worked for the Wayncrofts for twenty-five years: for Mr Robert, then Mr Hugh, then Mr Robert again.'

Georgia was fully alert now. 'What sort of person was he?' She'd heard his name often enough, but not much about the man himself.

'A hothead when he was younger, so Dad had heard. When he went into the army for the war, he was as full of himself as young Sebastian is now. Dad started working for him right after the war, but the war had changed a lot of people, and Mr Robert was one of them. His father had died way back, and his grandad, Mr Alfred, was running Chillingham when war broke out. Then he died in 'forty-two and Mr Robert – lieutenant he was then – came back to Chillingham on compassionate leave. Whether it was that, or the war itself, he became broody and preoccupied. He was out at Dunkirk, then later got posted to the Desert, then Italy, then Germany. Won himself a DSO, he did. He never did settle down here again after the war. Came back regular to see his Mum, while she was alive, but Mr Hugh managed the estate until Mr Robert handed it over to him. All Dad would say was that it was his belief something happened to him during the war that changed him, and I reckon Dad knew what that was. He never told us though. He'd stayed close to Mr Robert though, especially when Dad knew he hadn't got long to go. Very set he got on that towards the end. "I got to," he said to me. "It's only right. It's his."'

'What was?' Georgia was on tenterhooks. Could this be the key to the whereabouts of St Thomas's bones?

'He never said, but one day I remember Dad was near to tears. "What's wrong, Dad?" I said. "Wrong?" he asked. "Murder's wrong, that's what."'

'Whose murder?' Georgia asked sharply.

Molly sighed. 'Again, he never said. Dad was like that. But he and Mr Robert got even closer, if that were possible, and Dad seemed happy enough. One of the last things he said to me was, "You go on looking out for the Wayncrofts, Molly girl. They're good people at heart. It's just the heritage. They can't escape it. I did wrong, but it's been put right now, so don't you worry." Now, Georgia m'dear.' Molly grew brisk. 'I've been telling you this in case you can make head or tail of it. I can't. I'm taking a risk, speaking out, but we can't have no more murders.'

'You mean that Anne Fanshawe might have known what your father meant?'

'If anyone did, I reckon it was her.'

The Becket Shrine, which John Painter had taken so much time in restoring, was not as Georgia had imagined it. She had followed Molly's directions and gone out through the French windows to the terrace, in front of which was a sizeable garden, chiefly given to trees, bushes and grass. On the right she could see the path she had taken last night, but that had led her only along one side of the garden. Becket's Shrine was to her left, however, where there was a row of separate self-contained accommodation apartments, converted from the old stables, and one or two modern outbuildings. The Shrine looked so insignificant that she passed it by at first, but eventually found it tucked back between the main house and the stable rooms.

It was hardly in the ancient monument league. It was about six foot square, with a modern door and tiled roof. Molly had told her that the door was unlocked, and at first Georgia could see only a jumble of tools, which looked as if they had been accumulating since the house was first built. Old hoes, rakes, spades and forks, a pile of seed boxes – garden junk, in other words. The modern garden mower that this garden surely required must be kept somewhere else. Then she saw that the 'shrine' must once have served another purpose. Amid the jumble was an old chair, and a small grimy window with an ashtray on its sill suggested a hideaway, rather than an outside toilet.

Could this building be holding Becket's bones? It would explain Painter's closeness to Robert Wayncroft, and why Jessica and Val were so interested in it. Excitement began to stir inside her. It was a credible theory, surely? The more natural place for them would have been in the chapel, perhaps in front of the altar, or in the well, but this building was near enough to them to have formed part of the Becket complex. He might even have owned a house of his own on this site, a forerunner of Becket House. Steady, she warned herself. Not too far too quickly.

Without much hope, she peered behind the tools to see if there were loose stones, although other investigative hands would have found anything obvious. The roof? She peered upwards, but there seemed no possible hiding place, and in any case, the roof had been constructed by John Painter.

Only the floor remained as a possibility. It was covered with old lino, but she managed to lift one side of it an inch or so. There seemed to be flagstones underneath it, perhaps to match the terrace, and there was no way she could get any further. Under them, buried deep, might indeed lie the bones of St Thomas, and John Painter, Robert Wayncroft, Jessica and Val might have come to the same conclusion. If so, where did that lead her? Given the remote chance that they were indeed here, what would the result if they were exhumed? Apart from years of discussion by experts on their provenance, and publicity for Chillingham, could they have had any bearing on Hugh's murder? In 1967, Becket House had still been part of the Wayncrofts' estate.

She wondered very much what had sparked off Jessica's interest in this Shrine.

Jessica welcomed her like the first day of spring – clad in bright green, with a jaunty vivid bow to set off her white hair. 'Molly tells me you're staying at Becket House,' she began as she led Georgia into her living room. 'Such a fascinating building. When I first came to live in Chillingham Place, Hugh's mother moved into Becket House, as she was by then a widow. She never remarried, and nor have I. Now do tell me how can I help you.' Not waiting for an answer, Jessica swept on, 'Are you attending the play tomorrow night? I've decided to go after all, despite my earlier misgivings. Val would be so disappointed if I missed it.'

No mention of Julian being disappointed, Georgia noted. 'Yes. Peter, Luke and I are all going.'

'Dear me. A statement, you might say. We must all guard our tongues most carefully.' She giggled. 'Always so difficult with someone so pleasant to talk to as you are, Georgia. Now, what was it you wanted to ask?'

Flattery? Georgia smiled to herself. Obvious though it was, it still smoothed the path. 'Molly Jones was telling me of your interest in local history, and I've just been looking at the little outbuilding that her father restored at Becket House. Have you seen it?'

Jessica looked mildly surprised. 'Indeed I have. Val and I popped down to see it one day. It's one more site that we would like to add to the official village tour, which we shall be organizing. There's not much to see, but Vic Painter believes there is a case for claiming St Thomas might have once lived on the site.'

Georgia awarded Jessica full marks for quick recovery, but decided to go for gold. 'Especially if that could include the legend of Becket's bones being buried there.'

'Ah.' Jessica looked pensive. 'Now that it is a *big* question. Has it occurred to you that Anne had a good reason for leaving us the chapel and well in her will?'

'It has.'

'And that the reason might have been because she'd discovered that the bones were not in the well or the chapel ruins, but in Becket House?' Jessica was smiling blandly at her as she delivered this head-on punch.

Georgia pulled herself together. 'It hadn't,' she admitted, speedily running the possibilities through her mind. 'I can't see how that ties in however. Robert, who was so keen on the Wayncroft heritage, had sold Becket House to John Painter, and he would surely never have done so if he had believed the bones were hidden there.'

Jessica had an answer for that. 'Perhaps because *he* believed that the bones were in the chapel.'

'Like Valentine? He didn't find anything there last night, did he?'

A mischievous smile at this turning of the tables. 'Ah, he did mention he'd run into you. I told him it was unwise to go exploring there as yet, but the dear boy is so impetuous. He takes after his father, and the special forces were chosen for their fearless nature. I told Val he has only a month or two to wait until probate is granted and then he can go there any time he likes. He's gone to Canterbury today, of course, to join the others, as foolishly he decided not to do the walk yesterday. Julian would not be pleased, nor dear Tim, to hear of his clandestine activities. Please don't tell them.'

Georgia skirted round this request. 'Will you drive there tomorrow?'

'No. I do get tired in the evenings,' Jessica admitted. 'Simon has kindly said he will drive me over.' A pause. 'The police came to see me this morning, and it rather upset me.'

'To talk about Anne's murder?'

'Of course. Because Julian is inheriting the ruins, they seem to assume we Wayncrofts must have hastened her on her way. How short-sighted of them, not to mention annoying. We had no idea of her intentions.'

'She didn't consult you or Julian about it?'

Jessica sighed. 'No. Anne was a very private person. Furthermore, she was only just over fifty and could hardly have believed she would die so soon. She might have been assuming that Sebastian would inherit them, not Julian, and that he, in time, would change his views.'

The theory she had had herself, Georgia remembered. Could that indeed be the answer? She could not convince herself of it – it was too risky, and Robert Wayncroft did not strike her as a risk-taker where family was concerned. 'Sebastian came out in favour of abandoning the play at the meeting,' she said, 'so have his views on development changed too?' It was worth asking.

'Absolutely not.' Jessica sat ramrod still, very much the insulted grande dame. 'I too, if you recall, would have preferred the play cancelled. But that is a long way from being opposed to ensuring Chillingham's future. That is something I would never endorse, and nor, I trust, will my sons or grandson.'

*   *   *

When she returned to Becket House, Georgia was surprised to see Peter's car parked there, but then she remembered that when she had rung him earlier he had expressed great interest in coming to see the Shrine. She tracked him down to the rear garden, where she saw him sitting in his chair at a garden table, drinking coffee, presumably courtesy of Molly.

'What brought you here?' she asked.

'Escaping Janie.'

'Oh, *Peter*.'

'Joke,' he said hastily. 'She can't come to the play tomorrow night. I did ask her.'

There was a note in his voice that said step no further, and she obeyed it. 'Want a pub lunch?'

'Sounds good. I want to see this so-called Shrine first.'

'Over there.' She escorted him back there, and he peered into it with great curiosity.

'Shrine, eh?' he said, at last. 'It would take a Becket miracle to make this into one.'

'What did you think of my bones theory?'

'I'm nothing if not gracious. Brilliant, but theory only.'

'The only place would be under the flagstones, and we can't prise them up on mere conjecture. I can't see any sign that there's been any recent digging there.'

'Even supposing we did dig up a casket of bones, would that advance our case much further?'

'No,' she agreed, somewhat reluctantly. 'But it was surely the reason that Jessica and Val were interested in it, and the reason that Val was prowling around the Becket ruins last night. If the bones were found in either place, the very idea that they might be Becket's would bring Val the publicity he's so eager for.'

'Glad you said *might*. Becket's bones are one of those never-ending puzzles like the *Marie Celeste* and Jack the Ripper. There are so many theories that the true one could lie nestling amongst them and never be proved or even be generally taken as "the truth". In Becket's case, it's not even certain that the bones of St Thomas were *in* the shrine when Good King Henry's Commissioners came to destroy it. They were generally quite careful over bones, but even if those they found *were* Thomas's, they could have been burnt or reburied somewhere by the Commissioners themselves. If the monks themselves spirited them away, they could still be in the Cathedral crypt, where bones were discovered in 1888, or countless other places.'

'What are the odds on their being at Chillingham?'

'Very long, but you never know. The monks might have decided to get them right out of the Commissioners' way, and quite apart from the Wayncrofts, Chillingham church has always had a link with what is now the Cathedral and once an abbey church. Chartham had one too. The snag is that there's no evidence, save family tradition and legend, that these stones were anything to do with Becket lore – and yet dear Val is sniffing around so eagerly that he can't even wait for probate.'

'He's the type . . .' Georgia began, uncertain where this was going.

'What exactly would you say *is* Val's type?' Peter shot back.

'Ruled by self interest alone.'

'How would you define his self-interest in relation to Thomas Becket?'

'Money for the estate . . .' She pulled a face. 'Oh.' False step.

'Precisely. For the estate. Which only indirectly means his mother, and thus even more indirectly means Val.'

'And Val and brother Julian don't exactly hit it off. So his self-interest presumably lies in keeping a roof over his head, and a possible income through tourism and the planned theatre.'

'I agree. But is Val really trying to keep on good terms with brother Julian? We haven't seen many signs of it. He, Julian, Aletta and Jessica are an unlikely collection of ingredients to make a successful pudding.'

'That's very culinary of you.'

'But good observation?'

'Yes. Although Aletta, Julian and Seb are his alibi for Anne's murder.'

'It's Hugh's we're investigating.'

'He has an alibi for that, too.'

'Provided by his mother. Keeping it in the family, eh?'

'Very much so,' she agreed. 'But there are other families: the Painters, the Moons, not to mention Tim and Simon. They're all sticking together.'

'Like the Glueman's game in the Michael Powell film about Canterbury that Lisa mentioned to you,' Peter said. 'Everyone has his or her own quest where the Old Road and Canterbury are concerned.' He paused. 'Switching subjects, I haven't yet told you about Mike's visit. He brought Will Whitton with him.'

'How are they getting on?'

'Some good news, some bad. The only DNA evidence they recovered is hers. Will's team is pursuing a local man slung out of a pub for being drunk about that time, but he hasn't taken his eye off the ball so far as Anne Fanshawe's legacy is concerned.'

'And the good?'

'That *was* the good news. The bad is that, interesting though that battle royal Anne Fanshawe had with the Wayncrofts is, it doesn't seem to be relevant, as their alibis are backed up by plenty of other witnesses. Anne left, they stayed on. It's true that her departure seems to have sparked off a general drift towards leaving. She left about ten fifteen, but the land-lord confirms that his overnight guests were there until last. The place seems to have emptied not long after ten thirty.'

'And the camping ground that the youngsters were using was to the right of the pub, back towards Wrotham. Anne turned left.' Georgia frowned. 'You said no DNA but hers?'

'Yes.'

'But her credit cards were missing. You'd think there'd be some on her bag if the cards were pinched.'

'That's the other news. Her anorak and credit cards were found by Will's team, hanging in that corridor you told me about.' Peter's turn to frown. 'Even Suspects Anonymous can't make anything out of that.'

The Stour Theatre was not on the River Stour itself, but out near the ruins of St Augustine's Abbey – a good situation for producing this particular play, Georgia thought. She and Luke knew the theatre quite well. It mounted both professional and amateur productions, it was small, it had a bar, and it was welcoming. Tonight was, hardly surprisingly in view of the publicity, a sell-out. Georgia could see the Full House sign standing proudly outside as she drove past the theatre to the car park. Peter had driven here separately, and by a miracle she could see he had found the one disabled spot available.

By the time Georgia reached the theatre, though, having battled to find a space for herself, the idea of sitting through a long Victorian verse play was not an attractive one. She told herself that duty and loyalty were at stake here, but nevertheless she was glad that Luke was coming too.

'Like waiting for Godot, isn't it?' Peter said cheerfully as she joined him in the auditorium. She could see what he meant. There was a tension here far above the expectancy level of a normal first night.

Luke must have felt the same when he finally arrived. 'What are they hoping for?' he muttered. 'Just Becket's or another murder thrown in?'

She shushed him, as Lisa Moon was just taking her place in front of them. Jessica's white hair could clearly be seen in the front row; another reminder of why she and Peter were here. There was no rational reason that this play was going to provide any indication of why Hugh Wayncroft was killed so many years ago, and yet – as Peter had implied about the Michael Powell film – it was beginning to feel as if this were a pilgrimage of their own. But what pilgrimage? Even as she pondered this, Tim came on to the stage to make a brief speech about Anne's tragic death. And then the curtain rose.

Tennyson's play was not nearly as inaccessible as she had expected, and what was even more of a plus was that the standard of acting was exceptionally high for an amateur group. She became absorbed in the relationship between Becket (Val), the man of God, and the King (Julian), the power of the state. Julian was playing the King excellently, she thought, as an intemperate changeable man all too easily manipulated by the cunning of others. In particular he was at the mercy of the formidable Queen Eleanor, and torn between her and his beautiful mistress Rosamund, mother of his ten-year-old illegitimate son Geoffrey, whom Anne had played in the 1967 production.

'How dost thou know I am not wedded to her?' the King threw petulantly at Becket.

An interesting point. Georgia toyed with the notion that Hugh might have married Lisa, but had to discard it immediately, if regretfully. Jessica and Hugh had been married in 1956, when Lisa would have been in her early teens.

There were strong emotions between Julian and Val. Superb

acting? Or was their offstage relationship helping things along? A play, she told herself, a *play*. Where did Aletta come into this? She played the role exceptionally well, but that's all it was. A role. She had no offstage quarrel with Tess Moon, so far as Georgia was aware.

'What do you think?' Peter asked her when the interval arrived.

'Impressive.'

Peter waved this aside impatiently. 'No, the play itself. Tells you a lot, doesn't it? Just think about the 1967 production; think of Clive Moon as the King, of Val as chief murderer Fitzurse, and Hugh their victim. All that passion on stage. And then comes the cast party, when once again the row breaks out over development of the Becket ruins. And Hugh holds his ground. "I must die for that which never dies," he says in this play. He meant heritage, Georgia, heritage.'

'But Val's playing Becket now,' Georgia said uneasily. 'And Julian's the King.'

'The King, Georgia, the King. He who wields the power.'

'But is manipulated by others. Don't forget that.'

TWELVE

'The King's in residence,' Peter shouted over her mobile. Georgia's eyes were barely open as yet, and the glories of Becket House breakfast awaited. The King? Ah, she remembered Peter's proclamation of the night before. Now his phone call made some sort of sense. 'How about an audience this morning?' Peter continued.

'In Canterbury?' she asked, puzzled.

'No, no, no. Chillingham. He drove Jessica back last night.'

'I'm not sure.' Surely they wouldn't get anything of interest from Julian in the middle of the play's run?

'I am. We're already booked in. Eleven o'clock. I'll be with you fifteen minutes before.'

'He can't have been pleased,' Georgia demurred.

'He wasn't. Not at first, anyway.'

Her heart sank. She had originally planned to return to Medlars later this morning. Luke had left earlier for his office, leaving her asleep. Peter had suggested last night that she should stay on here for the week, and Luke had backed him up. She had agreed only very reluctantly, interpreting Luke's stance on this as wanting to avoid *the* issue. Peter's only comment on why she should stay on had been vague: 'Something might happen.'

Looking through her window at the village roofs, Chillingham seemed peaceful enough, sheltering in the lea of the Downs, and she tried to think of what it would be like visiting it as a tourist in future years. On a day like today, the summer sun would make the village seem so united and tranquil. She could imagine bowling up in a coach, stepping out in some future enormous car park, in happy anticipation of a pleasant stroll round the St Thomas ruins, a pub lunch and perhaps even a theatre visit. Her situation today was not quite like that. She was now enmeshed in Chillingham, and there could be no departure, at least mentally, until this case was solved. But what if it never was? She refused to face that possibility, because she and Peter had often been stuck in the doldrums over an unsolved case. It was too early to assume that there could never be a fair wind behind them, when it was less than three weeks since they had walked into the Three Peacocks and met the Chillingham Drama Group.

What, Georgia wondered, had Peter meant by his reference to the King wielding the power? And, come to that, what had *she* meant by her own instant response that kings could be manipulated by others? Was Julian a pawn in a chess game being played by others, and was that game the Becket development or Anne's death? It couldn't be Hugh's, because Julian played no part in that, except as Hugh's heir. It occurred to her that Peter might have meant something entirely different, however. In the play they had seen last night, the King had been driven to rid himself of that 'turbulent priest' Becket. Brother Val.

It was no use. She could not see what Peter's own game was. He duly drove up to Becket House at ten forty-five to pick her up, and she hopefully asked, 'Clarification, please. What are we looking for? *How* are we looking?'

'Don't ask me,' Peter replied happily. 'Something will turn up. There's something there. I know there is. It all comes back to that word "heritage".'

Julian's apartment was at the other end of the building from Jessica's, and fortunately, as there was no lift, it had a downstairs room, which looked as if it served both as reception room and study. Georgia noticed there was no sign of Aletta, who had probably stayed in Canterbury. Aletta, like T.S. Eliot's Mystery Cat Macavity, 'wasn't there' whenever there was trouble around. The power, in her case, stayed *behind* the throne.

'Good to see you. How can I help?' Julian asked heartily. He seemed to have recovered from his reluctance to see them – probably because, Georgia thought, of their genuine praise of the play and his performance. His tall and well-built figure seemed to dominate the room physically and mentally, a role he was obviously used to. 'My father's death again. That it?' he continued.

'It is,' Peter agreed.

'Not sure I can help, but try me.'

Peter did. 'As head of the Wayncrofts, you're still a power in this village, aren't you? Unspoken now, but generally the case.'

Julian looked taken aback. 'I'm honoured you should think so, and there's some truth in what you say. What bearing does that have on my father's death?'

'The path to solving it, perhaps. The link with Anne Fanshawe's death.'

'There is no link.' Julian's voice grew icier.

'I would say there is – the link is the Wayncroft heritage.'

Julian gave a theatrical heavy sigh. 'Not again. I've been through that with you, Georgia. Look, no one knows why my father was killed, and it's a rash assumption that because he refused to open the Becket ruins to the public, that is the reason he was murdered. It could have played a part, but that's as far as I or anyone else can go. There were other reasons – personal motives – that have to be taken into account. Because of the strong feelings over the ruins, the personal side gets overlooked.'

'And what was it?'

'Having grown up with the situation, it's always been my opinion that pure hatred was the reason for my father's death, with personal gain as an added incentive. One does not wish to speak ill of the dead, and so I will not name—'

'Fred Miller?' Peter suggested, to draw him out.

'No.'

'Then it was Clive Moon.'

'Yes,' Julian unwillingly admitted.

'Do you have evidence, or is it only your opinion?'

'He was the obvious candidate. He was a bad-tempered sullen man when I knew him, and I can't imagine he was much different at the time of my father's death. He certainly loathed him.'

'And he led the protest march, I understand.'

'In my opinion that's why he did it. He wasn't the sort of man to get worked up about the future of the village, especially as his trade would not be affected. But the chance of revenge on Hugh Wayncroft would be irresistible.'

'But why then and in such a public place?' Georgia asked.

'There had been an incident the night before at the after-show party when Clive perhaps thought he had been publicly humiliated. My mother's patience snapped, and she poured a glass of wine over Clive's wife, whom she saw as her rival.

Clive would not have taken that in his stride. So that, Peter, Georgia, is my view on my father's death.'

'Does your mother have the same view?'

'You may ask her, but please do not upset her. She may not talk of it, as I suspect she feels a degree of responsibility because of that incident. But I am as certain as I can be that it was Clive.'

'But partly linked to the heritage question, as you said.'

A fractional pause before Julian's reply. 'If I said that, I was wrong.'

Retreat was good, thought Georgia. It meant Peter could make the running.

'Can you talk about it openly?' Peter asked innocently. 'Or is it forbidden territory for non family members?'

This caught Julian on the raw. 'Yes – no. *Yes*. It's the eldest son's responsibility, and no one else's concern. I can only refer to it in the most general terms.'

'Responsibility towards whom or what? The Becket ruins?'

Julian seemed reasonably happy with this question. 'Yes, but in my case the situation was different. I was under two years old when my father died, and so my uncle resumed the responsibility until I was twenty-one.'

'And then he coached you?'

'Yes. Nowadays the heir knows in general terms what's involved, but when he inherits there may be specific instructions. In this case, came the shock that he'd left the ruins to Anne.'

'Without any intimation that they might one day return to you?'

'No,' he said shortly. 'And before you condemn me for supporting their development, I would point out that it is the only way of preserving them for the nation. And preserving Chillingham Place.'

Julian was in full lord of the manor flow, but too late he must have seen the pitfall ahead. 'And if you think this provides your *link* to Anne's death, you are mistaken, and furthermore my father's death is an entirely different situation.'

'In what way? The trouble is,' Georgia put in earnestly, 'there's a flaw in what you're saying. The heritage, as you describe it, is fairly straightforward, but the legalities surrounding it seem to imply a much more formal obligation.'

Julian managed a laugh. 'Believe me, Georgia, I'd like nothing better than to be able to tell you of priceless relics handed down in secrecy to the Wayncroft heir. Perhaps you'd like me to produce a golden chalice with St Thomas's DNA on it? Alas, I fear not.'

'I was thinking of something just as valuable,'Georgia said.

A raised eyebrow. 'And that would be . . .?'

'Becket's bones.'

That laugh again. 'The old chestnut. I told you my uncle believed the bones might be here, but he told me that with a pinch of salt.'

'Your half-brother seems more committed.'

A frown. 'Val? What do you mean?'

Georgia decided to forget Jessica's request for silence. 'I met him at the Becket ruins late on Sunday night.'

Julian looked astounded. 'What the hell was he doing there? What were *you* doing there, come to that?'

'I saw a light flickering and went out to investigate.'

'And you assume he was looking for Becket's bones? Did he say so?' Julian asked sharply.

'No, but it's possible. Finding them would be a linchpin for your publicity.'

Surprisingly, Julian did not shout her down. 'I'll ask him about it. Anyway, they'd be impossible to authenticate.'

'Like the remains of the wooden St Thomas figure I believe you have,' Peter said.

Julian stiffened. 'You're well informed on our affairs. They, too, I agree, are impossible to authenticate, but the wood is thirteenth or fourteenth century.'

'Have you ever had them looked at by the Church or British Museum?'

'No.' Julian was definitely holding back now, although he was not, Georgia thought, hostile.

'Could we see them?' Peter asked.

That produced a stronger reaction. 'No. They're with the heritage papers.'

A split second silence before Peter gently enquired, 'And they are?'

'Not for outsiders,' Julian blustered.

'Even if they hold the clue to your father's death?'

'They don't.'

'They might.'

A hesitation now. 'My father died over forty years ago. Let it rest.'

'It's rested long enough. And Anne Fanshawe died possibly as a result.'

'Keep her out of it.'

'The police won't,' Peter countered. Will was pitted against will now, and Georgia would not intervene.

'Are you threatening me?' Julian asked, almost wearily.

'No. Telling you that there really could be a link.'

'I will therefore tell *you* that I believe Clive Moon killed my father. I admit, however, that although personal motives were behind it, the Becket development might also have played a part. And for that I do have evidence.'

'Thank you,' Peter said simply. 'Can we see it?'

Julian wavered. 'I can't bring it down here . . .' He looked at the wheelchair.

'That's OK. I'm used to that. You go, Georgia,' Peter said. Thus boxed into a corner, Julian surrendered, and Georgia followed him upstairs to his living room. Peter was well used to such frustrations, but nevertheless Georgia felt for him as she saw his downcast face as they left.

Julian led her across the room to a small door at one end, so well disguised that she had not spotted it.

'It once served as a small chapel and priest's hole combined when religious times were tough,' Julian explained stiltedly. She could see that he was an unwilling guide. 'We Wayncrofts are good at surviving. We got through the Reformation and the Civil War. We lost the baronetcy, but kept our heads. The last baronet was Sir Bevis, in the mid seventeenth century. He began to get cold feet about where the family might be heading, so he decided to record the traditions, just in case the eldest son ended up on the chopping block. It was just as well because he was murdered by his younger brother. My father and Robert got on rather better, thankfully.'

The room was about ten feet square, and Georgia looked around it in fascination. Chapel it might once have been, but now it was a glory-hole of books, papers, and more paintings – a Wayncroft treasure house. Julian marched over to a

bookshelf on which stood a large wooden box, which he
brought over to a small table. He opened it to reveal what
looked little more than a collection of small branches and
pieces of bark at first glance. Then she noticed the wood-
worm holes as she picked out a piece that could have been
a thumb and part of a forefinger, then another that could be
part of a long robe.

'Do you think these are genuine?' she asked.

Julian hesitated, but must have decided he had nothing to
lose. 'The wood is. But they were Clive Moon's work.
Evidence, Georgia, the evidence you wanted. When we begin
our development it won't include these. Far too risky nowadays. My mother admitted they were fakes when I was grown
up enough to hear the truth. Clive Moon was a brilliant
carpenter, and he concocted these out of authentic wood, not
hard to get in a village of this age. They were all part of the
earlier development plans, but after my father's death and my
uncle's stance on the ruins, they were locked away. Now can
you believe how eager Clive was for personal revenge?'

'Did you ever talk to him in later years about these fakes?'

'I did. He told me with great pride that he'd used no tools
that weren't authentic to the period. The only modern addi-
tion was pesticides for the wormholes. When I told my
unscrupulous brother that these were fakes, however, he
suggested we ask Matthew Moon to produce a declared modern
replica of what the figure would have been like.'

'Hold on. There was no such figure, was there?'

'No. It would be a replica of a fake idea, and therefore I
have vetoed the suggestion. The ruins have plenty to say of
their own, without resorting to such means.'

'And the bones? He doesn't want to fake them too, does
he?'

'No. They will be declared as legend – unless, of course,
they really do turn up,' Julian replied.

'I take it there's no mention of them in the Wayncroft
papers?'

She had thought this would receive a prompt and dismissive reply, but to her surprise Julian beckoned her over to a
modern desk in one corner. He pulled open a drawer and withdrew a box file, inside which was a small pile of paper sheets.
'One of my ancestors fortunately made transcripts of the

papers, and the originals have now vanished. The transcripts themselves are locked away; these are photocopies taken ten years or so ago.'

'Could we take these down to show Peter?' she asked.

'No. They stay in this room.'

Co-operation was only going so far then. Julian was adamant, and there would be no point arguing about it. There were about ten sheets covered in copperplate handwriting, and with Julian breathing down her neck all she could glean was that they seemed to go on *ad nauseam* about the duty to protect and preserve the saint's memory, relics and buildings. There was nothing, as Julian had said, about his bones, unless they were included under 'relics'. Again, she could not see that, even if the bones were unearthed, it could help Marsh & Daughter's work. The last page ended up with: 'Your heritage is wisdom. Guard it and honour it until the true faith is restored and St Thomas returns to claim his own.'

A clarion call to the Wayncrofts, but she was no further forward.

'Pray tell me everything, daughter mine,' Peter said as soon as they were back in the car. 'Spare not a single word.'

'Clive Moon faked the medieval St Thomas figure remains. He admitted it to Julian himself, and I can't see any reason that Julian would be lying about it.'

'Which backs up Julian's theory about Moon killing Hugh Wayncroft, but doesn't prove it to the slightest extent.'

'It does hang together as a story.'

'Doesn't it just. Almost too well. He was very anxious to dwell on Hugh's death, not Anne's, wasn't he?'

'We let him,' she said in Julian's defence. 'We could have pressed him harder.'

'We could, though we would have got precious little out of him in my view. Did you see those heritage papers?' he asked, turning left out of the drive. 'Lunch, I think. The Three Peacocks. You do have something more to tell me, I trust?'

'Not much.' As he pulled into the car park, she described as fully as she could what she had read.

'Wisdom,' he said thoughtfully. 'Presumably wisdom in dealing with the ruins and/or simmering threats to the

Wayncrofts practising their faith. As regards the ruins, that wording might give them licence to restore and develop them of course, so why, I wonder, did Robert and Hugh so adamantly interpret it as leaving the ruins as they were?'

'Because of the bones?' she asked hopefully.

'That surely implies that the clue to where the bones are would be in the recorded traditions somewhere.'

'There didn't seem to be.'

'Leaving it to the heir to interpret as he will. The primal curse.'

'What is?'

'In this case, the curse of being the eldest son.'

'Relevance?'

'I don't know. There's always the primal curse of the murder of Abel by Cain in Genesis. Murder of the younger brother.'

'If you're thinking Robert killed Hugh, no way,' she replied. 'He was abroad.'

'There's our two half brothers, Val and Julian,' he ruminated. 'No love lost there.'

'Julian was in the dark over Val's excursion to the ruins on Sunday. He wasn't pleased.'

'Am I my brother's keeper?' Peter quoted with relish. 'Sibling rivalry breaks out no matter what Wisdom says.'

'Irrelevant, however, for Hugh Wayncroft's murder, and *that's* our focus.'

'As Julian is all too eager to make clear.'

'Could I remind you that all the Wayncroft family have an alibi for Anne's murder? They're known to have been in the pub long enough for Anne to reach the farmhouse.'

'Unless, of course,' Peter said, 'she came back to the pub. Let's go in and eat.'

'Been to Chillingham Place, I heard,' Lisa greeted them as she brought the menu over.

'News travels fast.' Georgia laughed, hoping the news did not include the discussion of Clive Moon.

'Vic's a speedy worker,' Lisa agreed. 'Went to see Mrs Jessica and heard you were with Mr Julian. He remembers the upset in sixty-seven, especially where Mrs Wayncroft was concerned. She was beside herself, he said. Natural enough because of Hugh's death – and what it meant.' Lisa grinned.

'The estate going back to Mr Robert. Couldn't have expected that, could she, him being the younger brother? Now, what can I get you?'

She busied herself with writing down their order, but Georgia could see there was something else on her mind.

'Anyway,' Lisa added, 'Vic says if you give him a knock, he'll take you into the church. That'll be a start. Takes his time coming round, does Vic.'

'And what's this in aid of?' Peter asked blankly when Lisa had gone, having said she knew no more than they did what Vic meant. 'Anything you remember in particular about the church?'

'Only the Wayncroft memorial chapel.'

'Well, we'll find out in due course. In the meantime . . .'

'So you've come then.' Vic nodded. 'Thought you would. I'll just get my pipe and I'll be with you.'

What was so special about St Thomas's that she hadn't noticed before? Georgia wondered as Vic helped Peter steer his wheelchair down the ramp. It felt wrong to be coming into this church with its vicar so recently and horribly dead. Whatever secrets the church held, however, Anne could well have known about. One she shared with Robert Wayncroft? Whatever it was, it wasn't in the chapel, because Vic was leading the way to the far aisle. He stopped in front of a brass plaque, one of the world war memorials.

Looking at it more closely than she had on her first visit, Georgia realized that it was unusual, in that it was dedicated specifically to the memory of those who died in the air raid on Canterbury, on the second of June, 1942. A list of names followed, the last two separated by a scroll ornament. These two were servicemen, the others civilians. At the foot of the memorial was inscribed the legend: 'The price of wisdom'. *Wisdom* again – a coincidence? She could not understand the context it was used in here, however. A terrible raid the price of wisdom? Did that make sense? She asked Vic, but he just shook his head.

Peter had his own questions. 'Why just that raid?' he asked Vic. 'There was a second one two days later and another one after that. Not so heavy, it's true, but nevertheless people died.'

It was Georgia who replied, however, not Vic. 'Perhaps it

was because Robert Wayncroft was caught in this one,' Georgia said. 'Did he erect it? And your father was caught in the raid too, wasn't he, Vic?'

'That's right.' Vic looked pleased, which meant they must be on the right track – to wherever this was leading. 'Dad saw Mr Robert struggling to restrain a soldier who'd gone wild, but before he could pull him away a wall came down on him and he was killed. Mr Robert was pulled clear of it though. Dad always reckoned it was one of these two.' He pointed to the last two names on the plaque.

'Shouldn't this memorial be in the Cathedral itself?' Peter asked. 'It seems strange to have it here.'

'Mr Robert lived in Chillingham. Seems natural enough to me,' Vic said non-committally.

'Why did you want us to see it?' Georgia asked.

'It could have been that raid changed Mr Robert for good, that's why,' he replied, and Georgia knew better than to push him. If the Painters or Moons had something to say they would do so in their own good time, not when it suited Marsh & Daughter.

Nevertheless, patience was not one of Peter's virtues – nor indeed one of hers, Georgia would admit.

'Did Robert get on well with Lisa and Clive Moon?' Peter asked Vic as they left the church. 'He obviously did with your family.'

'I'd have said that was their business, but seeing as how Lisa and Molly think it's time to speak out, I'll tell you,' he grunted. 'Mr Robert liked Lisa. Clive were a different matter.'

Georgia could not see that this was advancing Marsh & Daughter's case, but she supposed it was good that Vic at least thought he was contributing. Little by little she and Peter had tacit permission to dig away the layers of silence that led back to 1967. Or further, if this plaque had some relevance.

'Did you get on with Clive Moon?' she asked.

'I'd no time for the chap. Led Lisa a dog's life. Mind you,' he added fairly, 'it didn't help, her and Hugh being what you might call close. But even after Mr Wayncroft died Clive never let her forget it. Took it out on the kids, especially Matthew, until Lisa had it out with him. Said, Catholic or not, she'd leave him and take the kids with her. That shut him up, and shut up wagging tongues too. It was over. Done with.'

Georgia hesitated. 'Julian Wayncroft told me earlier today that Clive went overboard in pushing ahead the plans for the Becket ruins because he hated Hugh Wayncroft so much. Would you agree?'

''Course I would,' Vic answered with a snort. 'You've got to bear in mind that the police never knew about Lisa and Hugh. Even Mrs Jessica never told them, and whether Clive did him in or not, Lisa reckoned her kids needed a dad. One thing I can tell you –' Vic paused to cup his hands over his pipe as he lit it – 'Clive had it in for Hugh. I remember him clear as day saying he'd get him one day.'

'He threatened him to his face?'

'He did. I was there and told him flat: Clive, you've got a chip on your shoulder. Keep it for your woodwork. Reckon he did,' he added, giving them a sideways look.

Georgia grinned. 'I heard he's faked the wooden relics of St Thomas.'

'He was real annoyed that they got put away and never used. He was a true carpenter was Clive, and when he told me about it later, I reckoned I could see what he was after doing. There were those monks hiding behind the screen ready to pull the strings of St Thomas. One pulled the staff so it struck the ground for the water to gush out; another one pulled his hand up and down so it could bless any pilgrim who put his penny in the monks' slot. They'd all have been on their knees, young and old, no matter what in those days. No hip replacements then. Maybe St Thomas did something about hips too.' Vic cackled. 'Clive told me and Dad it had only been a bit of fun, but fun it weren't. We knew that. He was going to see Hugh Wayncroft done down, one way or the other.'

THIRTEEN

To Georgia's pleasure, Peter had elected to join her at Becket House, urged on by Molly. Perhaps this was only for extra trade, but it was also possible that Lisa's mandate about it being time to talk had been taken to heart. Peter was obviously convinced of the link between the two deaths, even if Clive Moon had been responsible for Hugh's. It was tantalizing that the missing clue could be within their grasp, but still eluding them.

When she came down for breakfast on the Thursday morning, she found Peter already at the table. The breakfast room was conveniently handy for staring out of the window towards John Painter's Shrine, and she noted that his table gave him the best view of it. As she arrived, he was taking full advantage of it. She was less sure than he was, however, that the Shrine had anything to do with the Becket story or had any relevance to Hugh Wayncroft's death. Whatever Val and Jessica might have hoped to find, it looked as if they had failed. Molly would surely have known if those flagstones had recently been moved, and there was nowhere else for anything to be hidden.

Molly came to serve her as she sat down, but Peter apparently had more important things on his mind than Georgia's breakfast. 'Do you have a photo of Fred Miller around, Molly?'

He had the magic touch with Molly, even if he seemed to have lost it with Janie, Georgia thought, seeing Molly beam as though fulfilling this request would make her day. She reappeared some minutes later with the photo and a cooling teapot.

'Fred Miller's been a silent witness for too long,' Peter commented as she handed him the photo.

'He's dead,' Molly pointed out cheerfully.

'Witnesses can speak from beyond the grave,' Peter replied portentously.

'True enough. Also true that there was talk at the time that Fred and Clive were in it together. They were very vocal in trying to get Mr Hugh to think different about St Thomas, and they were in front of him in the column.'

'Look at him, Georgia.' Peter handed her the photograph. 'Taken in 1965.'

'Not long after he took over the Three Peacocks,' Molly said. 'He was a cocksure lad. Eager to get ahead.'

'Did Fred do food at the pub, like Simon?'

'Not like nowadays. His wife did a bit, but most pubs didn't in those days. Fred wasn't keen because no one saw food as a way to get ahead. Jeannie did though. She was a goer.' Molly grinned. 'And one day she did go. A Frenchie came to the village, tracing one of his ancestors. Jeannie helped him out, and that was that. She flew the nest in the 1980s some-time. Served Fred right. He was all for development, but did he listen to her? No way. After Mr Hugh died, Fred thought the path was clear, but then Mr Robert told us there wasn't a hope of that. So Fred let the pub go to rack and ruin. No wonder she left. None of your hail-fellow-well-met about Fred. More of a surly glare. One word out of turn, and he'd kick you out, Vic said. Not good for custom.'

'Did *you* think Fred, with or without Clive, murdered Hugh?'

'All talk, no proof,' Molly said firmly. 'No one knew for sure, and that includes me. We all knew Mr Wayncroft was at the back of the column, but people were moving up and down all the time. Mostly though Mr Hugh, Fred and Clive were at the back and Mr Harper and Mrs Jessica at the front because they were all the stars of the show. Mr Hugh liked being at the back, so he could linger when he liked. He liked the peace of the Old Road. When we got near Chillingham, Mrs Jessica nipped back to tell us that the lute players would strike up when we'd nearly reached the village, then would come two of the villains, herself and Mr Val, then at the end would come Fred, Clive and Hugh in all their glory. She left to return to her earlier place, and I heard the lute players strike up. I looked round and saw Mr Hugh then ambling along behind Clive and Fred, quite happy.' A pause. 'But you'll be wanting your breakfast, Georgia,' she said point-edly.

'Yes please.'

Peter grinned as Molly went out to the kitchen.

'You look very satisfied with life,' Georgia said.

'I am. I spoke to Mike earlier.'

Poor old Mike. 'It wasn't even his case.'

'He rang *me*.' Peter was indignant. 'There's something new on Anne Fanshawe's murder.'

'What?'

'The landlord's wife remembers seeing her hanging up her anorak in the hall as she arrived that evening.'

'So? That explains why Anne wasn't wearing it.'

'She was behind the bar when Anne Fanshawe left, and shortly afterwards she went to the loo and saw the anorak still hanging there. She said she didn't worry about it as it was a warm night and Anne wouldn't have missed it. When she went to lock the outside doors however, twenty minutes or so later, it *wasn't* there, so she assumed Anne had come back for it.'

'But Will's team found it there the next morning.' Georgia had a sudden cautious hope that this might be leading somewhere at last. 'She's sure it was Anne's?'

'Yes. It was bright red, and she complimented Anne on it when she arrived at the pub.'

'And she wasn't wearing it when she was found. So that means—'

'She came back (as I said),' he added complacently, 'probably not for the anorak itself, but because her credit cards were in it. Her killer saw her do so and went out to talk to her. An unexpected opportunity for murder.'

'What about the torch that *you* said would require advance planning?' Georgia asked innocently.

Peter brushed this aside. 'In the killer's hotel room. He or she noticed the anorak still there, watched to see if she would return, saw her, came down, took the coat out to her, and accompanied her as she made her second trip towards the farmhouse. He'd then have to take the anorak back to the hotel, as he couldn't take the risk that someone had noticed the coat while it was still hanging there and so would deduce from its absence that Anne had returned. His luck ran out, because someone did. Nevertheless, where does this take us?'

'Alibis are blown to pot. Oh, Peter, are we there?'

'Mike thinks so. Now he merely has to find evidence.'

'Someone staying overnight.'

'The King? Becket himself? Both anxious to give his heartily disliked half-brother an alibi only because it also gave him one?'

'Could be. Or Seb or Aletta?'

'Seb was camping, which makes it less likely, but Aletta could have accompanied the killer – which would have given Anne confidence that she was in no danger. There's Tim and Simon too, who have to be considered, tough though that would be for Luke. All the main pub bedrooms are all over-looking the front of the pub, and I'm sure Will Whitton is well aware of it.'

Georgia contemplated the days ahead. It was countdown. The last performance of the play would be on Saturday, and on Sunday the group would return to Chillingham along the Old Road. Just as it had in 1967. Every time she thought of that it grew more ominous.

Peter was watching her. 'Don't worry, Georgia. There has to be a resolution soon.'

'Yes.' Was he talking of Hugh's murder though, or of her IVF treatment, or of Janie? All problems for which there had to be some cure.

'Meanwhile, it's time,' he continued, 'that we had a thorough look into the Shrine, or the Poo-House as it was elegantly nicknamed.'

'You're fixated on that. Why not the St Thomas ruins if you have the bones in mind?'

'Because of the ease with which Anne Fanshawe signed the ruins back to the Wayncrofts. Almost, don't you think, as if she knew they would find nothing.'

It was hard to judge Molly's reaction when they approached her about the 'more thorough' look at the Shrine. All she said was: 'I've been expecting this. I suppose it has to happen, no doubt about it.'

'You think there's something still hidden there.'

'I don't know nothing of the sort, but Vic and I can't keep putting you off trying to find out. Not now. We always reck-oned Dad had a reason for staying out there so much. When do you want to do it?'

'Now?' Peter asked.

Molly grinned. 'How about tomorrow? Vic's up at

Chillingham Place today, and my Bill's at work in the morn-
ings. Matthew's popping back from Canterbury tomorrow.
He's handy with a pickaxe and that.'

'What about the play?'

'He'll get there in time,' Molly said firmly. 'He don't need
to be in Canterbury till the evening.'

Matthew had obviously received his instructions because at
breakfast on Friday morning Georgia saw him outside on the
terrace unpacking tools and chatting to Vic. She and Peter
hastened to join them, and Molly followed them out.

'What are you hoping to find?' Matthew asked bluntly.

'Not sure,' Peter replied truthfully. 'A hiding place perhaps,
ideally with its contents.'

'St Thomas's bones, for preference,' Georgia added.

Matthew took his time to consider this. 'Good,' he said
finally. 'Best to get it over with then. Ready, Vic?'

He pulled the door open, and he and Vic began dragging
the contents out, while Georgia and Molly formed the end of
a chain to distribute them on garden tables and the terrace
flagstones.

'Lot of junk in here, Molly,' Vic grunted.

Georgia could see he was right, and removing the contents
one by one was a time-consuming task. At last – with the
chair removed and, one by one, the old boxes – the end seemed
in sight.

'Remember Dad sitting on that chair, don't you, Vic?' Molly
said.

A nod. 'Wearing that old panama of his. Don't know why
he bothered. He had enough hair on his head for the sun to
do him no harm.'

'He said Mr Robert gave it to him.'

'Did he come out here too?' Georgia asked.

'Not that I remember,' Vic answered.

'Might have done that day not long before Dad died.
Remember that, Vic?' Molly said. 'Dad told us he wanted to
be left alone with Mr Robert, so Bill and I came over to you
for the day.'

'Now you mention it, yes. He was doing lots of odd things
then though.'

Matthew was working onwards, beginning to pull off the

carpet, which was so rotten that it tore off in pieces. When, at last, the flagstones were laid bare, there was a silence as Vic and Matthew studied them. Georgia could hear her heart thumping, Molly looked tense, and Peter was drumming his fingers impatiently on the arm of the wheelchair.

Georgia was almost beginning to believe that the bones of St Thomas were indeed secreted under this flagstone floor. Watching Matthew and Vic alternately heaving at the flagstones, she felt first apologetic at the labour involved in what might be a fruitless venture and then caught up in a wave of hope and curiosity. It took an hour and two cups of coffee before the flagstones were removed and the sand and grit beneath them revealed.

'Ready, Vic?' Matthew asked again.

'Yup.' Vic took over for the next stint, but that didn't take long, because almost immediately he struck something underneath the sand.

'Concrete, blast it,' he grunted. Neither he nor Matt looked fazed, however, as they took it in turns to prod the bedding inch by inch to see if the concrete covered the entire floor. Matthew was a good man, Georgia thought, apropos of nothing. Lisa might not have been blest in having Clive as a husband, but she was in this son, at least, and probably in Derek too.

'Try here, Vic,' Matt said. 'There seems to be a hollow patch by the window.'

Vic took over, and Matthew emerged to allow him room to manoeuvre.

'Any idea what it is?' Georgia asked him. 'Just sand?'

'Maybe.' Matt remained his usual calm self.

Vic was hard at work on scraping away the sand, with Matt reporting progress from the doorway. At last a breakthrough. 'Something metal,' Vic called. 'Could be a box.'

'The Crown Jewels,' Molly joked, but even so she looked excited.

'Yup,' Vic called. 'Stand back, coming out.'

Now that there was really something to be found, Georgia realized how little she had expected it. Peter, however, was looking as though he had been right all the time – deservedly so, she acknowledged.

Between them Vic and Matt tugged their find free of its

surroundings, and out on to the terrace. It was a tin box about two feet square. 'You look, Molly girl,' Vic said gruffly.

Georgia held her breath as Molly lifted the lid and peered inside. And then a great cry of disappointment. 'It's empty,' Molly said indignantly.

Georgia's hopes plummeted down into anticlimax. There was indeed nothing in this box, nor anything to show what it had once held. Surely no one would have buried something so securely for no reason at all, however? The let-down was hard to take, especially since she had come so close to believing that St Thomas's bones had indeed lain beneath in that box. The box itself, of course, was modern, but who knew how old its contents might have been? Their original covering could have rotted away, making their rehousing imperative.

'Was there ever anything in it, do you think?' she asked.

'I reckon so, don't you, Vic?' Molly said. 'Something important to Dad that made him sit out here day after day.'

'If it's bones you're after, Georgia,' Vic said, 'they've gone long since, and nothing here has anything to do with Mrs Fanshawe's murder.'

Peter was keeping very silent, but Georgia could see the obstinate look on his face. He *still* didn't agree.

She reasoned that Vic and Molly must have expected to find something too, or they wouldn't be wasting their time humouring Marsh & Daughter. Or perhaps, she thought with sinking heart, that's exactly what they were doing. They could have been hoping that the sight of an empty hole would lay the story to rest.

Peter did not seem as daunted as she did, however. 'This link between your father and Robert Wayncroft,' he asked Vic and Molly. 'Did it begin with the 1942 raid or had he met the Wayncrofts before the war?'

'Began with the raid,' Molly answered. 'That's what he said. Then he came to work at Chillingham for Mr Robert after the war.'

'Those two servicemen listed on the monument, Vic. You thought one of those was the soldier Robert tried to save in the raid, but failed. What about the other one? One was French, wasn't he? What was he doing in Canterbury?'

'Plenty of Free French servicemen were around in the years after Dunkirk, waiting their chance to get back home,' Vic replied. 'I told you about that night of the raid that turned Mr Robert's head. Now I'll tell you a bit more. Dad heard Tugboat Annie – that's what the special inner warning system for the city was called. It usually came a while after the sirens, to warn folks the raid was nearly at the city. That night the sirens and Tugboat Annie came more or less together, and then the whole city seemed alight. Mr Robert was caught in it. I wasn't born then, but I listened to Mum and Dad telling us about it later. How they thought the end of the world had come with all those bombs and incendiaries. Dad was near the Cathedral library when the fires started – it was hit to blazes. He and the other guards were in there trying to throw out the incendiaries so they could save as many of the papers and books as they could.'

'Which of the soldiers was the one Robert saw die?' Peter asked. 'Private John Wilson or the Frenchman? That was Lieutenant Christophe Bonneur, wasn't it?'

'That's it,' Molly exclaimed. 'Bonneur. That was the name of the French fellow Jeannie Miller married. Not a Christophe, but the surname was Bonneur all right. He came over looking for information about his dad or uncle. He'd heard about the memorial, came to see it and asked for Robert Wayncroft. Mr Wayncroft was away so he never met him, and he ran off with Fred's wife instead.'

Bonneur. That name now rang a bell with Georgia too, and she scrabbled in her memory.

'Isn't that the family Valentine Harper married into?'

FOURTEEN

The end of the pilgrimage. Canterbury, and the last night of *Becket*. Georgia found it hard to believe that this was the same play, the same actors and the same production that she had watched only a few days ago. The cast must have sunk deeply into their roles in the course of the intervening performances in order to give such a mesmerizing performance. The battle between the King and Becket, Julian versus Val, dominated the play to such an extent that, for the first time, Eleanor's part in the conspiracy seemed almost a sideline, good though Aletta and Tess were in their roles.

After Tim had said his few words in memory of Anne, the play had taken off right from the beginning, and as it reached its final scene she almost wanted to cry out, 'Look behind you!' as Becket entered and the knights, led by Seb Wayncroft, advanced. The King himself, the main enemy, was not present in that scene, but his power was evident. As she watched them on stage, it was not hard to see both the love and hatred between them, locked into an impossible situation that ended in murder, and nor was it hard to see the parallels in today's Chillingham – save that love did not seem to exist between Julian and Val.

'Into thy hands O Lord . . .' Val was a superb actor. No doubt about that. Becket's last words jerked painfully and movingly from his mouth. Playing Becket had been Henry Irving's last performance on the stage, and he had died very shortly after those final words. And Hugh Wayncroft had uttered them in 1967 and died the following day. Hugh had been gentle by nature, but strong when it came to defending the Wayncroft family. She had seen few signs of gentleness in Julian or Val. Which would win if Armageddon had to be fought in their power struggle? Val, she decided. He had cunning, whereas Julian had only strength – and Aletta. Which way would Jessica jump, however? To her beloved Val or to the Wayncroft heir?

'Quite something.' Luke drew a deep breath, after the curtain had fallen and Tim had added a few more valedictory words on Anne.

'Seconded.' Peter was as impressed as Georgia was.

Outside in the small foyer, Luke managed to collar Tim and congratulate him. He seemed in such a daze that it was even an effort for him to say thanks. The strain of the last few weeks was still visible, but he looked genuinely happy at the way the play had gone, and Georgia was glad. He deserved it.

'Come along to the party,' Tim managed to add. 'It's at Seymour House, further along this road. Can't miss it. Stands in its own grounds with a whacking great forecourt.'

'Sure?' Luke queried. 'Not just a cast thing?'

'Everyone's welcome after a success,' Tim said happily.

Peter elected to go straight back to Becket House, but Georgia could see Luke was keen to attend. It might even help, she thought. Tongues might be loosened as the cast relaxed, and she'd be a fool to miss the opportunity. The party was being held in a ground-floor room at the front of the house, and as Luke parked and they walked round towards the front door she could see Julian and Aletta inside, and Val's tall figure moving around. The cast must have changed into party gear quickly to get here so soon, no longer delayed by having to remove the lashings of stage make-up that she dimly recalled from her own youthful acting. The smell and the way it had clung were with her still. Atmospheric perhaps, but today's lighting had done away with that.

Luke was driving, and so there was the added inducement that she could indulge in a glass or two of wine. By the time they entered, the party had spread outside at the rear of the house on to a paved area and garden lit by lanterns, which gave the effect of presenting another stage for another play. Ideal for an after-show party, as it continued the make-believe, she thought. Unfortunately, that wasn't possible for her.

At first it seemed pleasant enough as, with Luke engrossed in talking to Tim and Simon, she wandered round on her own.

'Enjoy the show?' Seb was grinning at her with his arm round Tess.

'Terrific performance – and especially by Fair Rosamund and Reginald Fitzurse.'

Another grin. 'Not bad, are we, Tess? I'll get to play the king once we put it on in Chillingham.'

'No aspirations for Becket?'

'No way. We Wayncrofts like doing the regal stuff.'

'So the Chillingham theatre project is going full speed ahead now?'

'Nothing to stop us once we get planning permissions and all that dreary stuff. There's the matter of funding of course, but Val's got his head round that. Lottery money, community grants and stuff.'

Tess pulled a face. 'Don't be too sure, Seb. Big plans can hit the dust. The opposition's still strong.'

'You'll all come round, sweetheart.' Seb hugged Tess. 'The plans are already drawn up for submission.'

'That was quick work,' Georgia said. 'You've only had a week.'

'Did them ages ago. And for the ruins too.'

'But you only knew about the legacy a week or so ago.'

Seb shrugged. 'Val got cracking on them as soon as he knew Robert had died. It all got put on one side when he found out about Anne having inherited them, but once she told us the happy news about her legacy—'

'*Anne* told you?' Georgia asked. 'When?' She could hardly believe what she was hearing.

Seb looked surprised. 'At the pub that night. They were all talking about it when I joined them just before she left.' Seb must belatedly have realized how this could reflect on his parents because he flushed, muttering, 'They probably knew already.'

The damage had been done, however. Seb had obviously thought that this was general knowledge and must be grappling with the fact that his parents might not have mentioned this to the police. So that, Georgia realized, was the reason the table where Anne was sitting had gone very quiet after the row had finished. Anne had been telling the Wayncrofts that the ruins would eventually come back to them. The *eventually* must have struck home to Julian and Val – and Seb himself. Too late, perhaps, to save Chillingham Place.

Seb made his escape with Tess, and Georgia sympathized. It was easy at his age, especially with drink loosening tongues, to say too much and even to distort the truth. She shouldn't place too much reliance on what he had said. That was what she told herself, but she could not help doing so. What Seb had said fitted in all too well with what she remembered of that evening. And what a motive if, driven beyond endurance by Anne's intransigence, one of them had seized the opportunity to force the issue.

Georgia retreated into the house to find a drink and some food, still wrestling with Seb's information. Anne hadn't apparently cared about development in the long term, only in her lifetime. Which pointed surely to her desire and Robert's to skip a generation. She wondered if Jessica, too, realized the implications, as Julian or Val must surely have told her about Anne's disclosure. Georgia could see her sitting alone in a corner, looking rather white, and went over to her.

'Are you all right, Jessica? Can I bring you a drink?'

'It's good of you, but no.' She did not sound well. Then, out of the blue, she added, 'My boys don't always see eye to eye.'

However true, that seemed an odd statement to make at such a time. 'Tonight's success bodes well for your proposed theatre and other plans. Your sons are united over them.'

Jessica smiled. 'In theory. But which one has the prize?'

It seemed unfair to take advantage of Jessica in a rare moment of weakness, but Georgia could not miss the opportunity. 'You mean the Becket bones,' she said flatly.

Jessica stared at her vacantly. 'It's not about theatres or bones. Perhaps it was once, but not now.'

To Georgia's frustration, just as Jessica seemed about to continue, Julian arrived with a look of thunder on his face. 'I hope you're not pestering her with questions.'

'No,' she retorted. 'Your mother looked ill, so I came over to see if I could help.'

'I heard you talking about the Becket bones.'

'And why not?' Jessica roused herself indignantly. 'Val says you have our jewel in the crown.'

Julian went white with fury. 'I do not. My darling brother has. Why can't you see that? And you –' turning to Georgia – 'stop meddling. You're upsetting her.'

'Not me,' she replied firmly.

'I agree, Georgia.' Val appeared from nowhere at their side. 'It's you, Julian. Don't you have any sense of restraint? This is hardly the place to be brawling over our family affairs in front of poor Georgia.'

'Family affairs?' Julian's eyes glittered. 'What family? You're not a Wayncroft, remember? You're an unwelcome guest at that party.'

'Julian—' Jessica said sharply.

'It's no use, Mother. I've had enough. You can get out, Val. We don't need you. Seb and I can run things very nicely without your destructive input.'

Val's face turned a sickly colour, but before he could speak, Jessica intervened. 'Enough,' she said. 'Nothing changes *yet*. You understand me, both of you? We can't afford it. Either you or Val have the answer, and Chillingham needs one.'

There was a dead silence, then Julian, completely ignoring Georgia and Val, helped Jessica up and escorted her away. Val took one look at her. 'I need a drink,' he said.

'Please do. I'll be fine on my own.'

Val looked ill at ease, but without outright rudeness could hardly leave after that.

'I was looking at the memorial in the church, the one to the victims of the raid in 1942, and I noticed the name Bonneur,' Georgia said chattily. 'I remembered Anne telling me that you married into that family.'

'Not the same family,' he said too quickly for credibility.

'Someone said a relative of his came to Chillingham in the 1980s asking for information about him. Then he ran off with Fred Miller's wife. I thought it might be through him that you met your wife.'

'It wasn't. It's a common enough name. My ex-wife had no connection, so far as I know. If you'll excuse me . . .' He walked away without a glance back at her, which told her that she had rattled not one, but at least two cages this evening.

As was often the case with after-show parties, she could see that by now there were two distinct groups, the outsiders and the insiders, the latter being the cast and stage staff. It was almost as if the insiders were declaring themselves a united family for the last time. From her own knowledge of drama groups, once everyone had resumed his or her daily life, the sense of unity would vanish. The walk back to Chillingham would postpone that for a day, however, and tomorrow she would be walking with them. For tonight, however, she had had enough, and when Luke came up to join her, he made no demur when she suggested leaving.

Luke had decided to stay over at Becket House, but again he left early on the Sunday morning, promising to be back to meet her as the pilgrims arrived home. When she went in for breakfast, Peter was waiting for her, but before she could even begin to tell him about the previous evening, he said, 'You've heard?'

'Heard what?'

'Julian Wayncroft.'

'He was there last night and—'

'Attacked last night.'

Her head began to reel. *Julian*? 'What happened? Is he dead?'

'No, but critical, so Molly says. She had the news from Lisa. He was run over.'

'How? Where?' she asked.

'Apparently while walking to his car, where Jessica was waiting for him.'

'Accident?'

'No one stopped. Jessica didn't see what happened, and so the next person out had the happy surprise of finding him.'

Georgia tried to cope with this new horror. An accident would be pushing coincidence to its extreme. She could not face a heavy breakfast and so compromised with a slice of toast and tea. Then Luke rang her mobile.

'I've had Tim on the phone,' he said.

'We've heard about Julian.'

'He's beside himself, poor chap. Kept saying it couldn't happen again. It couldn't be one of them.'

'Is the walk still going ahead?'

'Believe it or not, yes. Don't know about the celebration.'

'But Aletta and Val—'

'Aletta, Seb and Jessica are at the hospital. It seems Val has nobly offered to lead the triumphal walk back for the rest of them. Tim asked me to tell you it's leaving from the cathedral as planned at two p.m.'

Georgia switched off her mobile with mixed feelings. Half of her wanted to go nowhere near the Old Road, and the other half knew that Peter would point out that that was all the more reason for her to do so.'

'I take it from your expression that you don't want to go,' Peter said.

'No, but I should. I haven't told you yet what happened last night.'

A keen look. 'Do so, and make it good.'

His eyes gleamed as she related Seb's staggering information. 'I'll ring Will Whitton with that. It takes us a whole lot further.'

'You mean Will.'

'And possibly us as well.'

When she went on to tell him of the spat with Julian and Val, Peter almost crowed with delight. '*Yes*.'

'I'm glad you're pleased,' she said drily. 'Val wasn't. He had to contend with the threat of being evicted, plus my bringing up the subject of the bones again.'

'Tell me the exact words Jessica used, if you can.' When she did so to the best of her ability, he continued, 'The references to "the jewel in the crown" and "the answer". Answer to what?'

'Both refer to the Becket bones, I presume.'

'Really,' Peter said with satisfaction, 'this case is *most* interesting.'

'Which case?'

'You do right to remind me. But Bonneur, Georgia, Bonneur.'

'Val didn't like my bringing up the name one little bit.'

'Understandably so, I believe. I have not been idle,' Peter announced. 'I researched army records for Private J. Wilson. Not an uncommon name, but I think I have the right one. Went with the Royal Engineers in the Expeditionary Force to France in 1939; based in England in 1942, having been evacuated from Dunkirk in 1940. As was Robert Wayncroft,' he added.

'And as were well over three hundred thousand other men,' Georgia pointed out.

'That is true.' Peter looked complacent. 'I would suggest that if Lt Christophe Bonneur was alive and well in Canterbury in June 1942 then it's odds-on that he was in the Free French forces also evacuated from Dunkirk.'

'As were roughly twenty-five thousand of his countrymen.'

'Wilson and Bonneur died in the raid. Robert Wayncroft survived.'

'Which only means that he felt that his fellow servicemen deserved a memorial.'

'But why were they all in Canterbury in the first place? Robert, I understand, but neither of the other two was stationed nearby.'

'On leave?'

'Perhaps. It'll take more time to get at the Free French force records, but the same question mark hangs over Bonneur.'

'Where's this going, Peter?'

'Like all good journeys – to Canterbury. I also did some research into the Bonneur family. Did you know that it goes back to medieval days?'

'So do all families. They're just not all on record.'

'Kindly be constructive, Georgia. In medieval times the head of the Bonneur family was very close to the kings of France. It supported the king at all times. It shot to real power under King Louis VII, who seems to have been devoted to pilgrimages. He was also the first husband of Eleanor, who later married Becket's adversary Henry II of England and a large part of France. Both Henry and Louis did penance at the tomb of Thomas Becket.'

'So?' A few bells were beginning to ring in her mind.

'Big shot Henry II decided it would be fun to extort that huge ruby, the Regale, out of Henry VII as a donation to the shrine, which helped save his own pocket.'

'Isn't that the jewel that disappeared into the King's coffers in Tudor times and not long afterwards disappeared for good?' She stopped as Peter's implication hit her. 'Do you mean,' she asked incredulously, 'that the jewel in the crown Jessica was talking about was *that* and *not* the bones?'

Peter nodded. 'I invite you to consider that possibility. Also, I recall you told me that the Wayncroft papers contains the injunction that "your heritage is wisdom", and the Bible tells us that the price of wisdom is above—'

'Rubies,' she finished for him.

Peter sighed with pleasure. 'Consider, therefore, that the heritage of the Wayncrofts might actually be to protect that ruby and not the bones?'

'But—' She was instantly springing to the defence of her own interpretation and took a deep breath. 'A long shot, Peter. All sorts of questions. It's a big jump from our guess to assuming that Julian has this jewel—'

'Or Val, according to what you told me. They each assume the other has it.'

'That doesn't make sense.'

'No, but I really smell rubies. That *does* make sense. Think of all that lovely money Val could make just for himself if he had it, without Julian having any legal claim on it. And Julian the same.'

'It's too way out.'

'Is it? Val married into the Bonneur family. There would be a big market for the jewel in France if he has it, together with provenance for it. It would have not only the value of the jewel itself, but also the accompanying prestige of France having regained its own. Val needs money for himself, not for the Chillingham estate.'

'I accept that, but Val denies his wife was part of the family.'

'He would, wouldn't he?' Peter said reasonably. 'And remember a Bonneur came over in the 1980s to hunt for an ancestor. He might also have been looking for the jewel.'

'So what's your thesis?' Georgia was slowly beginning to think Peter could be on the right track.

'More of a hypothesis than a thesis. A thesis suggests evidence, and ours is heavily circumstantial. The Regale seems to have disappeared from the public record after the reign of Queen Mary, and it is presumed to have been sold amongst other crown jewels when the monarchy was hard up in the seventeenth century. Queen Mary was a Catholic, believing devoutly in the need to restore the Roman Catholic faith to England, together with St Thomas and all his brother and sister saints. Now if you had a big jewel like that, which had been stolen from a saint's shrine, might you not want to bequeath it back to its home?'

'Yes, but I'd send it straight back to Canterbury Cathedral.'

'Mary wouldn't. She would have been all too well aware that Elizabeth would succeed her and not turn the country back towards Rome. If Mary sent it to Canterbury, Elizabeth might well pinch it back again. Where, therefore, would Mary send it?'

'To France? That was still Catholic enough, and it was the Regale's original home.'

'Perhaps. But the Bonneur family thinks it's here with the Wayncrofts. Let us theorize that, in the mid twentieth century, Christophe heard a rumour of its survival and whereabouts and tried to claim it or steal it, according to your point of view. He was killed in an air raid and no more was heard of him. Forty years later his son or nephew came over to check this out and was told about the war memorial in Chillingham church. Robert Wayncroft was away, and whom else he met apart from Jeannie Miller is unknown, but Val comes to mind. Christophe and Jeannie are no longer alive. Natural causes, I'm sure.'

'If you're right, Peter, where is the Regale now? Either Julian or Val is lying – or both, in which case it's still hidden. And it's not in the Shrine, even if it ever was.'

'It should have gone to the heir after Robert's death. I doubt very much if he would have given *that* to Anne for safe keeping. But it doesn't seem to have done so. Hence Julian's fury yesterday evening. In his view the Regale is his heritage, and not to be sold by Val to the highest bidder.'

FIFTEEN

Canterbury had always been a gathering point, the end of the quest; once for pilgrims, now tourists. Just as the pilgrims before her, Georgia walked through Westgate towards the cathedral, in pilgrim times the abbey church of the Augustinian monks. There had been many changes to the building they knew, through fire and reconstruction, and today's cathedral was vastly different to the one St Thomas had known. There were still guided tours around the cathedral, however, even though tourists no longer had to kneel at the appointed stations on their way to the shrine, each stop heightening expectation of the final 'show', the shrine revealed in all its glory.

Including the Regale.

Georgia was still unsure about Peter's theory, tempting though it was. It hit most of the right buttons, and yet not quite all. The religious war between the Roman Catholic and Anglican church had passed with the advent of freedom of worship, so the Wayncrofts' duty would be to hand it back, not keep the jewel for 'protection'.

As she turned into Mercery Lane she could see the group waiting outside the gatehouse into the cathedral complex. Some were sitting, some standing, but most preparing to leave, removing sweaters and putting on backpacks. The weather couldn't be helping the general mood, she thought. Hazy sun might seem ideal for walking, but today it felt oppressive, hindering not helping. As she approached, with retreat impossible, her stomach knotted up with more tension than the hurried cheese sandwich that she'd had for lunch would have generated. Val was clearly in charge here, but unsurprisingly seemed to be having difficulty in assuming his usual leadership role.

'I'm so sorry, Tim,' she said as he came over to greet her. 'How's Julian?'

'I'm told he's pulling round,' he said, 'but not yet out of the woods.'

That reminded her unpleasantly of Peacock Wood, which she would have to walk past this afternoon. Some triumphal return home this would be.

Val turned round to add, 'There's a couple of nice policemen guarding him, so that might be holding his progress back.' He must have seen her expression because he continued, 'Sorry. Not quite myself.'

'Understandable,' she said, forcing herself to be 'normal'. 'How's your mother coping?'

'Not well. She insisted on staying at the hospital with Aletta and Seb, but the shock's beginning to tell. Excuse me,' he said pointedly, 'I should do my bit now, and then we can leave.'

His bit? Georgia realized he must mean an announcement, although she would have thought that would be Tim's job. From the look of it, however, Tim had no problem in Val taking over from him, and called for silence. 'I'm sure I'm speaking for my brother and mother,' Val began, 'when I say that today isn't the last lap. It's the first step to a new era for Chillingham, and if my brother were here he would be the first to say so.'

He received a dutiful but lacklustre reception, which he deserved, Georgia thought, considering he knew well that this group held many who did not support his plans for the village. It was a bad mistake, in her view, to move straight into the assumption that the plans were going ahead, especially with his brother so ill.

'Turning our back on St Thomas,' Matthew said firmly as they moved off, but his words were picked up by Val.

'Nonsense,' he declared. 'The very opposite. He's given us his blessing to put him on the map.'

'Looking at this place,' a wit grunted, 'he's already there.'

Val ignored him, this time with a certain dignity. 'I suggest we begin our march today with a short silence praying for my brother's recovery.'

It did seem to have some effect, for the group seemed to pick up spirit as it moved into St Peter's Street to walk out through Westgate. Even by the time they crossed the river, Georgia was wishing she'd worn shorts, rather than trousers, and her backpack began to feel sticky. She dashed into a shop to buy a bottle of water, and when she came out she was surprised to see Aletta hurrying towards them from the station car park, with Seb loping along in front of her.

'Good. We thought we'd missed you,' Aletta said.

'How's Julian?' Georgia asked.

Aletta looked shattered, unlike her usual self. 'They think he'll be OK. He's awake anyway, and he wanted Seb and me to come. He said it was important,' she added. 'There had to be an end. I don't know what he means, do you, Georgia?'

Aletta seemed to be appealing to her for help, and Georgia was taken aback. She did her best, however. 'Just the pilgrimage, I expect.'

'Thank you,' Aletta said gravely.

As they walked along the old Watling Street and up towards the downs, Georgia began to feel better, either because she was out in the open or perhaps because of the pull of the Old Road. Her companions, too, were chatting more freely now, as though everyone had broken out of some kind of chains, at least temporarily. Nevertheless, she was not looking forward to the rest of this stretch of the Road. Tim told her that Simon had driven back to Chillingham, rather than walk with them, so that he could help Lisa prepare for the 'celebration' this evening – although that was hardly the right word in the circumstances. She was relieved that Peter and Luke would be at the pub this evening. It was something to cling to, once she had faced the ordeal of passing the spot where Hugh Wayncroft had died. She knew from experience, however, that there must be a good reason for Peter being so insistent on her coming.

'Bigbury, folks, said to be Julius Caesar's camp,' Val called out as they entered the first woodland stretch of the walk. On the way to Canterbury, the group had been in too much of a hurry to stop here, but now Val seemed determined to assert his leadership. 'Plans are afoot to make more of it; not much to see now.' A footpath led up from the Old Road track to the camp itself, and from the highest point there was a steep drop down to the valley below, where the sight of Canterbury ahead would have greeted the eyes of pilgrims. Today, the camp itself looked only a bed of leaf mould, although its shape among the trees suggested something of importance might have happened here.

She could hear the rooks in the trees, much as Hugh Wayncroft must have done. Much as Julius Caesar must have done when he arrived in this alien land with his legionnaires, intent on conquering this wayward island. Not knowing what lay ahead of him, this must have seemed the perfect stop. The river ran along the valley beneath, and there would be a clear view of any imminent attack. Legend had it that the Romans fought at Chilham, a few miles further on, before turning back. What made Caesar decide on retreat? Defeat by the natives? A message from home? She thought fancifully that Bigbury could have been a turning point for Julius Caesar, as it was in a way for Marsh & Daughter. She and Peter, like Caesar, were inching along the Old Road towards a goal, but how it was to be achieved was still a mystery.

Rubbish, she told herself, although not totally convinced it was. This track had a way of bringing about solutions, no matter whether it was Caesar's troops involved, pilgrimages to St Thomas or a case for Marsh & Daughter.

Georgia told herself this was the twenty-first century. Problems were solved by people, not by ancient roads. Problems such as whether it was in her stars to have a child, or how Peter was ever to live with himself if he could not accept that Rick was dead – or problems such as who killed Hugh Wayncroft. Nevertheless, out here on the Old Road it was easier to understand what had brought people to St Thomas's healing well in earlier times. They'd had physical or mental problems, and in such a place of peace and quiet it would have been easy to think that the saint himself had guided them there, that he had appeared in person to them and that the water had blessed them with a cure.

Almost reluctantly, Georgia turned away from Bigbury Camp to rejoin the track. The group had moved on, and she had to hurry to catch it up. Tim was walking at the end of the group, alone, and still looking despondent.

'What's wrong, Tim?'

He just shrugged, and so she tried again. 'You had a success this week, and none of the horrors you've been through can affect that.'

'Can't they? I'm not so sure, Georgia. It all seemed plain sailing. We have a good reception for the play, we go back home, celebrate it, then get together to plan the next stage and how it's to be financed. Val was talking about setting up a trust, which seems a good idea. The path ahead looked paved

with gold – *yesterday*. Today – I just feel there's too much
fighting against us. Julian's accident – if it was – is the last
straw. Why's it all happening?'

'It's old Tom's fault.' Seb, walking in front with Aletta and
Val, turned round to grin at them.

'Don't be ridiculous, Seb,' Aletta said wearily.

'I'm not, Mum.' Seb looked affronted. 'Dad was murmuring
about it while he was only half awake.'

'Murmuring about what?' Aletta asked sharply.

'Well, Becket, and stuff. And something about a ruby.'

Georgia froze. Peter's theory could be right. She waited on
tenterhooks to hear Val and Aletta's reactions, and she saw Seb's
expression change to realization that something was wrong.
Aletta's face, however, registered nothing but polite interest, and
Val remained silent. Nevertheless, Seb's flippant side had
vanished, and Georgia could see the Wayncroft in him now.

'Dad told me about that old ruby a week or two back. Is
that the reason he's in hospital?' he threw at Val. 'He said
you'd got it.'

Val retained his control remarkably well. 'Julian had an
accident,' he said gently, 'so don't let's make it worse. The
ruby's not important, whatever it is.'

'Isn't it?' Aletta asked woodenly.

'Aletta darling,' Val said sadly, 'it's Wayncroft business. I
only know about it because Robert told me.'

Georgia found that hard to believe.

'Julian overheard a private conversation between my mother
and myself,' Val continued. 'But don't upset yourself, please,
Seb. Julian doesn't have the ruby, and I don't either.'

Seb stared at him in contempt. 'You expect me to believe
that?'

'If I'd inherited it,' Val retorted, 'it would no longer be in
my possession. It belongs in France, and I would, unlike the
Wayncrofts, have delivered it to its rightful owners.' He tried
a laugh. 'Believe me, I'd have been out of here and living in
the lap of luxury again, instead of facing the prospect of having
to work for my living in St Thomas's cause, noble though
that is, and willing though I am. As you see, however, I'm
still here.' He sounded bitter. 'You may, therefore, all assume
that I don't have the Regale.'

*　　*　　*

The heat and tension began to mount, and Georgia stopped to take a drink from her bottle of water. The path was running through a public orchard now and would soon lead the pilgrims down to the village of Chartham Hatch. The pilgrims of the past must have looked forward to convivial drinks of ale in the local taverns, but convivial was the last thing Georgia felt today. Let this ordeal be over *soon*, she prayed.

In the pubs they went by, people still seemed to be enjoying the aftermath of Sunday lunch, but the Chillingham group was marched relentlessly past on its way to rejoin the Old Road track that would take them on to Chillingham. Georgia felt a terrible sense of inevitability now that she and her fellow travellers had crossed the lane leading down to the Canterbury Road, and thus were committed to going onwards. That meant passing Peacock Wood.

Val had done a good job in protesting his innocence over the Regale ruby. Did she believe him? Yes, oddly enough, at least as far as the Regale was concerned. The clash between him and Seb did not bode well, however, and she could see a tight-lipped Seb with his arm firmly round Tess and not his mother. Wayncroft he might be, but he had his own mind. As for the celebration that lay ahead, the only thing Georgia wanted to celebrate would be seeing Medlars again.

And yet Peacock Wood could surely hold no threat for her now . . . or could it? Hugh Wayncroft's murder was still unsolved, and although she felt she and Peter were inching their way closer, that did not yet mean success. She thought of how this scene would have looked in 1967. A younger Val would have been prancing along; so would Lisa, Jessica, Clive and Fred.

The Old Road was taking them past farmland and orchards, with views far out over the Weald, and she could see the River Stour snaking its way through the valley to their left. On their right, the appositely named Fright Wood was coming to an end, and then there would be only one stretch of open land before she had to face Peacock Wood. She could almost hear the tramp, tramp, tramp of Caesar's legionnaires as they marched on Chilham; she could hear the trotting of pilgrims' horses and the crunch of the rough boots of those who could not afford to ride as they inexorably made their way to an unknown fate. There was a sense of 'what will be, will be' about the Road, because of its antiquity. Had Hugh Wayncroft felt it as he walked along here in 1967 – that just as nothing could change the Old Road, his job must remain to look after the estate and the St Thomas ruins? And the Regale too? No, he would probably not have had the custody of that. Robert would probably have had it. But what had happened to it when he died? Only Julian could have it, surely.

Ahead, Georgia could see Tess and Matthew walking together. From behind Tess's long blonde hair made her look just as her grandmother did forty years back. Lisa Moon had been in front of Clive and Fred, with Jessica leading the column with Val. Today Aletta was there with Tim – or was that Val? Georgia was feeling dizzy with the heat and all too aware that Peacock Wood was coming ever closer. She could no longer think rationally as to which was 1967 and which was today. Ahead of her she could see the front of the column had reached the wood. It was disappearing round the corner, while she herself was at the rear, just as Hugh had been. Hugh, who had had so little time left to live.

The plan was being drawn up in front of the column for the ceremonial arrival. Now or then? She could hear the lutes and the wooden balls rattling on the staves of the pilgrims. She knew Becket and the King were at the rear, as was she. Jessica had taken the news of the plan down the column right to the very end where Hugh was. She had then returned to the front, so who had come next? Who else brought Hugh news? Either Clive or Fred had killed him, or someone else must have dropped back to speak to him, but who? She could not see the picture in her mind, and her head began to swim again. Nothing had changed here. Just as before she was reaching the spot where Hugh had died.

She forced herself to halt and walk on to the scrubby ground to the side of the path as it entered the wood. There were bushes there; passers-by could easily not have seen the body. The column was nearly all into the wood now, and so his killer would be alone with Hugh. She began to realize that the dizziness she was experiencing was unlike the 'fingerprints' she had endured three weeks ago. Today it was only the heat, surely. Didn't that mean that the solution to Hugh's murder was close at hand? She looked up, startled by movement.

Val Harper was blocking her way back to the path.

'It was here,' he said pleasantly, 'if that's what you're wondering. I know that because I found the body.' There was no emotion in his voice at all. She was gripped by terror for herself, but he grinned. 'Give up,' he said. 'You'll never prove it.'

As she pushed past him, she was afraid he would catch her arm, but he didn't. He let her pass. It had been he who came back to Hugh right at the end of the pilgrimage. Told him to stay back, and that other principal players would be joining them. But Val had an alibi, didn't he? She made a grab for memory. Yes. He'd been with Jessica. She stumbled along the Old Road through the wood, catching up with the rear of the column, forcing herself not to look back. Val would be following her, he must be, but she would not look behind her.

And then came the blessed sight of Chillingham, nestling at the foot of the Downs. There was only the slope to walk along, and then she would be on the road that led into Chillingham village. Georgia could even glimpse a welcoming party, waiting for them where the path ended. She could see cars parked, and she hoped desperately that Luke's would be one of them. Luke, all she wanted, all she needed. As she emerged into the open again and followed the group down the slope to the road, she could see no Luke, however. Only Peter, two police cars, and some curious onlookers.

The police were there, Peter told her, to arrest Valentine Harper for the attempted murder of Julian Wayncroft.

The Three Peacocks was humming, but not for the expected reasons of celebration of the play. The whole of Chillingham seemed gathered here. Those who knew talked, those who didn't speculated and pestered. Georgia had managed to find a table in the corner of the conservatory, but only because of consideration for Peter's wheelchair, and when Luke at last came in he looked completely bewildered at the maelstrom around them.

'What on earth's going on?' he asked. 'I couldn't park. I had to drive back to Becket House and walk here.'

'You can have a drink then,' Georgia said shakily, hardly able to believe she was safely here.

'Thanks. If I can fight my way to the bar, I will.'

The table was barely large enough for two of them, let

alone three, but Luke managed to squeeze in with his drink. After Luke had been given the news of Val's arrest, he asked the obvious question: 'What about Anne Fanshawe, and, come to that, Hugh Wayncroft? Is it just that attempted murder of Julian is the easier charge to hold him on?'

'Good thinking,' Peter said. 'But you're wrong. Who isn't here?'

Puzzled, Georgia looked round the sea of faces. 'Stella, Tessa, Seb.'

'And who else?'

Then all was clear, even in her fuddled state. 'Aletta.'

Peter nodded. 'Not forgetting Julian.'

Georgia looked at her celebration drink, which no longer seemed so enticing. Her stomach began to churn. 'Anne's murder?' she asked. 'They did it together?'

'Will Whitton is sure that's it. After I told him the full story of what happened at that table before Anne left, he began to take a closer interest in Lady Macbeth and husband, as he called them. He thinks much as we did. They – or probably Aletta – saw Anne's anorak still hanging there when they left the bar and kept an eye on the window from their room in case she decided to come back for it. Even if they had her mobile number they wouldn't have been able to risk ringing it, because she'd simply tell them to hold on to the anorak until the next day. It was her bad luck that they did see her return. So easy for them then to come downstairs, take it outside for her and even insist on walking back with her to express their gratitude over the proposed will bequest. They may or may not have intended to kill her. Macbeth could have hoped that one last quiet appeal would work and that she'd agree to open up the ruins after all. But, if so, she didn't oblige them, and Julian, whose temper is erratic, lost it – with or without his Lady's encouragement.'

'And the Regale?' Georgia asked, no longer able to bear the thought of Anne's last moments.

'My theory is that when Robert wrote his will, I don't think that came into it. Robert was not only firmly set against development, but also highly suspicious of Julian's character, not to mention Val's. So, as we said earlier, he could have decided to skip a generation and leave it to Anne either to bequeath them back to the Wayncrofts or if Julian predeceased her to

give them back to Seb straight away. Seb might be of a
different calibre than Julian, so Robert took a chance.'

Georgia forced herself to think his through, but still wasn't
happy with it. Chance didn't sound like Robert. 'There's a
hitch. What's happened to the Regale?'

'It's a loose end,' Peter admitted, 'and I'll have to leave it
dangling, I suppose, but—'

'I hate to come the heavy publisher,' Luke said politely
when Peter came to a halt, 'but the proposed Marsh & Daughter
book is about Hugh Wayncroft.'

'Patience, patience,' Peter said crossly. 'I'm getting there.
That has something to do with Becket. It has to.'

'Val?' Georgia said. 'The problem with his motive is that
he was young enough in 1967 to have the world before him.
If the Becket development idea didn't work, he'd find something else. As he eventually did – a well-connected wife. He
had no need to kill Hugh.'

'No, not Val,' Peter said, deep in thought. '*Becket* not Becket.
That's the answer,' he cried, crashing his fist on the table.

'Very clear,' Luke observed.

'*Becket* the play, not the man. *That* was the motive.'

'What was?' Georgia was lost now.

'There were personal reasons for killing Becket, as well as
the power struggle. It was sheer hatred.'

'Val's hatred of his stepfather? Just as he tried to kill Julian
for hatred?'

'No, no,' Peter said impatiently. 'He did that because he
saw his last lifeline – living at Chillingham Place disappearing
after Julian's threats.'

'But are you sure he didn't kill Hugh? I know he had an
alibi, but he practically told me he'd done it. He said I'd never
prove it, but—' And then Georgia saw. 'Of course. He meant
his mother. Jessica killed Hugh Wayncroft.'

Jessica Wayncroft had aged since Georgia had last seen her
at the after-show party, even though only a few days had
passed. She looked her full years now. The lively eyes were
indifferent, her movements those of an old woman.

'Come in,' she said, and she took them into the living room.
She might be dressed in bright yellow, but it did her no favours
today, Georgia thought. It was Jessica who had asked to see

them, so it would be a difficult meeting from all points of view.

'How's Julian?' Georgia asked. He was still in hospital, but under arrest and about to be charged when fit enough. Aletta had been released on police bail, and so had Val.

Jessica looked surprised, as though Georgia's question had no relevance to her. 'He seems to be recovering well,' she replied. 'However, I wished to see you for another reason. I suppose you still intend to write a book about my husband's death. In it you no doubt wish to blame poor Val.'

'No,' Peter said. 'He isn't guilty of that.'

The eyes flickered slightly. 'I am much relieved. He has enough to contend with, merely because he gave way to impulse after Julian's vile accusations. I take it, therefore, that you've decided who did kill my husband?'

'Yes,' Peter said quietly. 'You.'

Jessica's only reaction was surprise. 'I had not thought you were so intelligent.'

'Thank you.' Peter's voice held no hint of sarcasm.

'I gave Valentine his alibi, of course. Which made him *my* alibi also. I thought it out quite carefully. I told you about devising the order of arrival, which was true. It was also true I returned to join Val. However, I then slipped back again to join Hugh at the right moment. At that point the path is enclosed as it goes through the wood, but the tree line on the right between it and the orchards is, or was then, thin, and it was easy to take the field path unnoticed to reach Hugh at the end of the wood, draw him on one side and kill him. It was all so very quickly done. Val never even noticed I was gone because he was talking to the musicians.'

'But why, Jessica? Why kill Hugh and not Lisa if you resented their relationship so much?' Georgia was incredulous that she could be discussing her husband's murder so calmly. She showed no sign of fear, no sign of the enormity of what she had done.

'I had nothing to gain from killing her, Miss Marsh. That's why.'

'And you did for killing your husband?'

'I *thought* I did. It was the worst mistake I ever made. When we were married in the 1950s it was a different world to today. At Hugh's level of society, at least, women were not permitted to trouble their pretty little heads with business affairs. They should sit in a parlour and sew a fine seam. No one, not Robert, not Hugh, not my solicitors, thought to mention to a mere woman that in the event of Hugh dying before Robert not just the ruins but the whole estate went back to him – or rather what was left of it after Hugh's mismanagement. His stupid idea of management was to change nothing, repair nothing, let it all be. The fool. Gallivanting around with a girl half his age, when he had me. He wouldn't let me run the estate. I could have made it profitable. I asked Robert to let me run it after Hugh's death, but he turned me down. He referred so little to Hugh's murder either to me or publicly that I sometimes think he might have suspected me of Hugh's murder. Even if he did, he was a fool not to let me manage the estate. It has grown poorer and poorer.

'Then I found out about the Regale ruby from Val after Robert's death. Robert had that ruby all the time. A fortune, and he just sat on it. And now it's vanished. Julian's a fool; he takes after his father. He must have it, because Val hasn't, but still Julian denies it. Can you wonder Val lost his patience? Tell me,' she added, when neither Peter nor Georgia spoke, 'how did you come to the conclusion that I had killed Hugh? Unusual for a woman to strangle a man, isn't it? I imagine a jury would never believe it, especially without evidence.'

'Your first husband was in the Special Forces, Mrs Wayncroft,' Peter said, 'and that you told us you met him in the services, which I presume would be the SOE. I believe the training, even for women, included methods of instant killing.'

'Another silence. Then: 'A jury still wouldn't believe it.'

'No,' Peter agreed. 'And there's no evidence, as you say. I imagine, however, that a life sentence for one son and a long jail term for the other is life sentence enough for you.'

A pause. 'Julian's a weakling,' she said scornfully. 'He takes after Hugh. He's a weakling, and he's stupid. But Val, ah, my Val, he takes after his father.'

They left her there in her chair, unbending and ramrod straight.

SIXTEEN

'**D**o you fancy a trip to the Old Road, Georgia?' Peter asked.
            'At Chillingham?'
'Yes.'
'Work or pleasure?'

A pause on the phone. 'In-between. Private business. I'll stand you and Luke lunch. You and I can have our trip and leave Luke in the pub with a drink. If he doesn't mind, that is.'

'Which bit of the Road?' she asked, after she'd parked the car as near to the Old Road as she could get it. 'I don't have to go past Peacock Wood again, do I?'

'No. The other way is flatter. It will take this old bone-shaker. One of these days,' Peter ruminated as he manoeuvred himself into the chair from the car, 'I'm going to invest in one of those new thingummy machines that take inconvenienced folks like me up mountainsides and so on. I could even go to the Himalayas.'

'Good idea, but today you only have me. Sure you don't want Luke to come with us?'

'Not today. Do your best. We'll just go a little way.'

At first the path was quite wide and flat, but the further they got from the road the narrower it became, and finally, as they skirted round some woodland, Peter said, 'This is far enough. Just wanted to see the view from up here and feel what it was like for myself.'

'Can you smell the Old Road?'

'Oh, yes. I can even hear the pilgrims.'

'I can too. I can understand why they believed in miracles.'

'Did we achieve anything in this case, do you think?' Peter asked abruptly. 'The result seems to be one good woman murdered, three people in gaol as a result, and another killer probably dying of grief. An unlucky jewel it seems, the Regale, wherever it is. Not much of a heritage for the Wayncrofts.'

'No,' she agreed.

'Do people still believe in miracles, Georgia?'

'Yes, but they come in different forms.'

'Such as?' Peter asked.

'I suppose we begin to see things differently. Isn't that a form of miracle?'

'Coming to terms with illness and disability, like this?' Peter indicated the wheelchair.

'Yes. But maybe Rick too.'

A pause. 'You touch a tender spot, rightly, Georgia. That watch – if only I knew the truth behind that.'

'Then something else would make you unsure again. It has to come from you, not the watch.'

'That's what Janie said. She's right. You're right. But how does that help? How do I replace doubt? Does old Thomas have a cure for that?'

'You don't replace it. You look at your grief for Rick from time to time, dust it down, give him a loving kiss and put it aside again. And you take on something new—'

'Janie?' he interrupted. 'No, that was the mistake I made. She knew it. I knew it too. We both jumped too quickly. This David—'

'The museum trust manager?'

'He sounds a good chap. She agrees. That's all. I bow gently out.'

'So what's your "new" going to be?' Georgia asked.

His eyes turned to the Old Road. 'Even if I buy the thingummy to take me up mountains, it won't bring Rick back, but I can travel along this path to Canterbury whenever I like. What about you? What's St Thomas got in mind?'

'I have to discuss it with Luke, but I think St Thomas has already given me the answer. It's Luke. If we have children that's fine; if we don't, that's fine too.'

He laughed. 'Hand me that bit of wood down there, please.'

Puzzled, she picked up the branch and gave it to him. He promptly banged it on the ground at his side. 'See any gushing water yet?' he asked.

'Afraid not. Only a muddy puddle.'

'That's it. Thomas's miracle, performed on the Old Road, eh? An answer for both of us.'

When they returned to the Three Peacocks, Luke was nowhere to be found, but eventually he returned, after ten minutes or so.

'There's a house down the road for sale,' he said.

'You don't want to leave Medlars, do you?' she asked in alarm.

'Good grief, no. Um –' he glanced at her doubtfully – 'I forgot to tell you, Georgia. Mark rang me from the States. He's got a job down this way and said he fancied living in a village called Chillingham. He asked me to keep a lookout for a house.'

'That's really good news,' Georgia said warmly. 'How come you forgot to tell me though?' That wasn't like Luke.

'He told me Jill's pregnant,' Luke said awkwardly. 'The baby's due at Christmas.'

A variety of emotions swept through her: agony, jealousy, regret and then a sort of peace. It was done, the decision made; Luke would have a grandchild, and in a way so would she. 'Great,' she said, laughing and weeping at the same time. 'We can take him or her for walks along the Old Road. We can leave a heritage of our own after all, Peter.'

'That makes me a step great-grandfather. I wonder if he'd like the Himalayas? By the way, talking of heritage . . .' He looked at her meaningfully.

'The Regale,' she said in dismay. 'We'd forgotten it. If it existed, where is it?'

'I can make a guess.'

A ramp over the steps was already in place when Georgia and Peter arrived at Lisa's cottage the following afternoon. As they got out of the car, however, Seb and Tess had just emerged from her home and were walking towards them.

Seb stiffened. 'You walk on, Tess. I'll catch you up.'

What to say to him? Georgia wondered. His family life had disintegrated around him, his parents and, if he knew the truth, his grandmother all wearing faces he could not have dreamed existed.

Seb swallowed. 'I just want you to know . . .' He stopped and then tried again. 'I just want you to know that it's going on.'

'It?' Peter asked gently. 'The Becket development or . . .?'

'The "or". The Becket development is easier – I'm planning to call a village meeting about it. We'll discuss the issues and plans democratically before anything's decided. In any case, there may be inheritance problems now that my father . . .' Seb made a visible effort for control. 'So Stella and lawyers will have to be in on it throughout.'

'That's good.' Georgia approved of that, even though the task might be rather more Herculean than Seb was assuming. But he was young enough to weather it.

'As for this Wayncroft thing,' he muttered. 'I just want you to know . . . I'm a *real* Wayncroft. My job to put things right, yes? Tess has just told me she's off for the rest of the summer and then it's university in the autumn. She's going to make her own life, and so shall I. I'll need a mission, so Becket will do me very well. OK by you?'

Peter nodded. 'OK.'

Visibly pleased, Seb raced after Tess, just as Lisa opened the door to them.

'You come in, both of you,' she said. 'I'll get tea. And a nice slice of cake.' The traditional welcome, as though nothing out of the ordinary had or would happen. They had expected to be alone with Lisa, but awaiting them in her parlour Georgia saw Molly, Vic and Matthew, crowded together on upright chairs as if assembled for a business meeting. As perhaps this was.

Lisa opened the proceedings after tea and cakes were distributed. 'Now, you said on the phone, Mr Marsh, that you wanted to talk about the big raid in the war.'

'Yes. In its various ways it's affected the Wayncrofts, the Moons and the Painters deeply. It was the night John Painter met Robert Wayncroft.'

'Let's get down to it,' Lisa said practically. 'This is about the Regale ruby, isn't it? Well, we're all in the picture now. Vic's come clean about it. Even Molly didn't know. We knew there was something John was keeping to himself, and it seems he told Vic and swore him to silence. It stops with us though. That agreed? Not to go into none of your books, Mr Marsh.'

'Agreed,' Peter said.

'And,' Lisa said earnestly, 'that goes for my Hugh's killer too. I always knew who it was. No reason, just knew. We were both so close to him, see.'

'I think so,' Peter said gently.

Molly cleared her throat and looked at her brother. 'You tell the whole story now, Vic. They're all dead, so no one will be hurt by it.'

He nodded. 'I told you all true enough, but there's more.

Dad saw Mr Robert struggling with that soldier who was yelling his head off. Panic, Dad thought, and who could blame him? But then he saw the soldier chuck something, a stone it looked like, into the burning library, which was in ruins by that time, and then the wall came down on both the soldier and Mr Robert. Mr Robert was staggering around moaning afterwards, so Dad took him to the ARP centre. Well, he was still raving, but not much physically hurt, so after he came off duty Dad took him to where he and Mum were living in Canterbury, till he came to his senses. That's how Dad came to work at Chillingham Place after the war. And that's how he came to know the story of the Regale, because Mr Robert was out of his mind for a day or two while he recovered. Kept thinking Dad was St Thomas himself, so bit by bit Dad got the story. Not that he cared. They were rough times, and Dad had seen and heard worse than Mr Robert's tale.

'It seems that Mr Robert had been at Dunkirk, and life seemed short on those beaches while they were waiting to see if the Germans or the rescue boats got them first. He started boasting about a legacy he was going to get when his grand-father died, the Regale of France. It was going to be his duty to look after it for the Pope, he said. He wouldn't know where it was hidden until his grandfather died, and he had a letter given him by the solicitors. Well, Mr Robert was chattering on about this to two chaps with flapping ears. One pair belonged to Private Johnnie Wilson, and the other to the Frenchman whose name you saw on that memorial.

'Mr Robert thought no more about it after he got back to England, but Johnnie and the Frenchie remembered and kept tabs on him. When they knew his grandfather was dead, they managed to get themselves to Canterbury. Chillingham Place had been requisitioned by the army, so it turned out the grand-father had hidden the Regale in St George's church in Canterbury for safety, the vicar being a chum of his. Robert came to pick it up, not knowing the Frenchie and Johnnie Wilson were dogging his footsteps. Then, just as he found the ruby, the big raid started, and the church was in darkness as the bombs began to fall. The two other soldiers were after the ruby, grabbed it from Mr Robert and began to fight over it. In the darkness, Mr Robert realized that one of the two chaps was dead, he could feel his blood on him, and knew that the other one had murdered him and stolen the ruby. That was Johnnie Wilson. So he chased him through the city, caught him up at the cathedral, but Johnnie refused to give him the Regale back. Seemed he had a conversion, like, and thought Mr Robert was only out for himself and didn't deserve the jewel, so he chucked it into the burning rubble of the library, crying out that St Thomas could have the Regale back. Then when Johnnie was killed by the wall, Mr Robert blamed himself for pushing him. Whether that's so or not, I couldn't say, but Mr Robert devoted the rest of his life to doing good. Then in 2002 back he comes to say sorry to St Thomas in Canterbury Cathedral and to live out his last years.'

'But the Regale was lost to him,' Peter prompted him.

Silence.

'Your father found the Regale, didn't he?'

Vic nodded. 'He guessed what it was all right. Kept it in the Shrine, he did, not knowing what else to do with it. Ashamed of that, he was, not to have told Mr Robert or the Cathedral. But he loved it. When he knew he was dying his conscience really got to him, and he want to see Mr Robert, to make his peace and ask him what he should do. Mr Robert thought awhile, and then said he'd come down to Becket House for it in a few days to fetch it.'

'That must have been the day he got rid of us. They dug it up between them,' Molly said, 'and he only told Vic the whole story when he was dying.'

'Mr Robert said he'd bequeath the ruby as the heritage demanded,' Vic went on, 'which we took to be the heir, so you could have knocked me down with a feather to hear Mr Julian hadn't got it. We knew Mr Robert was going to leave the ruins to Mrs Fanshawe, but she never had the ruby, I'm sure of that.'

'So where is it?' Georgia asked, catching a glance exchanged between Molly and Lisa.

Lisa got slowly to her feet. 'It's time, son,' she said to Matthew, who obediently rose.

'Happen you'd like to see my workshop,' he said. It wasn't a question.

Georgia was completely at sea now, but clearly she and Peter had been summoned. She doubted whether the wheelchair would go in through the workshop door, but perhaps the doorway had expanded, or St Thomas had given it a shake, because it slid in quite easily. There was little natural light inside, for the blinds were down, but she watched Matthew go over to the cupboard, from which he brought out the same wooden box as Lisa had shown her.

'The living wood,' he said softly, running his hands lovingly over it.

Georgia caught her breath. 'And inside?'

He unlocked it and briefly opened the lid, with just enough time for her to see a jewel lying on a black velvet cushion; its red glow illuminated the whole box and spread outside into the dimly lit room.

'There was a description,' Matthew said, 'by someone who saw it in its proper place honouring St Thomas. What he said was: "When we went to see it, the sun was near setting. Nevertheless, I saw that ruby as if I had it in my hand." And here it is, glowing still.' Matthew gently closed the box and went to put it safely away.

'But you,' Georgia asked him, when she had got her breath back. 'Why?'

Matthew did not reply, just smiled.

Peter cleared his throat. 'Forgive me if I'm wrong, but the Wayncroft heritage had to be left to the eldest son. Robert had no sons, so it had to be left to Hugh's eldest son.'

'You mean . . .?' Georgia looked at Lisa in amazement, and Lisa blushed, not with shame, but with pride.

'Matthew, my dear Matt. He's Hugh's eldest son, aren't you, my love?'

'But even so – I'm sorry – why you, Matt?' Georgia asked.

'Because he's a good man and a carpenter. What better safeguard,' Peter said.

'Mr Robert told me,' Matthew said, 'that it was to go to St Thomas when the true faith is restored. I thought he meant the Catholic faith coming back to the Cathedral, or Rome perhaps. But maybe he didn't.'

'So what do you think he would want you to do with it now?' Georgia asked. 'Hand the responsibility to Seb in due course?'

'I'll have to wait for St Thomas to tell me, won't I?' Matthew said seriously. 'One of these days I reckon he'll call me up to the Old Road for Canterbury, and then I'll find out.'